I0680757

The
Lost
Colony

Kelly Cheek

© 2017 Kelly Cheek

All rights reserved. No portion of this book may be reproduced, stored in a retrieval system, or transmitted in any form, or by any means, electronic, mechanical, photocopying, recording, or otherwise, without the express written permission of the author, except in the case of brief excerpts in critical reviews or articles.

This is a work of fiction. Names, characters, places and incidents are all products of the author's imagination, or are used fictitiously. Any resemblance to actual events, locations or persons, living or dead, is entirely coincidental.

Cover and book design by Kelly Cheek

ISBN: 978-0-9909982-9-7

Fiery Muse Publishing
Littleton, Colorado 80129

Printed in the United States of America

Also by Kelly Cheek

All We Hold Dear

Trial by Fire

JackSimile and the Phantom Fury

Profile

Private Messages

Poked

The tiny ship rode the wave to the crest, then tipped forward and plunged violently into the trough. The canvas had been furled before nightfall, but there were a few clews of sail that had worked loose and were being whipped back and forth by the gale.

And the rain! The torrents of rain fell so hard, it was difficult to distinguish it from the waves washing over the bulwark. By now, there was nothing left on deck that had not been lashed down.

It was black. The occasional streaks of lightning that slashed across the sky did little to ease the unsettling fear now gripping the new captain's chest. Not to mention the queasy feeling in his stomach.

Captain Christopher Cooper had never felt such violent pitching.

Part of that was likely due to the size of the ship. The pinnace was just too small to be very stable on seas this wild. He had sent his First Mate, John Spendlove, below deck, ostensibly with the mission to calm the passengers. The fact was that there was nothing he could do on deck anyway. At this point, it was all Cooper could do to keep the bow turned into the storm.

He had tied himself to the helm to keep from being washed overboard, and he could feel the lanyard biting into his back with the rolling of the ship. He gripped the wheel tightly, making adjustments as necessary, but there was no controlling it. The little ship rolled and pitched at the whim of the mighty storm.

He could only imagine the terror of the passengers. And the bruises. They were packed in so tightly, along with a few head of livestock. But as another wave crashed across the ship's bow, Cooper realized that he could spare no time worrying about the passengers' discomfort.

So this be the end, he thought. *An attempt to return home leaveth us dead in the sea.*

The pinnace rode another wave down into the trough. Over the roaring of the wind and sea, Cooper heard a cracking sound. He thought the hull had been compromised, until the next impact. The cracking sound was much louder this time, as the main mast broke about twenty feet up and plunged over the port bow into the sea in front of him.

Attached only by the cordage now, the mast and partially furled sail hanging over the side caused greater drag. The little ship was now even more difficult to control.

Cooper struggled with the helm, feeling her trying to pull to port.

He hadn't heard any sounds other than those of the storm, so he was surprised when Spendlove appeared at his side, to the left. He was holding on tightly to anything that would keep him from being swept into the sea, but his feet were slipping on the deck.

Cooper glanced at him and, with a lightning flash, saw that he was looking at him expectantly. It was only then that he realized that Spendlove had said something. Cooper shook his head and turned a little to try to hear better.

"What might I do, Captain?" Spendlove shouted.

"Pray!" Cooper shouted back.

"Everyone below deck art already doing so. I only hope the Almighty may hear it above the storm."

After less than a minute, Spendlove noticed how much Cooper was straining with the wheel.

"Thou must be tired, Captain," he shouted into Cooper's ear. "Might I take over for a bit?"

Cooper thought for a moment. As the senior seaman on board, he had the most experience at controlling the ship in dire weather. At the same time, he had no experience in weather *this* dire. And no amount of experience would save them if his strength gave out.

He nodded to Spendlove.

"Keep her bow running straight into the wind." Spendlove nodded in response.

While still holding the wheel with one hand, Cooper braced himself and squirmed downward a little, pulling the rope up over his head, no mean task with the ship pitching and rolling as it was. He held the rope out for Spendlove and started to step aside.

At that moment, a wave broke over the bow, catching the mast and sail, trying to turn the ship to the side. Cooper, while not in the best position, tried to compensate by turning the wheel against it. John Spendlove, knocked off balance, grabbed for the rope but missed, and instead got hold of one of the spokes of the wheel. With his feet washed out from under him, he went down on the deck, clutching desperately at the wheel.

As Cooper was holding it with only one hand, he had not been prepared for the sudden additional force against it, and it jerked out of his hand. The ship turned with the force of the wave. The next wave struck them athwartships, completely engulfing the deck.

When the water cleared, Cooper was down on the deck, his arms hooked through the rope. Spendlove was nowhere to be seen.

Cooper knew that if another wave struck them broadside, it could capsize the ship. He struggled to his feet and tried to turn back into the waves.

The little ship was responding sluggishly, but Cooper finally got her turned. He was attempting to step back into the rope and pull it up around his back as a flash of lightning illuminated the wave in front of them, a wall of water thirty feet high.

God help us.

Holding the wheel steady, he braced himself as the ship was submerged under the unbelievable force of the wave. Cooper figured that this was the end, that he would now ride his craft to the bottom of the sea, holding fast to its wheel.

But to his surprise, they bobbed to the surface again. No doubt the passengers were getting soaked below, but so far, the little ship remained buoyant.

She was turning around and around, caught in a maelstrom between the waves. Cooper wrestled with the wheel, trying to regain control. He breathed a sigh of relief as the ship steadied, her bow once again pointed into the storm.

Cooper saw a dim light in the sky ahead, as if the storm was beginning to clear. That glimmer, along with the next lightning flash, showed him that it wasn't over yet.

Another wave was heading his way. It was not as large as the previous one, and Cooper began to feel confident that they might get through this.

As he leaned back against the rope to remove any slack, the wave struck. It caught the mast and sail dragging through the water along the port side of the ship, swinging them out and around, which affected the little ship's balance. Listing to the port side now, she was pulling in that direction. Cooper struggled to get her turned back to starboard, but before he could, another wave shoved the ship's hull, threatening to tip her over. With the help of the rope around him, Cooper managed to stay on his feet.

The wave tipped the ship over more than forty-five degrees. The mast, dangling on its web of cordage, was sent swinging away, splashing into the sea for a moment. Just as the ship was starting to settle back into an upright position, the broken mast was snatched out of the water and swung back like a pendulum, skimming just over the top of the waves, its momentum intensified by the pull of the rocking ship. The jagged broken end of the mast crashed through the weakened hull.

Through the deafening roar of the storm, Cooper thought he heard the muffled sound of screams coming from below.

Clusters of bloated cumulonimbus clouds perched far out on the western horizon, bright white against a cerulean sky. The clouds created a boundary between the sky and the sea, reflecting the morning sunlight from the east. Their presence heralded the possibility of rain later in the day, but for now, the sky overhead was clear.

A gentle breeze made its way across the water from the west like the relaxed exhalation of an ancient sea goddess, languidly stretching as she awoke to a new day. Audible only in the soft misting of the crest of the waves, the breeze gradually warmed itself as it continued its persistent journey toward the direction of the sun.

Seabirds traced wild, swirling paths through the sky, vocalizing their endless raucous entreaties. Magnificent frigatebirds, their black feathers reflecting an iridescent purple and green in the sunlight, soared in endless patterns over the water, their wings spread to their full eight or nine feet, their eyes constantly alert to the next morsel to be snatched from the surface. Royal terns would occasionally dive down into the water, reappearing soon after with a small fish clamped in their bills.

The clear turquoise water undulated gently, constantly kneading the white sand of the beach. As it washed back out, it pulled with it a small trickle of blood, which dispersed rapidly, leaving no trace. Another drop fell and merged with the water on the beach, quickly seeping between the grains of sand by capillary action, then was washed away by the next receding wave.

Cutting off the dead iguana's head, the man placed it in the sand as if it were looking skyward. He muttered some ancient words of thanks, then tied the still-bleeding carcass to his belt.

The man was brown and wore only a small skirt-like garment about his hips, and a few feather and bone items which pierced his ears. Long, shiny black hair hung down his back, but was cut straight across over his eyes.

As he looked up, a spark of light caught his eye far out on the distant horizon. Narrowing his eyes under his dark brows, he waited, watching the line between water and sky. A minute later he saw it again. He could not see any details, only the briefest flash of light, then it was gone.

He picked up his bow and slung it over his shoulder, wiped the blade of his knife in the sand and slipped it into its scabbard, and with one more look at the horizon, he turned and vanished into the dense forest.

§

Jax Malone throttled back and the diesel engines quieted down as the *Camilla* continued drifting a little ways under her forward momentum, finally coming to rest, rocking gently on the turquoise waves. North of the Dominican Republic and Puerto Rico, there was nothing but ocean for many miles in all directions.

Using his hand to shade the screen mounted just to the right of the wheel, Jax tried to interpret the shapes that were being outlined on the ocean floor. The image flickered a couple of times, then reappeared, but it was not clear. Jax could still see the image that he saw before, but it was snowy, filled with static.

I'll have to have Ron take a look at the side-scan sonar, he thought with an annoyed sigh, *see if he can find the glitch. It's brand new – it shouldn't be acting up already.*

He took note of what appeared to be rocks and coral, mapping their relative positions to the shapes and shadows he saw in the sand. He glanced at the GPS display and compared the coordinates with the notes he had.

The location is about right.

The GPS flickered too, then displayed an error message.

What the hell? 'Can't find satellite'?

His confusion and irritation were interrupted by a voice behind him.

"What's up, you damn hippie?" Jax looked up and saw Beau Bannister climbing up to the bridge. He often called Jax a hippie, or some variation, as Jax liked to wear his hair longer, in contrast to the military issue crew cut that Beau still wore. Jax usually ignored it.

"Not sure," Jax replied, "but I think I may have found something. Have a look."

Beau looked at the screen, shading it from the bright sunlight as Jax had done just a moment before. Again, the image flickered, then became somewhat clearer. Beau stood up quickly, almost as if he were shocked, and looked at Jax.

"What the hell was that?" Beau asked.

"I don't know," Jax said. "It's been doing that."

Beau bent over again and studied the image for a few seconds. He glanced up at Jax with a sardonic grin, then looked back at the screen, shaking his head.

"I think you're just a little too enamored with your new toys."

"Oh, come on," said Jax. "You can't see anything?"

"I don't know. If there *is* anything there, it's pretty much buried."

"Well sure, but that's usually the case. What do you think of this?" Jax pointed to a series of faint lines on the display.

"It's kind of hard to tell through the static. But I suppose these parallel lines *do* look a little too regular and evenly spaced to be a natural structure," Beau admitted.

"Yeah, that's what I thought. Let's go take a look."

"You're the boss, boss."

Jax dropped anchor, then they went below to the main deck where the others were gathered. The boat, formerly a Navy supply vessel, had been drastically modified to accommodate vast research and laboratory areas. So far, much of it was still unused.

But Jax had made sure that there was a comfortable living area as well, and the rest of his small crew was relaxing there.

Brit Malone was Jax's sister, a pretty blonde sitting sideways in her chair, with her shapely legs dangling over the left arm. She was wearing a bikini, a wrap skirt and flip-flops, and was reading a *Smithsonian* magazine.

Sitting at his work area was Ron, a geeky young man with his head buried in his laptop computer. His hair, as usual, was disheveled, not really styled at all, but just sort of there. It was as if Ron had more important things to think of. He didn't have time to waste on styling his hair.

Then there was Allie, an attractive brunette who assiduously hid her looks behind her large, out-of-style plastic-rimmed glasses and her oversized, baggy clothes, usually including a pair of cargo pants with lots of pockets. She wasn't quite disheveled, like Ron usually was, but just seemed to like to be considered one of the guys.

"Arr, why have we stopped, Cap'n?" asked Brit, squinting one eye closed and badly imitating pirate speech she had heard in a movie. Jax took a moment to sneer at her before answering her question.

"Beau and I are going down to have a look at something. We may have found a wreck and we just want to check it out."

"Cool," she responded, as she cast a smile and a lingering glance toward Beau.

"Ron," Jax said, "the sonar was flickering a little bit earlier, and I was getting errors on the GPS. Can you see if you can find anything wrong?"

"Sure, boss," Ron replied distractedly. Finally, he pulled his attention away from his laptop. "I've been having some trouble with my computer too. I can't seem to stay connected to the internet."

"Well, Ron, we *are* in the Bermuda Triangle," said Allie, trying to hide her smile. "The aliens are probably blocking your signal."

Ron looked at her for a moment as if he might be seriously considering the possibility. Jax and Beau smiled and shook their heads as they continued on their way back to the stern of the vessel and donned their scuba gear, picked up metal detectors, then slipped into the clear water.

§

The man and two of his friends gathered on the beach, looking northward. Like their friend, they were nearly naked, wearing only a small skirt-like garment, their brown skin decorated extensively with intricate tattoo designs and piercings. They muttered between themselves, punctuating their conversation with shakes of their heads. Though they scanned the horizon, they saw nothing.

The first man seemed unhappy with what the others were saying. He gesticulated wildly as he spoke, his voice raised in exasperation. He left the group, selected a particularly upright palm tree and easily climbed to the top. From there, swaying slightly just beneath the fronds, he looked out to sea.

He called down to his companions. They looked up at him as he described what he saw, though even from there, it was still just a faint dot on the horizon. They turned back to the sea, trying to see what he described but, the sun having moved since the first man sighted it, it was just out of reach.

The two men on the beach turned toward each other, discussing what should be done as their companion rejoined them. While they each apparently had different opinions, they reached an agreement, then turned toward the forest and disappeared into the foliage.

§

The water was as clear as glass. Convoluting reflections of sunlight rippled across the sand from the surface of the sea, only about thirty feet above, unusually shallow for this area.

Faint, ghostly images of Mahi-mahi and blue marlin could occasionally be seen in the distant deeper waters. Several yards away, shimmering schools of silvery bar jack glittered back and forth, while up close, brilliantly colored chromis and damselfish curiously inspected the two divers heading downward from the boat.

Jax could see the rocks and coral formations that he had noted on the sonar screen and using those landmarks, quickly located the slight ridges in the sand. He and Beau first looked around the area for any exposed relics, and finding none, began sweeping the site with the metal detectors.

They found a few heavily encrusted metal items just below the seabed and gathered them into a nylon mesh bag for later study. After this, they approached the ridges in the sand that they had seen on the sonar image. The ridges looked like little more than ripples in the sand, casting only the slightest of shadows in the morning sunlight, but to their practiced eye, they knew there was something below the surface. As Beau had observed, they were too evenly spaced to be a natural occurrence.

They brushed away some of the sand, then fanned the area with their hands which caused the grains of sand to become waterborne and move out of the area as if blown by a wind. Within a minute, they had exposed an old, disintegrating timber.

Jax looked up at Beau and, in spite of the regulators in their mouths, they both grinned. They repeated their motions in adjacent areas, exposing more rotted timbers, gradually moving to their sides, separating and spreading out their enterprise in opposite directions. By the time they had nearly depleted their oxygen, they could see a sizable portion of the ribs of an old ship.

Just as they were about to leave the area, Jax noticed a dark crusty shape partially buried in an area he had just exposed. He paused and repeated his previous movements to free it from the sand. It was nearly four feet long and five to six inches in diameter. Though all he could see was corrosion and mineral deposits, he knew it was still too straight to be natural and that there could be something inside that could help them determine the identity of the ship. It was too large to go into the bag with the other relics, so with the object in hand, he and Beau headed back toward the surface.

As they surfaced, Brit was waiting for them with towels on the diving platform at the stern of the boat. She helped them up onto the platform and out of their tanks.

"What did you find?" she asked.

"There's definitely a ship down there," Beau responded. "But it's not in very good shape. What's left of the timbers is pretty delicate."

"Yeah," Jax added. "It's been down there a long time, which is encouraging. It could be what we're looking for. But the water here is relatively shallow, compared with the surrounding seabed, so it may have been beaten and sandblasted by a lot of storms and rough seas before finally being buried." He picked up the bag and the long, crusty mass that he found. "I did find these, though. Why don't you see what you can find inside."

"Sure," she said, and she took the things from him and headed toward her lab space.

"So, what do you think?" Jax asked, looking at Beau.

"I don't know," he responded. "I didn't see any sign of gold, but it could be buried fairly deep where the ship's hold used to be. Or, being as shallow as it is here, it's possible that somebody already found the wreck and stripped anything of value before we ever came along. Or that it was scattered by storms over the centuries."

"You think it could be the *Maria del Gracia*?"

Beau shrugged and shook his head. "I don't know, you damn hippie," he said with a smile. "That's more Brit's department; or yours. You're the history geeks. I'm just the salvage guy."

"Maybe I'll get on my computer and have a look in the library, compare what we know about her with what we saw down below," Jax said as he stood up and finished drying off.

Beau followed him up onto the main deck where everyone was busy in their respective work areas. Jax settled in his chair and woke up his computer, while Beau headed toward Brit's area. He had been noticing her attention toward him lately and was feeling a similar attraction to her.

He came up behind her as she was working and tried to focus his attention on what she was doing, looking over her shoulder. But his eyes kept being drawn down to her breasts, covered only by her skimpy bikini top. He playfully poked her in the shoulder with his finger, and she smiled up at him, pushing him back with the same shoulder. Then she directed her attention back to her work.

As she worked with a combination of solvents and her arsenal of precision power tools, she carefully dislodged the majority of the crust of deposits from the long object that Jax had found. Beau whistled as a large chunk of crust came off in one piece and he saw what was inside.

"Jax, come have a look," Brit said.

Jax and the others got up and crowded around. On her table in front of her, still partly encrusted in the mineral deposits, were the remains of a musket.

"The wooden stock has long since disintegrated," she explained, "but the barrel and the wheel-lock firing mechanism are still in relatively good condition."

"Nice work," Jax commented. "Do you happen to know anything about it?"

"Not yet," she said, "but give me a little while."

The crew began dispersing back to their respective work areas.

"Well, good luck. I still haven't been able to connect to the internet," Jax said.

He turned and looked at their resident geek who had gone back to his computer where he was listening to assorted, seemingly unrelated sounds. Ron had been working on a side project, involving the relationship between various dissonant and harmonic sounds, and their effects on human listeners. This usually resulted in the irritation of his impatient coworkers who were frequently asked how the sounds made them feel.

Ron was often surprised that "annoyed" was the most frequent response.

"Ron, have you had a chance to check out the equipment yet?"

"Yeah, boss," Ron replied without looking up. "I checked them both out. There's nothing wrong with them."

"What the hell do you mean, 'there's nothing wrong with them?' They're not working."

"We were talking about that while you and Beau were diving," Allie said as she settled down behind her computer. "I've got the beginnings of a theory about what's going on.

"We're very near where the southern edge of the Atlantic tectonic plate rubs against the Caribbean plate. I've read reports from several sources who have discovered and studied electromagnetic phenomena related to tectonic activity along these joints. Since there's apparently nothing wrong with the electronics, with the machines themselves, maybe they're just being affected by EMF interference."

"EMF interference from amorous tectonic plates?" Beau asked.

"That seems kind of science fiction-y to me," said Jax.

"I know," Ally said, "it sounds farfetched, but it *is* an effect that has been studied by numerous scientists. Maybe it's a harbinger of some kind of seismic event or something."

"An electromagnetic field *can* disrupt electronic activity," Ron confirmed, finally allowing his attention to focus fully on the conversation. "Whatever's causing this, the good news is that at least it's not affecting the equipment itself, just communications – your sonar, the radio, the internet. But the computers themselves still work."

"Which means you can still access all the information in our database," Allie said, "since that's right here on the ship's server."

"Well, that's better than nothing," Jax said as he headed back toward his work area. "Brit, let me know if you find out anything about that gun."

"Will do," she responded. Everyone settled back down in their work areas and busied themselves in their respective tasks.

§

Jax had begun assembling this team a few years before, though the setting was decidedly different. Working from a 45-foot pleasure cruiser, the equipment had been relatively old and the accommodations cramped. But despite the comparatively humble beginnings, he had come from a somewhat privileged background.

Born thirty-eight years ago to a conservative upper-middle-class family in Boston, Jaxon Malone was seldom in want of anything.

His parents, Everett and Barbara, had their fingers in several pies and worked together in their various business ventures. That often involved traveling around the country, engaging in business meetings with accountants, executives and other button-down types, something that bored Jax to tears. So it was to be expected that he took his life in a completely different direction from theirs.

Jax's sister, Britannia, was born when he was seven years old, and despite their difference in age, they were close and often found themselves interested in many of the same things. So it was no surprise to anyone that a major milestone in their lives occurred at the same time.

Their family had taken a week to visit Jax and Brit's grandfather, Josiah Malone, the last keeper of the Fairhaven Light, on the southern coast of Massachusetts. The Coast Guard was soon going to be taking over the lighthouse, as they had others along the New England coast, and within a couple of years, the lighthouse would be completely automated. But that week that they spent with him was a changing point in their lives.

Formerly a sailor, Josiah Malone was a colorful, crusty old character. The stories that he had related to them in his vivid way had ignited something, in Jax particularly. The exciting and romantic – though likely embellished – historical tales of danger and shipwrecks, of lives saved and valuables lost, related in a way that breathed life into long-dead characters, were ultimately what led Jax to pursue a career in shipwreck hunting.

Frequent trips to the library continued to fuel his fascination with history, especially early American history. Besides the hardy settlers who crossed a vast ocean to come and settle a new and unknown land, he found he had an even greater interest in those who were already here, the first Americans. As a boy, he was enthralled by imagining the everyday lives of the natives who lived and died there long before white people ever showed up and drastically changed their way of life.

Graduating high school a year early, his further education included a history major, a couple of years at MIT and some post-graduate work at Woods Hole Oceanographic Institution, as well as a few other scattered programs. Brit followed him a few years later with similar studies.

Diving was one of his greatest passions, and he demonstrated a real facility with it, even without an air tank.

On one occasion during his time at Woods Hole, while snorkeling with friends, Jax came upon what looked like a silver coin in a cramped, narrow space in some rocks. He could not reach it with his mask and snorkel on, and even after removing them, and examining the space to be sure there was nothing dangerous lurking within, it took him quite a while to get into the area. His efforts were rewarded with the discovery that the coin was in fact just a discarded wad of aluminum foil partially buried in sand.

When he finally surfaced, he was surprised to find that his friends were in a panic, thinking that he had drowned. After this, at their encouragement, he dabbled in freediving, and while he found that he didn't enjoy the experience enough to pursue it as an avocation, he did set an unofficial free immersion record of 122 meters in a dive time of 4 minutes and 20 seconds. He enjoyed the adulation of his peers, but the experience did little more for him.

After graduation, Jax acquired a job on a research vessel working out of Woods Hole, and gained experience while mapping and studying the ocean floor. Al-though the purpose and direction of the research did not interest him much, he could foresee its application in hunting for shipwrecks. So while working his job, in the back of his mind, he was already assembling his own crew.

Beau Bannister was working at Woods Hole at the same time that Jax was, but had come from a much more humble background. Born and raised in Joplin, Missouri in the early seventies, his mother was single, his home life was destitute and the conditions often quite squalid.

His parents, Jenny and Joe, were high school sweethearts. They had quickly and impulsively gotten married a couple of weeks before Joe shipped out to Vietnam.

Jenny thought it was romantic being married to a soldier who was away defending his country. The romance, however, was lost on Joe who spent a year in combat, but then during a two week leave he returned home for a visit. Jenny got pregnant, and this visit home turned out to be Joe's last. Just a few days after his return, he was killed in Cambodia. Beau was born just over eight months after his father's death.

His impoverished childhood proved to be an uncomfortable ordeal to say the least. His mother, being unskilled, worked a long string of low-paying jobs, sometimes two or three at a time, which barely paid the bills. Though she accepted welfare programs for which she was qualified, Jenny was nevertheless conscientious about working and providing for her small family, and this meant that Beau spent much of his time with a babysitter, or by himself when he was older.

Jenny eventually remarried, but not until Beau was in his teens. Having apparently been influenced by her discipline, Beau was conscientious himself, and he did reasonably well in school, but even better in sports.

His route to the east coast had been somewhat meandering. First of all, he acquired a football scholarship for college in Houston, Texas, where he discovered an interest in diving. He followed his college time with numerous and assorted odd jobs along the Gulf coast, many of which required diving experience.

He spent a year in Tampa, Florida, working for a marine salvage company, before he heard from a coworker about a position opening up at Woods Hole, Massachusetts for an underwater salvage expert. With a referral from his supervisor and some brazen self-promotion, he got the job. He moved there in January and immediately commenced complaining about the cold.

Beau's expertise in underwater salvage was one that Jax knew would come in handy should he get his business off the ground. They had become good friends there and had remained so afterward.

Though Jax had become more liberal, polarized from his Republican parents, Beau remained true to his conservative roots. Coming from a more destitute background, too, Beau's interest in shipwreck hunting often leaned more toward fiscal remuneration, while Jax was more concerned with historical enlightenment and preservation. This difference of opinion admittedly resulted in numerous arguments between them, but still their friendship persisted.

One late summer morning in 2001, Everett and Barbara Malone were involved in meetings with a company in New York City whose business involved offshore oil drilling. They had asked Jax to join them, to lend his thoughts and expertise, but he had begged off, saying that he knew little to nothing about drilling.

The truth was it just didn't interest him. In fact, it bored him like most of the business they were involved in. Besides that, having witnessed more oil spills than he cared to recall, he wanted nothing to do with offshore drilling.

So he made his excuses, boarded his sailboat and went sailing out of Boston Harbor.

It was on that beautiful sunny Tuesday morning that a group of radical Muslims from Saudi Arabia overtook two airplanes out of Boston, crashing them into the World Trade Center in New York, the very building where his parents were having their meeting. Brit, having remained closer to her parents than Jax had, was living at home as she completed her studies in Boston when this happened.

By the time Jax came ashore, Brit had already spent the majority of the day immersed in a major panic attack.

He spent the following days with her, trying to keep her calm, reminding her to take the antidepressant and antianxiety medications that her doctor had prescribed, and trying to acquire conclusive information about his parents. After they had not contacted him on the first day, though, he was already sure that they were dead.

In severity, the survivor's guilt that afflicted Jax rivaled Brit's anxiety and depression. He knew that he was supposed to have been at that meeting with his parents, but blew them off instead. Jax and Brit each endured months of medical and psychiatric treatment, supporting each other in their troubles, and growing closer than ever.

Beau reacted to the terror attack in a much different way than Jax did. Enlisting in the Navy less than two days later, he excelled in his training, eventually becoming a Navy SEAL with special training in demolitions.

He had served nearly three years when he was wounded by shrapnel from a grenade in Afghanistan, with several fragments lodged in his lower back and legs. Some of the fragments were removed before he was flown back to the states, where he underwent additional surgeries in Maryland. By the time he began the extensive rehabilitation therapies, his discharge papers had arrived.

Beau arranged to be transferred to Boston, so he could be closer to the friends that he had left there. He suffered some nerve damage from the wounds and rehabilitation was slow and painful, but with the encouragement and support of his friends, he made progress.

Jax and Brit, weighed down by their depression, had allowed themselves to become isolated shortly after the attacks. It was only with the help of friends and family that they began a gradual reintegration into society, battling constantly against the guilt and despair.

When the siblings *did* go out, it was usually just for small gatherings in the homes of others for quiet evenings.

Occasionally they yearned for a night on the town as they used to enjoy, but small doses seemed to be more than enough. Together, they had inherited almost the entire family fortune, but given their now quieter lifestyle, even after over three years, the fortune remained intact.

The first time Beau saw Jax after returning to the states, he hugged him.

"I'm sorry I wasn't here for you, man," he said.

"You did what you had to do," Jax replied simply. He was happy to see his friend again, but the happiness was tempered with a deep sadness lingering just below the surface.

Beau, recovered now from his wounds, soon found Jax and Brit's quieter lifestyle boring and encouraged them to go for excursions on their boat. Since it was a somewhat isolated activity, it was fairly easy to convince them. Reigniting Jax's old love of history and shipwrecks, they eventually began doing research about lost treasures and started going out in his cruiser, coming up with theories and investigating them.

Their first outings were weekend trips, and it was little more than a hobby. But as they focused more on research, with their combined efforts, within a month they found their first wreck. It was a sailboat that had gone down fifty years before off the coast of New York, and while it was not a glamorous or lucrative find, still it sustained their enthusiasm until their next find.

They began attracting attention when they discovered the remains of a British frigate that was sunk during the American Revolution. Due to a fortuitous combination of physical circumstances, the ship was in relatively good condition. With funding from individual members of the Royal

Historical Society in England, a conglomeration of other vessels, and with the help of some of Beau's salvage contacts, they were able to raise and reconstruct the framework of the ship, along with twenty of the cannons and various other arms and miscellaneous items.

As their reputation grew, they were able to add more advanced equipment to their arsenal, at which time they began hiring Ron Rushby on an as-needed basis, to keep their electronics in top working order. An MIT alum, he was trying to start his own electronics consulting business, but though he was brilliant with technology, he was struggling since he was not much of a businessman.

Jax had met Allie Worthington at Woods Hole, and she had a deep interest in marine archaeology too, with a background in oceanography and tectonics. Jax knew that her enthusiasm and area of expertise could help them a great deal in their searches, and she joined the crew after about a year.

Working was difficult in the cramped spaces of his old pleasure cruiser, so Jax decided that it was time to upgrade when he found and purchased the former Navy vessel in Miami. The boat was fast, stable and had plenty of work space, both on deck and below. In fact, the boat could accommodate a much larger crew than his current little group, so they had plenty of room to grow.

Jax closely supervised the customization of the boat, adding all the technology that he thought they might ever need. This included a small mainframe computer, which he immediately started filling with the data that they had already accumulated up until then. It was at this time that Ron joined them full-time.

They christened the boat *Camilla*, after an Amazon queen in Roman mythology, famous for her speed and for her ability to run across the water. This was *Camilla's* first outing with her new crew and new trappings, and while Jax was not happy that their communications systems were already experiencing problems, he was consoled by the fact that it was because of external influences rather than hardware or software malfunctions.

From Miami, they headed southeast to break in the equipment with a project north of Puerto Rico and the Dominican Republic. Using money from a research grant, a professor at the University of Miami had hired them to look into a theory he was developing about the possible location of an eighteenth century Spanish ship that had disappeared somewhere in the Caribbean.

Studying a combination of current and tide charts, weather history and local oceanographic characteristics, and backtracking to the date that the *Maria del Gracia* was thought to have disappeared, he wanted an area examined for wreckage and treasure, as the ship was supposed to have been loaded with gold from Veracruz. That they had found wreckage on their first day examining the assigned grid was either a testament to the accuracy of the professor's studies, or an incredible coincidence.

§

"It's not the *Maria del Gracia*," Brit said. Jax got up from his chair and went to her workspace. She positioned the musket where he could see it better. "I continued cleaning the musket and was able to clear off a lot more of the encrustation. I was able to identify the gun itself. It's an arquebus."

"Arquebus?" Jax echoed.

"Yeah, it's an early form of musket. The arquebus originally had a matchlock firing mechanism."

"I've heard the term matchlock," Allie said from her work area, "but what is it?"

Brit turned to address her, and the others who were also listening.

"A matchlock gun had a smoldering fuse or 'match-cord' attached to it to ignite the powder. This, as you might imagine, had a number of disadvantages. Damp weather, for instance, made it difficult to light the match or to keep it lit. Also, when using it in night-time combat, the smoldering match could potentially be seen by the enemy, or even smelled, giving away the gunman's position."

At this point, Beau spoke up to contribute to the conversation.

"Not to mention the danger of having a lit match around gunpowder. When a soldier had to refill his powder horn, he had to be extremely careful about where his gun was in relation to the powder store."

"Right," Brit continued. "But in the latter half of the sixteenth century, the arquebus started being made with a wheel-lock mechanism, which used a friction wheel to ignite the powder." She picked up the relic. "That's what this is."

"Okay," Jax said, "so this is from the late fifteen hundreds."

"Right. And I'm pretty sure it's English-made."

"Hmm," Jax pondered. "Well, I guess finding the Spanish treasure ship in the first few hours would have been too much of a coincidence. And way too easy."

"Well, there's more," Britt added. She turned the barrel of the arquebus to show Jax the other side of the breech. There was an engraving of an ornate set of letters surrounded by a delicate leaf design.

"AD?" Jax read.

"Yeah, I don't know if it's part of a date, or initials or something else altogether. Could mean anything," Brit said, rubbing her fingers lightly over the engraving. "I just haven't figured out that part yet."

"Well, it's a start. And at least we already know that this isn't the wreck we were sent to find."

"So where does that leave us?"

"It leaves us with a footnote for a personal project. We know that there's a wreck we can investigate after we've finished this job. But for now, we have to continue looking for the *Maria del Gracia.*" He sighed. "I guess we better get started." With that, Jax turned and went above to continue examining the grid.

He went to the bridge and was about to start the engines when he saw something in the distance. He watched patiently as the boat rocked gently on the waves, and as it rose on the crest of a wave, he saw, to the south, what appeared to be an island. He puckered his brows in confusion. The nearest land he knew of was the Turks and Caicos, nearly two hundred miles to the west.

He pulled up the charts for the area on the bridge computer from the database, confirming what he was already certain of. Nothing but open ocean. He found his binoculars and looked through them toward the island. He could not see much detail, but he could see that it was heavily forested with a low mountainous area in the center.

Still at a loss, he went back down to the communal lab area. Ron was still there, puzzling out something on his laptop.

"Ron, is there any chance that the GPS could have given us an incorrect location?"

"Not likely," Ron said, scratching the side of his head as he pondered the possibility. "I checked it earlier, and it was having trouble staying connected to the satellites. That could prevent it from providing coordinates, but I don't see how it could give *false* coordinates. Why?"

"To the south of us is an island where there should be open water. I checked the charts and there's not supposed to be anything to the south until the Dominican Republic."

"Well, let's go investigate," said Beau. "Maybe we can have a luau tonight."

"Right," Jax replied sardonically as he walked back toward the stairs up to the bridge. "I don't know if you've noticed, Magellan, but we're in the wrong ocean for a luau."

Beau, Allie and Ron followed him up to the bridge while Brit continued working at her table. Jax pointed ahead and as they rocked up again on the crest of a wave, they saw the island.

While Ron checked the instruments again, Jax carefully took down an old-looking brass device that was hung securely on the wall, and he went outside to the railing.

"I thought that was just for decoration," said Beau. "You actually know how to use that thing?"

"Yes, I do," Jax replied. "My grandfather taught me how to use this sextant. He used it during World War II. He left it to me when he died."

Jax sighted through the device's telescope, then moved the arm until the reflected image of the sun lined up evenly with the horizon. As soon as he finished taking his sightings, he made note of the time and came back inside and looked at the charts, comparing it with the readings he had taken on the instrument.

"Well, I'm no master with a sextant, but as close as I can tell, these readings match the coordinates on the GPS." He looked again toward the island and shook his head. "I didn't think there were any uncharted islands left anymore."

Beau had been looking up something else on the computer as Jax was taking his readings. "This could *partly* explain it," he said, pointing to a map with numerous overlapping lines of various colors. "I was curious about the location of shipping lanes in relation to the island. Looking at this map, it doesn't appear to be near any. Based on that, I suppose it's conceivable that it could have avoided detection for this long."

"Well yeah, but satellites have pretty much mapped the entire globe. How could a satellite photo miss this?"

"I don't know, boss," said Ron. "Maybe it has something to do with those wonky EMF conditions we've been experiencing."

"I suppose," said Jax distractedly.

"Do you think there might be dinosaurs on that island?" Ron asked, straining to see the island better. When everyone looked at him in disbelief, he got defensive. "What? That's really not so farfetched. I'm just saying that, isolated from other land masses and human interference, it might be possible. There could be a little evolutionary pocket there."

"Sure," Allie replied, "and a giant gorilla who gets a virgin every full moon."

"I imagine *those* are becoming kind of rare by now," Beau said with a crooked grin. "Virgins, I mean, especially on a little island like this."

"Let's go check it out," Jax said.

§

It only took a few minutes to raise anchor, move closer to the island and drop anchor again. Now that they could see the island up close, they were impressed by its unspoiled beauty. There was a long, white sand beach stretching out in both directions, backed up by a dense jungle. That lush forest climbed part of the way up the hills, terminating a short distance below the largest peak, perhaps two thousand feet high.

"It's beautiful!" said Brit, who had joined everyone else on deck. "You know, it's kind of late in the afternoon. Why don't we pick up scanning the grid for the *Maria del Gracia* tomorrow?"

"Good idea," said Allie. "Let's relax and build a fire. We can have an early dinner on the beach. What do you say, boss?"

"Fine with me," Jax said. "I wanted to see this up close anyway. I've never discovered an uncharted island before."

In just a matter of minutes, they had transported what they needed for the evening in their inflatable hulled Zodiac and had set up a camp on the beach. Jax and Beau had gathered dead wood from the fringes of the forest and got a blazing fire going.

Ron had a collection of music stored on his phone and had hooked up a small speaker to play it. Brit and Allie busied themselves with getting some swordfish steaks ready to grill over the open fire.

Beau took a swig of beer and then smiled when the next song started playing.

"Mary Jane's Last Dance!" he said enthusiastically.

"Tom Petty and the Heartbreakers!" Jax added.

Brit looked at them and shook her head as if she didn't know what the fuss was about.

"This song was on the charts when we were just starting at Woods Hole," Beau explained. "Kim Basinger was in the video. Jax kind of had a thing for her."

"Yeah, you did too, as I recall," Jax replied.

"She was hot!" Beau shrugged and made a face as if that explained it all. "Of course, she was dead, but she was still hot!" The others laughed, but Jax and Beau were both quiet as the song played and they nostalgically listened to the churning guitars and harmonica. As it faded out, a reggae beat began and they heard *"I Can See Clearly Now,"* by Jimmy Cliff.

"Hey, I remember this one too, and also from Woods Hole," Jax said as he looked at Ron.

"All this music is from 1994," Ron replied.

"You keep all your music categorized by year?" Beau teased. "Can you get any geekier?"

"Leave him alone, guys," Brit said. "You know Ron can find any file on his computer or online faster than the rest of us combined." Closing and snapping the metal baskets around the seasoned steaks, she looked at Beau and said, "Why don't you make yourself useful?" Her tone was serious, but the flirty look in her eyes made Beau smile as he got up to arrange the steaks over the fire.

"You know, I could get used to this," Allie said. "The warm breeze, the beautiful, clear water, the white sand. Good discovery, Jax. I heartily approve." He smiled in response and raised his bottle of beer toward her in a toast.

"I hereby claim this island," he said in his most comically officious-sounding voice, "and I shall christen it Jaxonville."

"That's kind of already taken," Allie laughed.

"You're right. How about Malonetown?"

"Well, it doesn't quite roll off the tongue as easily as Jaxonville, but if it's here, I think I could learn to live with it."

"Better not let word get out," Beau said sarcastically. "A few other people might come and enjoy it. Might mar its unspoiled beauty."

"I didn't say I was going to tell anybody about it yet," Jax replied. "Who knows what there is to discover here."

"Yeah, God forbid somebody might be able to make a little money from discovering a new island. Sure can't have that."

"Not at the risk of the discovery itself," Jax said, feeling the indignation rising.

"Alright, you two," Brit interrupted. "Let's not spoil our time here, okay?" Jax and Beau looked at each other, both still simmering in their annoyance. "We already know your respective opinions, so you don't have to share them with us yet again." Jax and Beau smarted under the scolding, but they let it go.

Allie, in a meek voice, looked over at Brit and changed the subject. "Is there time for a swim before dinner?"

"A short one," Brit replied. "The steaks will be ready in a few minutes."

With a nod, Allie stood up and pulled off her baggy T-shirt and cargo pants, revealing a fair-skinned, shapely body in a swimsuit. She slipped the sandals off of her feet, placed her plastic-rimmed glasses on top of her clothes and ran toward the water.

Jax, his irritation suddenly gone, watched her retreating figure with a bit of surprise and fascination. Allie would never dive with them, saying that scuba and claustrophobia don't mix well. She even coined a word for it: claustroscubia. She was happiest plying her specialties of marine archeology, oceanography and tectonics using her electronic equipment from the safety of the boat.

Jax had only seen her in her baggy wardrobe and glasses. He was startled, now, to see this attractive nymph splashing into the water. He found himself intrigued, wanting to get to know her better, but then he silently rebuked himself for being so shallow that it was only the discovery of her physical appearance that had awakened that feeling in him.

Still, he watched with interest as she swam through the waves a few yards out from the beach.

The swordfish steaks were grilled perfectly, the corn on the cob was juicy and sweet, and Brit and Beau had concocted a quick and easy Mai Tai which everyone loved. They were busy mixing up another batch as *Breathe Again* started playing over the speaker.

"I loved Toni Braxton's voice," Allie said as she smiled at the memory.

"Would you like to dance?" Jax asked her. Allie was surprised out of her reverie, at least as surprised as Jax himself was, but she accepted his offer. They stood and began a slow dance in the sand. Brit and Beau exchanged surprised glances as well.

Allie had liked Jax for as long as she had known him, and more recently had begun feeling a deeper attraction. As his employee, however, she had been apprehensive about broaching the subject. She also feared his rejection.

Allie had always known that she possessed some attractive qualities, but had never exploited them, enhanced them, or even allowed herself to recognize their value. She had endured an unhappy childhood in Portland, Oregon, raised by a cold, demeaning mother and a weak milquetoast of a father. Over time, the frequent criticism from her mother gradually caused her to withdraw into numerous "safe zones."

While growing up, those safe zones included her schooling, and she excelled in most subjects. When she graduated from high school, without consciously planning to, she chose one of the most distant colleges she could find, ending up in Boston, followed by Woods Hole. But though she managed to escape from her overbearing mother, she took with her the emotional scars and the safe zones that had become part of her psyche so many years before.

In her adult life, her safe zone was bounded by her total immersion in her continued schooling, then her secular work, and by a protective layer of figure-hiding clothing. She didn't like to be noticed and often seemed embarrassed when she was. Shedding her inhibitions an hour before with her clothing had been uncomfortable at first, but also oddly freeing.

She was wearing her glasses again, but had not put her baggy clothing back on. As they slow danced in the sand, their bare thighs would often touch. That, and being held close to Jax, his hand on her bare back, were causing some intriguing feelings within her.

But the idyllic surroundings of a tropical island, the sun slowly going down in the west turning the sky a million shades of orange and crimson, the soft whisper of the waves on the sand – it was like paradise, and Allie didn't want this to end. She was actually feeling comfortable being herself for the first time in her adult life. She leaned against Jax, put her head on his shoulder and sighed.

As the song ended, she opened her eyes and looked at Jax. He was smiling at her. "Thank you," they said simultaneously.

Directly behind him, in the forest, a movement caught her eye.

"What is it?" Jax asked when he heard her sharp intake of breath. He felt her stiffen in his arms and the startled look on her face made him turn and look behind him.

Beau and Brit had also noticed, and they all gathered closer together.

A man with medium brown skin was slowly emerging from the forest, and shortly they saw others with him. Many of them had impressive tattoo markings, and all were armed with bows and arrows. Ron unplugged the speaker and turned off the music.

"Hello," called Jax apprehensively, putting one hand up, trying to appear unthreatening. He had turned toward them and, with his hand on her hip, had unconsciously placed Allie behind him, shielding her with his own body.

"Jax," Beau said, "do you know of any kind of protocol for this?"

"No, I don't," Jax replied quietly. "But they just seem curious. Maybe they've never seen white people before. Let's just try to be friendly and we can be on our way. Let's slowly pack up our things and get back on the *Camilla*."

"Works for me," Brit said.

The first native spoke, waving his bow.

"I don't suppose anybody understands what he said?" Beau asked. Everybody silently shook their heads.

The man began speaking again, and seemed more impatient or irritable.

Ron, curious about the language, saw the possibility of its addition into his private sound project. He found and tapped an icon on his phone, starting up a recording app, to get some samples of the speech for later study. He quietly stood and, positioning himself in the space between the two couples, held the phone out in front of himself, to record what the man was saying.

When the native saw the glowing thing in Ron's hand, he stopped. In fact, all of the natives stopped and were looking at the glowing phone. A few of them looked at each other with expressions of wonder, others with trepidation.

Suddenly without warning, almost before anybody could see the motions of the first native, he pulled back the arrow and let it go. There was a moist cracking sound as Ron fell down onto the sand with an arrow through his chest.

Allie screamed and pressed closer to Jax. Everyone stared at Ron for a moment in horror.

"You son of a bitch!" Beau yelled at the native. Jax reached out and held Beau's shoulder, trying to keep him from acting rashly.

"Take it easy, Beau. We're unarmed."

Allie knelt down beside Ron, hoping he was still alive, but the bloody arrowhead protruding from his back, and his complete stillness, seemed to suggest otherwise.

"Okay, everyone," Jax said quietly, his voice quivering as he struggled to remain calm. "Let's gather up our things and get out of here."

The natives were pressing closer now, and were nearly surrounding them.

"Hey, Jax," said Beau, "I don't think we're going anywhere."

Jax followed Beau's gaze behind them and saw two natives at their Zodiac, knives in their hands. The inflatable hull had been slashed to ribbons.

"Oh my god," Brit whimpered, as she leaned against Beau, watching for any signs of movement from Ron's body lying face down in the sand. When she saw Allie shake her head with tears in her eyes, Brit began to cry, too.

The natives continued advancing upon them and were now surrounding them at a distance of about twenty feet. Some seemed more aggressive than others. The first native was still speaking, and he seemed irritated at Brit's crying. He yelled something at her and waved his bow toward her, and Beau moved between Brit and the native.

The man fitted another arrow to his bowstring and pointed it threateningly toward Beau. Suddenly, two small explosions in quick succession, which Jax recognized as a musket shot, sounded from the forest to the east of them and the threatening native let go of the bowstring as he fell dead. He also let go of the arrow. Though not pulled all the way back, it still sped past Beau, slicing his upper arm before embedding itself in the sand behind them.

With the report of the gun, the remaining natives scattered and disappeared into the dark forest to the southwest.

What came into view next was even more surprising than the primitive natives.

§

The foliage parted and a group of Caucasian men emerged from the forest, dressed in what seemed to be an old style of clothing, and carrying equally old fashioned muskets. They ran toward the visitors on the beach, running in single file, keeping their eyes on the forest where the natives had disappeared, while the man in front separated from the formation.

"Pray, quickly gather thy necessaries," said this man in the lead, speaking with an English accent. "We must away before the Indians return."

Beau looked over at Jax, his face puckered in a tangle of shock and disbelief. The men were closer now, most of them fanning out between the visitors and the forest, their muskets aimed toward the dense jungle, forming a protective barrier should the natives make another appearance. The leader made a beckoning motion with his hand.

"Make haste, man!" he said impatiently.

"Let's go," Jax said with a nod. They left the folding chairs and the cooler in which they had brought their food, but Jax knelt beside Ron and, after checking for a pulse, winced as he broke off the arrowhead and pulled the arrow out from the front. He picked up Ron's body, while Allie, tears trickling down her

48

cheeks, picked up his phone, and then she donned the T-shirt and baggy cargo pants that she had left on the sand.

The sun was very low in the west as the strange group entered the forest, a few errant rays of sunlight following them briefly, before darkness closed in around them. After a few seconds, their eyes adjusted to the dim light from the twilight sky filtering through the foliage overhead, and they had an opportunity to examine their saviors.

The men were dressed in strange clothing that appeared to be a hybrid of tropical plantation and Renaissance era garments, consisting of breeches and vests made of a light brown colored fabric, possibly linen. The breeches, rather than being gathered at the knees as in depictions and artist renderings that Jax and his group had seen before, were worn loose, presumably for greater comfort in the tropical heat. The necks of most of their vests had a somewhat ruffled design, but were worn open. Their shirts with full, billowing sleeves were constructed of a lighter-colored and lighter-weight linen.

The guns they carried resembled old-fashioned muskets, but they looked different somehow, as if modifications in design and manufacture had taken place at some time in the past. Besides the muskets, they were all also armed with swords and daggers, both of which hung from scabbards attached to their belts.

Nearly all of the men wore mustaches and beards, also in an old, but somehow different, style. They all appeared to be in their thirties or forties, though the facial hair made it difficult for Jax's party to tell for certain.

"Where are you taking us?" Beau asked, his left hand clamped over the wound in his upper arm.

"Does it matter?" asked the leader of the group. "Aforetime, thy safety was in question, but now, if we hurry, it is assured."

"Who are you guys?"

"I apologize, good people, that we were unable to make appropriate introductions. However I assure thee, sir, that unfortunate situation shall, without fail, be remedied once we reach the safety of our fortress. Until that time, we must maintain vigilance and quiet."

They continued marching through the forest as the darkness intensified. After a half hour, they could see glimmers of a gibbous moon through the foliage overhead which helped to light their way.

The moonlight, as they moved through the forest, gave a shimmering effect to Ron's pale, upturned face, and Brit found her eyes often fixed on his relaxed expression, and she silently wept. Allie was crying too, and even Jax felt tears welling up at times. He forced himself to not look at Ron, but to keep his eyes straight ahead.

He was beginning to walk unsteadily, stumbling at times under the added weight of Ron's body, and his arms were aching. Just as he was about to ask if they could stop to rest, they emerged into a clearing, the moon fully illuminating the massive structure that rose before them.

Apparently constructed of logs sunk upright in the ground, the base of the fortress was thickly coated with a material that looked like adobe or concrete, but with the upper portion of the logs exposed and sharpened to points.

Dimly lit by torchlight at various points inside along the top of the thirty to forty foot tall structure, were sentinels dressed and armed similarly to their escorts, watching from the platform behind the battlement. There were also cannons every twenty or thirty feet, facing out through gun ports cut in the wall.

As they approached, a large portion of the wall began to open out toward them.

"Maybe that giant gorilla idea wasn't so far-fetched after all," Beau said to Allie, though he immediately regretted making a joke when he saw Allie's tears and Ron's dead body.

The men leading them began to hurry and ushered them inside the fortress, and then toward a building on their left. After they were all inside, the giant gate began to close behind them.

The expansive building they entered seemed to consist primarily of a large room with a few tables, some of which were strewn with maps and other papers. The room, lit by a few lanterns, was paneled with dark wood, and had numerous doors but no windows.

A few men looked up as they entered, momentarily surprised by the commotion, and one man of about fifty-five started toward them. The leader of the troop separated and consulted quietly with him for a moment.

One of the soldiers in their escort put down his musket, opened a door and led them into what appeared to be a barracks, with a row of beds down each wall. He turned to Jax and took Ron's body from him and laid it on a bed, while Jax bent and extended his arms repeatedly to ease the muscle cramps that were developing.

"My humble apologies, gentlefolk, for the mean informality of our meeting," said the man who had come from the main room to greet them. "I bid thee welcome. I am Governor William Payne." The man extended his hand.

"Jax Malone," Jax said, shaking Governor Payne's hand. "This is my sister, Brit, and our friends, Beau Bannister and Allie Worthington."

"I am very pleased to make thy acquaintance," the man said with a slight bow. Then he turned to look down at Ron. "And this poor, unfortunate creature?"

"Ron Rushby," Jax said quietly.

"May God grant him peace and rest." Payne placed a blanket over Ron's body, then turning toward Brit, he appeared nervous and spoke in a hushed tone. "I do apologize for my men's late arrival, and for the indelicateness of this question, but did the savages deprive thee of thy clothing, Miss?"

Brit looked down with some surprise at her wrap skirt and bikini top, then back up at Payne.

"No, I have my clothing." Payne seemed perplexed and was about to make a response but did not get a chance.

"What is this place?" Beau asked as he looked around. "Who are you people?"

"We are humble servants of the Queen," Governor Payne replied, "settled in this place by unhappy circumstance more than four centuries past."

"Servants of Queen Elizabeth?" Brit asked, trying now to focus on something other than Ron's death. "Wait a minute. You said, 'more than four centuries past.' You're talking about Queen Elizabeth the first?"

"How many hath there been?" Payne asked as he focused on her face, attempting to keep his eyes from wandering to all of the skin she was exposing.

"Two, so far."

Payne appeared taken aback by the statement. Shocked, even. He looked around at his men, who also seemed perplexed. But Payne quickly regained his composure.

"I am sorry," he replied. "Though logic dictates that the Queen's life could not have been sustained unto this era, still, it does give us a start to learn of our monarch's certain demise."

"You're not trying to tell us you're over four hundred years old, are you?" Jax inquired of him. Payne smiled, looking askance at him, then chuckled.

"Of course not, sir," he replied. "For a certainty, the selfsame logic that applieth to the Queen applieth no less to us." He became serious again, then continued. "No sir. Rather we are the descendants of those cast upon this shore so long ago."

The door opened and one of the men who had accompanied their group to this place entered the building once again. This time, he was leading another man who carried a small black leather bag with him.

"Ah," said Payne, turning to Beau, "Mr. Bannister, I present to thee Mr. Joseph Howe, our barber. If thou wilt kindly go with him, he will see to thy wound."

"Your barber?" Beau said, keeping his hand clamped tightly over his wound. "Don't you have a doctor?"

"A doctor, sir?" Payne asked, looking bewildered. "Why, doth thou feel ill as well?" Beau himself was now confused and was at a loss as to how to answer. Before the awkward silence continued any longer, Payne continued. "Mr. Howe will stitch up the gash in thy arm, and if afterward thou art still feeling ill, we will happily send for our physician."

Feeling apprehensive, but knowing that the wound needed to be closed, Beau allowed himself to be led to a table where the barber began unpacking the supplies he needed. They both sat down and Howe began working on Beau's arm.

Payne turned his attention back to Jax. "If I may be so bold, sir, thy speech soundeth different. Pray, sir, from whence dost thou hail?"

"Originally we're from Boston, but most recently from Miami," Jax responded. He knew as he said it that it would likely elicit the exact befuddled expression that now appeared on Payne's face.

"Indeed, I hath heard of Boston," Payne said, "a small seaport village in Lincolnshire, on the east coast of England. It is the home town of the forebear of a friend. However, I fear I am not familiar with a place called Miami."

"No, I don't suppose you would be. It's a city on the southern tip of Florida."

"Florida," Payne echoed and shook his head. "It appeareth that much hath transpired of which we are not privy."

"What about you?" asked Allie, wiping her eyes and speaking for the first time since their arrival. "Where are your people from?"

"Our ancestors were English," Payne said, "but came hither from Roonock."

Allie shook her head slightly, but Brit's head snapped up as she looked at him in shock.

"What is it?" asked Jax, noticing her surprise.

"Roonock?" she echoed. She looked at Payne with an incomprehensible expression, resembling shock, Jax thought. Payne looked back at her, apparently as startled by the intensity of her gaze as was Jax.

Then, with a bit of effort, Brit managed to turn from Payne and looked at her brother. "Roonock was the original pronunciation and spelling of Roanoke."

H old on," said Jax, looking at Brit through squinted eyelids. "You can't really be serious. Roanoke? You're talking about the 'lost colony'?"

"That's the one," confirmed Brit.

"What am I missing, guys?" asked Allie. "I know the name 'Roanoke' but what about it? What do you mean, 'lost colony'?"

"Sometime at the end of the sixteenth century," explained Brit, "the English settlement on the island of Roanoke, just off the coast of North Carolina, vanished, almost without a trace."

"Begging thy pardon, Miss," Payne said with a scoffing tone, "but I canst assure thee that it did not simply vanish. We departed, of our own discretion, in June of the year 1590. Art thou saying that our story is known?"

"Only bits and pieces. Nothing is known about what happened to the colony."

"Well, I should be happy to provide some illumination on the subject," Payne said, motioning to the room around them. "The building in which we stand is the Constabulary of our island shire, but it also beareth historical records and documents of times past. If thou wouldst like, I could find pertinent records which could fill in the areas in which thy knowledge is lacking."

"Yes, I *would* like!" Brit said enthusiastically.

"The hour is late and, having endured an ordeal this eve, thou shalt rest and upon my word, I shall relate our tale on the morrow."

§

The fortress was an enormous, fanciful thing, constructed on the extreme eastern side of the island. The original structure had been roughly a seven hundred foot square, but during the passage of many generations, additions and alterations were made, seemingly at random, so that the current haphazardly sprawling complex enclosed nearly twelve square miles of ground.

Though the original structure had been a simple square, the additions were styled after early construction in England, some with stone and some with wattle and daub surface treatments in the Tudor style. So the current colony appeared to be a version of an Elizabethan castle and village, with some buildings rising a few stories, complete with towers and turrets.

Inside the stockade, houses and other buildings had been constructed around trees and rocks that had been allowed to remain, all connected by winding cobblestone streets. What resulted was a quaint, organically arranged village that possessed an old-world storybook aesthetic.

It was more than a village, though. Despite its quaint appearance, the current colony was a small city, and the home of over a thousand people.

The tropical sunrise found the occupants of the new colony of Roanoke up and about, and word had spread quickly about the visitors. They had spent the night in the Constabulary and nobody except those men on duty the night before had actually seen them, but rumors were circulating about them. Some circles of lesser repute spoke leeringly about a blonde woman who walked about with her body shamelessly bared in the presence of all, like one of the heathen Indian women.

Most, though, were simply curious about these newcomers and were anxiously awaiting their appearance in public.

§

"We can't burn Ron's body," Jax protested. "He has family in Rhode Island. We have to take him back to the States."

"I do apologize for the misunderstanding, sir," Payne said. "But the deed hath in fact already been done. I am afraid that we hath not the space in our colony to allot for a burial, and the climate here is such that a corpse keepeth not for long. The body was burned shortly after thy party's arrival last night. It is our custom."

"Well, it's not *our* custom," Jax said indignantly. "It's our custom to return a body to its family."

"Please forgive me," Payne said humbly, placing his hands together under his chin as if he were praying. "Indeed, I should have consulted with thee first before giving the order."

A door opened and Brit and Allie came into the main room. Governor Payne had provided clothing for Brit, and out of respect for the modesty of the locals, she was now wearing a linen shirt over her bikini top and wrap skirt. Though they did not hear the preceding conversation, they could see that Jax was becoming very agitated.

"Look, I appreciate you putting us up here for the night," Jax said, trying to calm down, "and I guess I understand your reasons for cremating Ron so quickly, though I can't say I'm happy about it. But we do have to be on our way. And I promise that we will notify the authorities of your location so you can be rescued."

"I am indeed most appreciative of thy concern, sir. However, I feel obliged to point out that it is quite unlikely that thou shalt be able to return to thy place of origin."

"Why is that?"

"It is doubtful, sir, that thy vessel is still afloat. The Indians do have the curious practice of scuttling any waterborne craft that finds its unlucky way to our shore."

"Why would they do that?" Jax asked with growing trepidation.

"We do not know, sir," Payne said with a shrug. "They are wild savages and their actions are quite beyond any application of logic. Indeed, it is possible that they do it to prevent their victims from being able to escape their evil clutches."

"We need to get our boat!" Jax said firmly.

"But sir," Payne said, becoming agitated himself, "it would be a fruitless undertaking, endangering thy very lives!"

"We can't stay here," Jax said. "If there's any chance at all that the boat is still intact, I need to go get it, now!"

"Very well, sir. Allow me to assemble a guard to accompany thee. As I said, the Indians are savages and will not hesitate to kill thee."

§

They stood on the shore, at the site of their camp from the previous night. Their dishes and the cooler had washed away with the tide, as had the ashes and the unburned wood from their fire. The shredded Zodiac, now partly covered by sand, eased back and forth, weighted down by the motor, as the waves gently washed back out to sea.

The scarlet stain where Ron had fallen dead had been scrubbed away by the tide as well. Except for their vivid memories, there was little sign that anything had transpired here.

The armed guards were arranged between the visitors and the forest, guns at the ready, in a fashion similar to when they had been rescued the previous evening. Looking out to sea, there was nothing to interrupt their view.

The *Camilla* was gone. There was nothing but water for as far as they could see.

"What are we going to do, Jax?" Brit asked quietly, her voice tight, hinting at the fear and anxiety building inside her.

"God, I don't know." He rubbed his face in dismay, still looking seaward as if, somehow, his boat might have just escaped his notice. His life's work, a good deal of the family fortune, not to mention their transport off the island, now lay at the bottom of the ocean.

"Jax, we can't stay here!" Brit said.

"Well it appears we don't have a choice!" he snapped back. "Damn it! We should have taken it last night."

"We couldn't, man," said Beau. "The natives had already killed Ron, deflated our Zodiac and had us surrounded."

"Yeah, but the Indians ran for the forest when the colonists appeared."

"But we didn't know. They could have come back at any time. The men were urging us to get out of here, so we did what we had to do to stay alive."

"You seem particularly blasé about the loss of my boat!" Jax said as he turned quickly toward Beau. He impatiently pushed his hair back out of his eyes and glared at him, his breathing accelerated by his stress level.

"Easy, Jax," Beau said consolingly. "I'm not happy about it either. On the big list of things that suck, this is off the chart! But there's nothing we can do about it now. So I'm just trying to think of any other options."

"What options?"

"I don't know, I just got started. What about building a raft or a boat from materials on the island? I mean, how far is the nearest civilization?"

"Maybe a couple hundred miles to the west," Jax responded, pondering the possibility. "Over open ocean, across the gulf stream, and out of the shipping lanes, as you pointed out yesterday. If we miscalculate in the least, we could miss landfall and be on the water for weeks."

"Okay, so it's not a perfect plan, but it's something to start with. Nothing we can do about the *Camilla* now. She's insured, so if we get out of here, you can collect on her. The point is to get out of here."

"You're right." Jax sighed. "Let's get back." Then he looked down at the remains of the Zodiac. "You know what? If we *are* able to build a seaworthy boat, this motor could come in handy."

"We'll probably have to clean out the sand and salt from overnight," Beau said. "It was probably pretty much covered by the tide, but it's a good start."

He and Jax went to the shredded Zodiac and checked under the back seat. The tool kit was still there and they began disconnecting the outboard motor from the transom, while Brit and Allie kept a wary eye on the jungle.

§

They were back at the Constabulary, in a room at the back which they thought of as the equivalent of a modern day break room. There was a small kitchen behind a stone wall, and a dining room.

Despite their recent losses, they were enjoying a late breakfast of eggs, strips of some kind of fried fish, and a mixture of diced tropical fruits, including pineapple, mango, and some that they did not recognize. They had just begun eating when Payne entered, leading another man.

"My friends, I would like to present to thee my Lieutenant Governor, Mr. Thomas Dare," he said. The man to whom he motioned wore a pious expression on his face and actually bowed toward the newcomers. He seemed to be perhaps sixty-five years old and was dressed similarly to the others. "Mr. Dare is also our resident historian, one whose knowledge would be better able to satisfy thy curiosity about our past than would my own."

"Mr. Dare," said Brit. "Any relation to Virginia Dare?"

"Indeed, miss," he responded with a smile, delighted that Brit would know about Virginia Dare. "I am a direct descendant of her younger brother, William."

"I was not aware that she had a brother."

"Oh, quite so," he nodded. "William was born scarcely a fortnight after our unhappy arrival upon this island."

"Who's Virginia Dare?" asked Beau, apparently feeling left out.

"Virginia Dare was the first English child ever born on American soil," Brit replied, "born to Ananias and Eleanor Dare at Roanoke."

"Maybe you should start off with a brief history of Roanoke," Jax suggested to Dare. "Although my sister seems to know several details concerning your story, the rest of us are not quite as familiar with the history."

"An excellent notion," he agreed. "I would be only too happy to convey to thee that which I have learnt in my studies." He ceremoniously cleared his throat, then continued.

"It was the wish of Queen Elizabeth to establish a permanent colony in the New World, and to that end, she sent an exploratory expedition led by a man named Ralph Lane. This attempt turned out to be largely unsuccessful.

"Our ancestors were a group of people organized by a gentleman named Sir Walter Raleigh, also sent by Queen Elizabeth, in a second attempt to colonize the New World. The result was the colony of Roonock – or Roanoke as thou sayest. They landed in July of 1587, and less than one month thereafter, Eleanor Dare delivered Virginia unto her husband, Ananias.

"But relations with the natives were exceedingly difficult. They had enjoyed good relations with the natives of Croatoan Island, not far away, but the Indians at Roanoke were hostile and made much trouble for them."

"If I recall," Brit interrupted, "they were hostile because shortly before this, one of their villages was destroyed by the white settlers."

"Yes," Dare reluctantly agreed with some embarrassment, "in point of fact, during the expedition in the previous year, there was an incident concerning the theft of a silver cup. As an act of implementing justice, the men under the command of Ralph Lane did indeed sack and burn the village."

"Seems like rather harsh justice to me," Brit said critically.

"Well, be that as it may," Dare continued, apparently eager to change the subject, "the settlers had quite a difficult time of it. Some, in fact, were even killed by the Indians."

"Including George Howe," interjected Payne, looking at Beau, "an ancestor of Joseph Howe, our barber, who closed thy wound last night." Beau nodded.

"Yes," continued Dare. "Well, because they were having such a hard time of it, they were eventually able to persuade John White, the governor of Roanoke, and the father of Eleanor Dare, to return to England to bring back supplies, as well as more settlers to support them in handling the Indians.

"He was reluctant at first, but finally agreed, and he embarked upon his journey back to England a few months after landing there. But those who remained continued to experience quite a difficult time. Unfortunately, White never returned and the settlers, after enduring nearly two years of hardship, began to discuss the options available to them.

"One of those options was to move their settlement to Croatoan Island."

"That's right," Brit interjected. "White left them a pinnace, didn't he?"

"Excuse me?" Beau said with a sneer.

"Get your mind out of the gutter, Navy man," Brit said, rolling her eyes and shaking her head. "A pinnace was a small ship."

Dare seemed confused by their exchange, but then continued. "Yes, indeed he did leave them some smaller craft for the purpose of exploration of the coast, and a pinnace in case they did, in fact, decide to relocate the colony. Moving to Croatoan, it turned out, was the favored solution, and they began readying for this.

"In early June of 1590, they were in good spirits, as they were anticipating a better life. A large number of the colonists were onboard the pinnace, performing various tasks in readying it to set sail for Croatoan, when Indians attacked the colony, inflicting a very great slaughter."

"That's interesting," said Brit turning to Jax. "One of the theories about what happened to the colony is that Powhatan attacked and killed the colonists."

"Powhatan – why does that name sound familiar?" asked Allie.

"Powhatan was an Algonquian chief," Jax answered. "His name is familiar because everybody knows him as the father of Pocahontas."

"Right," Brit continued. "And some records of his later encounter with Captain John Smith report that he admitted to wiping out the Roanoke colonists, even providing proof in the form of some of the colonists' iron implements which they had taken."

"I know naught of these people of whom thou speakest," said Dare. "But some of the colonists had fled and hid in the woods when the Indians attacked, while others were out hunting for meat as they were planning a feast before setting sail for their new settlement. Those who were onboard the ship, or in the surrounding forest, returned to the village to find quite a gruesome scene. The able-bodied men who had remained ashore had put up a valiant fight, but many had been killed. The survivors were able to provide an account of what they had witnessed.

"The people were quite disheartened and called a meeting of their remaining number. It was determined that they had had enough of settling the New World. Rather than moving to Croatoan, they decided that they would all, instead, return to England, an option that had not been available to them before as the pinnace was too small. But now, in their violently reduced number, they determined that all would in fact make the trip which they set out to do in June of that year. They had found, however, that they possessed a particular lack of experienced seamen, for many had been slain by the Indians.

"As a result, their plan was to sail southward along the coast as far as possible, to allow their men to gain some experience before venturing forth into the open sea. Doing thus, unfortunately, resulted in their downfall, as they sailed into a storm, the like of which they had never experienced. The pinnace floundered and sank, and those who survived washed up on the shore of this very island."

"And you say they left in June of 1590?" asked Brit.

"Aye, Miss, that is correct."

"John White was unable to return," she said, "because by that time, England was at war with Spain. The Spanish Armada was sailing towards

England in 1588, and Queen Elizabeth needed all available ships to fight them. The following year, she organized a similar armada against Spain. White wasn't able to return to America for about three years, and when he did land again at Roanoke in August of 1590, there was no trace of the colonists. Every white person in the area had vanished."

"In August?" Dare asked with almost a tone of dismay in his voice.

"That's right."

"Thank you, Encyclopedia Britannia," Beau said. Brit smiled at him and stuck out her tongue.

"Well, miss," Dare said, bewildered once again by the odd interaction that had just taken place between them, "they were going home for good and they had taken all of their possessions with them. However, I feel I must make a correction to thy explanation, in that it was not *only* white people who left Roanoke."

"What do you mean?"

"It was a mixed company. There were a few Indians of a more noble and loyal nature who had formed alliances and friendships with some of the colonists, some even entering into matrimony with them. These were included among those who set sail from Roanoke.

"Sadly, in time, they too began to be suspicious of the white people, the same as those whom they had left in their homeland. Eventually, with a few exceptions, they left our company and joined forces with a tribe of natives on this island."

"They were the forebears of those who, unfortunately, attacked thy party and killed thy friend last evening," Payne said.

"You said there were some exceptions," said Jax.

"Quite right," Dare said. "And even now, there are descendants of those Indians living amongst us."

"Fascinating!" said Jax.

"You also said that William Dare was born two weeks after the shipwreck," Brit said.

"Indeed. For a fact, Eleanor was not very adept at appointing the birth of her children." Dare smirked at his joke. "However, to be fair, William's birth was quite likely precipitated by the shipwreck, for he did make his appearance earlier than expected. And sadly, poor Eleanor passed shortly afterwards. Ananias was quite beside himself with grief, and followed her within a few weeks. The children were taken in and raised by friends, Edward and Wenefrid Powell."

"Wait a minute," Brit said, her brows puckered in confusion. "One of the big mysteries surrounding the disappearance of the colony is the word 'Croatoan' carved in a tree at the settlement. Apparently this was an arrangement between the colonists and John White, to let him know where they went, if indeed they *did* decide to leave Roanoke. But they ended up not going to Croatoan."

"Yes indeed, except that it was carved into the palisade, not a tree. That was done after they had made the decision to move to Croatoan, but before the Indian attack. By this time, the people had lost hope that anyone was coming back, and they simply did not see any need to alter the carving or leave any other sort of message."

"Mr. Payne," Jax said, "you stated this morning that the Indians have the practice of sinking boats that come here."

"Yes, sir, that is correct," Payne replied.

"Based on that statement, I assume that there have been a number of occurrences. What has happened to the people? The survivors?"

"We can only assume that the Indians killed them," Payne said. "Indeed, they art a savage, warlike race. Cannibals, even, we suspect. Thou and thine art the first outsiders that we have been able to rescue from their hands."

"I'd be interested in seeing some of those historical documents you mentioned earlier," Brit said.

"Oh yes, of course, miss," Payne said agreeably. "I hath found some that may be of some interest to thee. They are stored within our archives for safekeeping. If thou art finished with thy repast, thou art welcome to view them there."

"Yes, please," she responded. She smiled excitedly at her companions, rubbing her hands together, as she rose from her seat. The others smiled back at her, but with varying levels of enthusiasm. With that, Payne and Thomas Dare led Brit across the Constabulary and through a heavy door while the others stayed where they were.

"Well, that was fascinating," said Allie.

"Yeah, it was," Jax agreed, his voice expressing a note of awe. "For a devoted student of American history, Roanoke is one of the biggest mysteries on the books."

"Hmm," Beau said. "Even bigger than who really killed John F. Kennedy? Or what the government is hiding at Area 51? Or even where they faked the moon landing?"

"You know what I'd really like, though," continued Jax, ignoring Beau, "is to talk to some of the natives that stayed on with them."

§

"The paper is quite delicate as thou mayest imagine," said Dare, "being, as it is, more than four hundred years old."

"Of course," Brit said, handling the documents only if absolutely necessary, and then, doing so very carefully.

"This room," Payne said with a sweeping gesture, "was constructed after we found that we had lost several documents to mold. In time, we discovered that by using certain porous building materials, and with vents placed in precise positions relative to the usual wind directions, we could control the level of moisture to an extent, thereby allowing a somewhat drier climate within."

Brit looked up at the walls he indicated and noticed that some vents were placed lower on one wall, with higher vents placed on the opposite wall. The air circulation in this expansive but otherwise enclosed room was actually good and the temperature was quite pleasant. She had only a passing interest, though, in the climate of the room and turned her attention back to the documents.

71

These documents, they told her, were stored, when possible, on individual shelves or drawers, allowing a space for air between the papers, preventing the growth of mildew. The room itself was long and narrow, with cabinets, drawers and shelves built into the walls, interspersed with an occasional table and chairs.

"Once we discovered these methods," Payne continued undaunted, "many of us adapted them for use in our homes, making for greater comfort in these warm, moist climes."

Brit nodded, already distracted by the first document before her. Dare noticed her interest.

"Ah, yes," he said. "Sadly, we were unable to save the entire book, but we salvaged several leaves from the ship's log, written by acting captain Christopher Cooper's hand." The paper was yellowed and brown around the edges, torn on one side where it had been salvaged from the book, and rippled as if it had once been wet. The ink was smeared but legible.

14 June 1590

Wee raised anchor at dawn on this warm morning, as the sun rose to shyne upon our uplifted faces. At long last, wee set sail for home, for wee admit that this place hath never been, nor ever shall be such. Indeed, it hath become the final resting place for many of our number, kilt by savages or by disease. And though our harts be heavie now for leaving their remaynes behinde in this wylde place of such dark and murderous beautie, they are jubilant at the thought of seeing deare England again.

Our goode mood was interrupted as we paused for the burial at sea of the most recent victims of the savages, as we decided to depart as quickly as possible rather than staying longer to excavate graves for all the fallen. As Captain, I spake some words and read verses from the Psalms, after which we committed their mortal remaynes to the deep. When the solemn event was finished, we got underwaye again.

Mr. Spendlove, my first mate, tells me our crewe is learning fast, and indeed I witnessed such with mine own eyes today. They respondeth quickly and with accuracy to commands, and though now lacking experience, I know that the season they gaine in these earlie days will see us home in goode stead. We made fair tyme this first day, with favourable winds southward. Keeping the lande in site on our sterbord side, our progress was visible to all, and the moods of crewe and passengers alike remayned high.

"Their optimism is almost heartbreaking," Brit said, "knowing how their journey turned out."

"Aye," Dare nodded sadly. "And indeed, the next page from a fortnight later doth present the trouble that they began experiencing."

28 June 1590

Our progress southward is still slowe, as wee continue to struggle with sluggish winds which are no match for the northward currents against which wee fight. Fewe are familiar with these seas and can but encourage us with speach unsupported by experience.

Wee hesitate to test the current's breadth, for feare of loosing site of lande on the one hand, and of crashing upon unseene rocks on the other. For now, wee keepeth England before us, and this sustayneth us.

The younge ones and the Indians in our companye, those who hath not seene or do not remember England, do not understand entyre, but our hope and tayles of home hath taken root in them, and they await site of our destination.

12 Julye 1590

I rite with difficultie as our vessel is shaken on the heavie seas. Wee hath lost site of lande as wee fight against the elements that are bent on destroying us. A fewe of our number, foremost among them beinge the Indians, hath broached the idea of going back to Roonock, but for now, the majority vote for going on.

17 Julye 1590

Two days hath past since our ship was lost to the depths. Sadly, 36 of our number are perished in the wicked storme, along with much livestocke and possessions.

Our first concern is for shelter, for though the storme hath past, the weather here is wylde and quite unpredictable. Also wee hath seene evidence of natives on these shoares and wee know naught of their disposition.

I can not saye with any certainty where we are, for our instruments were lost, but our last siting put us on a course for La Isla Española. Wee hath seene no other synes of a civilised population and spirits are very lowe.

Wee hath decided to name this place New Roonock, for apart from the warm climate, it doth remind us daily in very many other respects of that devilish place we left. Wee pray for the passing of a ship which might rescue us from this hell.

28 Julye 1590

A childe was added to our number this morn, as William Dare was borne to Eleanor and Ananias in a rough shelter near where wee were thrown upon this shoare. The babe arrived earlie but appeared to be in goode health. Sadly, the joye of the occasion was cut short by the passing of the new mother scarce 12 hours later, weakened by the ordeal and by the meanness of our conditions.

Wee hath seene fearfull-looking savages watching us from a distance in the forest, and though they hath made no moves against us, they do not seem friendlye in the least.

Many of the Indians in our companye hath begun turning on us, being short of temper and angrey about our situation since wee ignored their suggestions to turne back. Indeed, some hath even spake of seeking out the local heathens and throwing in their lot with them.

Though wee were only cast upon this island less than a fortnight ago, the moode of our solemn assemblie seemeth in the maine to be one of despaire.

"This was the last entry in the log," said Thomas Dare. "According to what we hath been able to piece together, Captain Cooper, who had assumed leadership on the island, was killed shortly hereafter by rebel Indians who then abandoned them to join the local savages." Brit saw a few other pages saved from various diaries and journals that seemed to support that conclusion.

She spent a good portion of the afternoon looking at what was available, supervised by Dare, though Payne had to take his leave to attend to his duties.

§

"We do not possess very extensive mining capabilities here, yet we are able to smelt and forge metals to which we do have access into useful items, including our arms and cultivation equipment." Justin Wilkinson, their guide, was showing Jax, Beau and Allie around the extensive grounds. He was an agreeable young man, the son of Payne's sister. He was in his mid-twenties and, like the others that they had met, very humble and friendly.

The day had grown warm and humid, with only the slightest breeze for relief. The compound was laid out much like an old, historic town, divided into residential neighborhoods and business districts. Almost every residence in the colony had a fenced-in area behind or beside it, enclosing gardens, compost piles and livestock, and in the warm sticky air, the smell was rather pungent, though Wilkinson did not seem to mind.

The main business district was arranged around a public square, and the signage and decoration reminded the visitors of a section of Disneyland or some other modern reconstruction of a medieval village. The effect was quaint and nostalgic. There was even a stream-fed pool of water with a hand-lettered sign that said, "Ye Watering Hole." The Americans had smiled at the banality of it, but their guide did not seem to understand the joke.

Governor Payne, as it turned out, had an office just east of the town square. This was in a row of structures whose backs were built up against a large rocky outcropping near the easternmost side of the compound. However, he seemed to spend most of his time at the Constabulary, on the north end.

The smelting area that Wilkinson was now showing them was a large stone structure, rising about three stories, but with several strategically positioned vents. Despite the torrid tropical temperatures of the afternoon, the heat pouring out through the door was even greater and easily discernible.

Wilkinson's mention of their arms reminded Beau of some things that had been percolating in the back of this mind, about their weaponry. "Where do you get your gunpowder?" he asked.

"We make it ourselves, of course," Wilkinson said. "Though I am not entirely knowledgeable concerning its manufacture, there are a few of our number who are quite adept at the process. There existeth upon this island several hot springs, around which we hath found sulfur in abundance. The other ingredients, charcoal and saltpeter are easily manufactured here as well."

"I noticed your guns," Beau said, "appear to be very much like the old muskets we know of from our history of hundreds of years ago, but somehow they seem a little different."

"Oh, indeed," Wilkinson replied enthusiastically. "Improvements hath been made on the arms of our forefathers. We found that a shorter length proved to be of greater benefit, particularly for ease of use and transport in this densely forested region. But one of the greatest advancements came about when Mr. John Endicott invented a method whereby we could load multiple rounds into a single musket, with a self-contained charge for each shot."

"You're saying your muskets are repeating rifles?" Beau asked.

"Repeating, sir? Yes, I suppose thou couldst call them that. Each cylinder contains powder and a projectile fitted to the end. We are able to fire six rounds without having to reload each time. Quite an improvement!" he stated proudly as if he were personally responsible for the advancement.

"Mmm," Beau grunted.

"Excuse me, sir," said a soft-spoken young woman who had approached the group. "Might I be introduced to our visitors?" This had become a common occurrence this afternoon, though some people only smiled and bowed their heads or tipped their hats in greeting.

"But of course," Wilkinson said with a polite head bow. "Miss Emily Viccars, this is Mr. Jaxon Malone, Mr. Beau Bannister, and Miss Allison Worthington." After the introductions, Miss Emily Viccars actually curtsied to them. She wore a long dress and a sort of bonnet made of the same linen fabric that the others had worn.

"I am so very pleased to meet thee," she smiled, "but I was given to believe that there were four in thy number."

"Actually," Allie said, "there were five. Ron was killed by an Indian last night." The statement registered in her mind as surreal, not only that he was dead, but that he was killed by an Indian. The memory of seeing his dead body, though, was still very real, and she felt tears well up in her eyes. Jax noticed her emotion and he put a protective arm around her shoulders.

"Oh yes, I heard about that poor young man," Miss Viccars said with such empathy that Allie almost felt like hugging her. "My sympathies to thee in very great measure."

"Thank you," said Jax with a grateful smile.

"Yes, and Mr. Malone's sister, Britannia, is at the Constabulary perusing our historical documents," Wilkinson said.

"I eagerly anticipate making her acquaintance as well," Miss Viccars said. "And I bid thee welcome to our home." The three of them echoed thanks to her. She smiled again and took her leave, and they continued on their tour.

"Do you have any ship building facilities here?" Beau asked Wilkinson.

"Ship building, sir? No, we have nothing of that kind."

"You don't use boats?" Jax asked.

"Some among our number do use small boats or rafts for fishing, but they hath only been manufactured by the individuals who had the specific need or desire for them. For a fact, we possess most everything we need on the island and seldom require to go out upon the sea."

"I'm surprised," Jax responded. "In over four hundred years, none of you have ever tried to get off this island?"

"Well, sir, there were some early on who did make the endeavor, but they were never heard from again. The seas about this island are quite treacherous, and they very likely perished in the attempt. In time, our ancestors did realize that they had everything that they needed here. Happiness and contentment hath kept us here on our island home."

"I don't know," said Beau, "I think I'd get tired of it after a while. I mean I love a tropical island getaway as much as the next guy, but I like to get back home afterwards."

"Oh, but this *is* our home, sir."

"None of you get tired of living behind this wall?" Allie asked. "It seems so confining to me."

"Oh, no Miss. Not at all. We simply recognize it as a necessary boundary for our safety and happiness, and are only too content to remain within its protective enclosure."

"Mmm," Beau grunted noncommittally.

They were nearing the Constabulary again when Jax remembered something. "Mr. Dare said earlier that there are still some natives living among you. In our tour of your colony here, I never saw any."

"Hmm," Wilkinson nodded thoughtfully. "Well, we met only a small fraction of our population in our brief turn about Roonock colony. Nevertheless, there are indeed loyal Indians mixed among us, though admittedly they are in much smaller number or proportion than we English."

As they arrived at the Constabulary, the sun was declining in the western sky, nearing the top of the island's central mountain, and was casting long, dark shadows. They were greeted at the door of the Constabulary by Payne.

"Welcome back. I trust thy tour was enjoyable and informative," he said.

"Yes, it was very interesting," Jax said.

"Excellent."

Wilkinson gave a brief bow of his head to the three of them, then turned to face Governor Payne.

"Uncle William," he said, "I must get myself home. Martha will have dinner ready soon, and I do not wish for her to throw my plate to the pigs."

"Very well, Justin," Payne said with a smile. "My thanks for thy help this afternoon. Give my love to Martha."

"As always, Uncle," he said, nodded a final time toward the three visitors, then turned and walked away.

"So," said Payne, resuming their conversation, "how dost thou like our colony?"

"Everyone has been friendly and welcoming. It's very nice," Jax replied.

"Good!" Payne said with a warm smile. "It is our hope that thou might experience a most happy and satisfying life among us."

"Not so fast, Governor," Beau said. "I mean thanks, and no offense, but we don't intend to stick around." Payne seemed confused.

"But where wouldst thou go? Forgive me for my lack of propriety, but the Indians were not so welcoming last night."

"We're not talking about moving to someplace else on the island," Jax said. "We want to go back to our homes."

"We have friends and family," Allie added. "We can't stay here."

"I am so awfully sorry," Payne said, looking at the three of them. "But how dost thou propose to accomplish this undertaking?"

"I was wondering if we might have access to whatever tools and materials we might need to build a boat," Jax said.

"Art thou boatwrights?"

"No we're not, but we know the principles behind making a boat seaworthy. We have to try! We need to do whatever we can to get back home."

"Of course, we are only too happy to share with thee whatever we have." Payne's expression turned grave. "However, I feel that I must warn thee that the seas round about this island are quite treacherous.

Many are those who hath attempted to sail away from here, to their detriment."

"So we've heard," Beau said. "We're willing to take the chance."

"Very well," Payne said, and appeared deep in thought for a moment, steepling his fingers under his chin again. "I shall ask about among some of our carpenters and see if any hath space in which ye might do thy work."

"Thank you so much," Allie said sincerely. "We don't mean to sound ungrateful for everything you've done for us." Again, her eyes filled with tears, and she felt irritated that she could not control her emotions better. However, she realized that she did like the soothing feel of Jax's hand on her back again in an effort to comfort her.

"Oh, no, certainly not, Miss," Payne replied warmly and sympathetically. "I do indeed understand completely. Meanwhile, other arrangements hath been made for thy comfort whilst thou art with us, for indeed I know that the Constabulary is rather mean lodgings for a longer span of time, and clearly no place for ladies."

"You really don't need to go to any trouble for us," Jax said.

"It is no trouble at all, I assure thee. In point of fact, upon hearing of thy appearance on our island, a number of our citizens demonstrated hospitality and offered rooms for lodging. I hath examined the offers and hath chosen two which I deem the most advantageous. My sister, Susan Wilkinson, Justin's mother, is a widow and will provide lodging for the ladies. And a young couple by the name of Hemmington has room for ye gentlemen."

"We really appreciate your kindness," Jax said, and Allie nodded a confirmation.

"Yeah, it's really good of you, man," said Beau. "Thanks."

"Not at all. It is my pleasure. And on the morrow, I shall begin my search for a site for thy boatwright enterprise."

§

"Good e'en. Please do come in," Susan Wilkinson smiled and nodded in greeting. Payne's sister appeared to be in her fifties and was an attractive, fair-skinned woman with graying auburn hair and a ready smile. Her relaxed demeanor put the girls at ease right away.

"Thank you," said Brit, looking back as Governor Payne led Jax and Beau a little further down the path toward the home of the Hemmingtons, located just next door. Brit and Allie entered the house and Susan closed the door behind them.

The home was simple and functional, but with a few purely decorative items hung on the walls. Brit was admiring several beautifully-crafted pieces of antique furniture before she realized that they could just as easily have been made yesterday in this old-fashioned colony.

"Your home is beautiful," Allie said. "It seems very comfortable."

"It *is* comfortable," she agreed, "though it be larger than that needed by a woman of my age with no family left unto me."

"Oh, yes," Brit said, "Governor Payne said you were a widow. I'm sorry." Susan smiled gently and nodded her head in acknowledgement.

"I was just about to sit down to my supper, and there is plenty for thee. Wilt thou join me?"

"Thank you," Brit and Allie both said together. They were led to a functional trestle table and chairs where they sat down, while Susan opened a door a few inches.

"Ruth, we are ready to eat now," she said. There was a muffled response from the other side of the door, and Susan sat down at the table. A moment later, an elderly native woman entered the room carrying a tray containing a ham surrounded by a variety of cooked vegetables and potatoes. "Britannia and Allison," Susan said, "this is Ruth, my cook."

Brit and Allie muttered greetings as Ruth curtsied, then turned and hobbled back into the kitchen. She returned with home-baked bread and white butter. She was seen a couple of more times during the course of the dinner as she brought more items or carried empty dishes to the kitchen.

"Ruth has been with me for all of my life," Susan said.

"Really? As your cook?" Allie asked.

"Well, no. When I was a young girl, my parents took her on as my governess, but as she hath grown older, she hath assumed other roles as my needs dictate and her health alloweth."

"What was it like growing up here?" Brit asked. Susan thought for several moments, seeming a little flustered, before responding.

"I apologize for my delay in answering. Verily, I hath never given it a thought, for everyone I know hath also grown up here in Roonock. Therefore, the question hath never arisen." She sighed, then continued, "I suppose it was pleasant. My parents were God-fearing people who trained my brother and me according to the way among us. They were strict but loving."

"And in all your life, you've never wondered about what life was like outside of this fortress?" Allie asked.

Susan smiled. "We hath found a happy life here, free from the fear of tyranny and persecution for our faith and way of life, where our children can grow and thrive in a healthful environment. Why would we fancy something else?"

"Do you have other children besides Justin?" Brit asked.

"No, I do not. Alas, my dear husband died many years ago, when Justin was a babe, before I could bear any more children."

"I'm so sorry," said Allie. "How did he die, if you don't mind my asking?"

"No, dear, I do not mind. Robert was a fiery man with rather a righteous temper. Several years ago, the Indians attempted a raid when a number of our people were outside the wall. Our safeguards back then were admittedly a bit more lax than they are now.

"According to what was related unto me, one of the savages layeth his hands upon a child and fled away into the forest. Robert had witnessed what had transpired, and he did shout out for help, but rather than wait for our forces to arrive, he took off after the offending Indian.

"Somehow, the child was rescued or escaped from the savage's hands and started back for the colony on her own. But by the time our forces arrived on the scene, my Robert lay dead, killed by the very Indian he had attempted to detain."

By now, they had finished their dinner and they continued visiting as Ruth came from the kitchen to clear the dishes. Susan smiled warmly at her and thanked her.

§

John and Mary Hemmington were in their twenties and married only four months. Their home was modest and, like most of the other houses in the area, was built in the wattle and daub style common in Tudor England.

The house had a nursery already prepared for the baby that was due in about six months. A wool-stuffed mattress had been placed on the floor of the nursery, and it was in this room that Jax and Beau would be sleeping.

The Hemmingtons were a sweet, innocent-looking, pink-faced couple, both blonde and good natured. Whenever Jax or Beau spoke, the couple listened with apparent wide-eyed wonder.

"Wouldst thou like some more roast mutton, Mr. Malone?" Mary asked.

"No thank you," he said. "I'm full. It was delicious, though. And please, call me Jax."

"Yes sir, Mr. Malone. And thou, Mr. Bannister?"

Beau snorted and laughed softly. "No thanks," he said. "So, what do you guys usually do in the evenings around here?"

"What do we do?" Mary asked with a blank expression on her face.

"Yeah, what do you do for fun?"

"We do, I think, what most everyone does," John said, seeming puzzled by the question. "We rest from our day's toils, converse with family, read the Bible or perhaps other books."

"I often do sewing or mending after dinner," Mary volunteered helpfully, her eyes sweeping from Beau to Jax and back.

"Hmm," Beau responded.

"I've heard there are natives still among you here in your fortress," Jax said, "but we took a tour of your colony today and I didn't see any."

"Oh, we hath one," Mary said. "She liveth here and worketh as our maid."

"Your maid?"

"Yes, many of us employ Indians who are willing to work."

"Not many are, I am afraid," said John. "Yahima, though, is a good worker. Thou wilt likely see her on the morrow, as she doeth her work about the house."

"Well, I don't know if we'll be around much tomorrow," Jax said. "We're hoping to begin building a boat soon."

"A boat, sir?" replied John.

"That's right. Apparently the natives sunk our boat, so we need to build a new one to get back home."

"'tis my understanding, sir, that the sea round about this island is quite treacherous and dangersome. We would hate for thee to risk thy lives and lose them in the attempt."

"We seem to be hearing that a lot," said Beau. "It seemed pretty calm when we were on our way here." John and Mary looked at each other and shrugged, and they seemed to have no response.

"Well, for now," said Mary, "I shall clear the dishes. Wouldst ye gentlemen care to join us as we read from the Scriptures?"

"Thank you," Jax said, "but if you don't mind, I've had a tough couple of days. I think I'm going to call it a night."

"Yeah, same here," said Beau. John and Mary's faces reflected perplexity at their words, though apparently they understood their meanings.

"Of course," said John. "Sleep well."

"Thank you," said Jax. "Good night."

He and Beau climbed the steep, narrow stairs up to the second floor of the house where the bedrooms were located. The second story was cantilevered, so the floor space was greater than that of the ground floor. They went into the nursery and Beau threw himself down on the mattress with a grunt.

"Not quite as soft as it looks," he observed.

Jax paced the room for a bit, apparently troubled by something. "What are your impressions of this place?" he asked.

"Kind of dull," Beau said after a moment of thought. "They spend their evenings talking, reading, mending, and they call that fun?"

"But what about the people?"

"Kind of dull," Beau repeated. "And pretty fixated on how dangerous the sea is. All very nice, though." He studied Jax through narrowed eyes. "What's up with you? I know how much you love history. I thought this would be right up your alley."

"Oh, believe me, it's fascinating. To be the ones who finally discovered what happened to the lost colony of Roanoke – I can't imagine anything we could do for the rest of our lives that would top that in historical significance."

"Historical significance?" responded Beau. "Think of how rich it would make us, solving one of the great mysteries, as you called it. We could do *The Tonight Show*." Then his face lit up. "Maybe a *National Geographic* special! Think of all the publishers that would be clamoring for our first-hand account of it. Assuming we could ever get off this damn island."

"But it just seems like something's not quite right," Jax continued, not wanting to get into one of their old 'history versus money' arguments.

"What do you mean?"

"I don't know. I can't put my finger on it."

"Maybe it's the whole Stepford mentality," Beau suggested. Jax looked at him, pondering.

"Well, not quite Stepford, but I see what you mean."

"You don't suppose they're all really robots, do you?" Beau said with a smile.

"No, I don't," Jax said with a chuckle, "but Ron sure could have run wild with that theory." They paused as they both remembered their lost friend. "I don't know. Everybody just seems so happy."

"And happy is bad?"

"No, of course not," Jax responded quickly. "And I don't mean to sound cynical or resentful of their happiness. It just seems so, I don't know, extreme."

"Well, think about it," Beau responded after a moment. "They don't have the news bombarding them every day. They don't know about Iraq, Afghanistan, Vietnam. Hell, they don't know about the world wars or any other war since the sixteenth century. They're on the barter system. Their lives are completely disconnected from the world economy and all the problems that go with that. I guess I could be happy with that too. Although I think a club or a movie or even TV might be nice once in a while."

"Yeah, I guess you're right." They were both quiet for a few seconds.

"What's up with that, though?" Beau finally asked.

"With what?"

"Well, they're so backwards here."

"They're colonial," Jax said with a snicker.

"Yeah, but think about this: both our culture and theirs branched out from the same place. But now, we have computers, cell phones, cars, an international space station. We've been to the moon and back several times. We've even sent probes to Mars and outside the solar system. And you mean to tell me that the biggest advancement that gets them all giddy is going from a single shot musket to a six round rifle?"

"Well, you said it yourself," Jax replied. "The disconnect from the world you mentioned also means that they were not involved in or affected by the Industrial Revolution. That's when technology started advancing exponentially. So that within less than a century, we went from driving a horse and buggy to flying to the moon."

"Hmm," Beau grunted.

"You know how easy it is for *us* to settle into a rut. Imagine how easy it would be when every day is essentially the same, with no outside influence from other countries or cultures. No new ideas or challenges from external sources. You settle into a routine and a way of life because it works for you and you see no need to change it."

"Yeah, I guess that makes sense." Beau was still pondering. "If that's the case, though, why do you suppose nobody's curious about our wristwatches, that cell phone you have clipped to your belt, or even Allie's big glasses? And I'm sure planes have flown over here from time to time. They have to be curious about things like that."

Jax shook his head and sighed. "I just wish we could get the hell out of here. I have millions of dollars' worth of equipment designed to find a sunken boat, but I can't get to it or use it because it's been sunk *with* my boat."

"Don't worry, man," Beau said. "We'll get back home. You heard Payne. We can start building a new boat soon."

"Yeah," Jax said and sighed again.

"Come on, big fella," Beau said, patting the mattress beside him. "Come lie down next to me and let's get some rest." He had a twisted smile on his face. Jax looked at him through narrowed eyes.

"If you try spooning with me, I'll punch you."

§

Phil Chesterfield sat forward at his desk, looking at the charts spread out in front of him. As a professor of marine archeology at the University of Miami, the rotund man had spent years studying charts of the ocean floor, of tides and currents, of weather patterns and of historically documented storms.

In his lab at Biscayne Bay, he had gradually put together a theory about the *Maria del Gracia*, and about what he thought was the likely spot where she went down. If his theory panned out, it would mean not only a coup for the university, but for him personally. He had already been thinking about how computer models could be constructed based on his methods and using known charts to find other high-profile shipwrecks.

But he was not able to concentrate on it now. Jax Malone had agreed to radio in every evening between 7:00 and 9:00 with their progress, and in the event that they were not able to, he would call by 7:00 the next morning. It had been three days since he had heard from them.

Phil had met Jax several years ago when he completed an internship here at the university. He knew Jax to be very responsible and trustworthy, and when he heard that Jax was going to start his own business, Phil knew he would be successful. This was not like him.

The Coast Guard had not been particularly helpful, though he understood their stance. But it still pissed him off. The area that Jax and his crew were investigating was outside America's territorial waters. And besides that, there had been no evidence of actual trouble, other than the fact that Phil had not heard from them.

Still, he had a bad feeling about it.

He picked up his cell phone and selected a number from his directory. The call was picked up on the second ring.

"Hi, Jerry, it's Phil. Listen, are you busy over the next couple of days? How would you like to go with me on a little excursion?"

Jax and Beau had been late to rise and found that John and Mary had both left for their various duties – John had gone to the metalsmith shop where he worked as a journeyman, and Mary had gone to the market to shop for the day.

Clean clothing had been left for them, and since they had been wearing their clothing for over two days, and Beau had bled on his shirt from the wound in his arm, they changed. Neither of them wore the vests but they found that the shirts and breeches were, in fact, quite comfortable.

In John and Mary's stead, breakfast was served by a lovely Indian girl. She seemed to be in her mid-twenties, with smooth skin the color of cinnamon, and she wore her thick black hair gathered loosely by a leather strip, to hang down her back. She was dressed similarly to the colonists, though with not as many layers, and she was barefoot.

"Good morrow," she said in precise English, but with a slightly different accent. "I am Yahima. Please sit thee down and I shall serve thy breakfast."

"Thank you," said Jax. "I was wondering when I would be able to meet one of the Indians we've been hearing about." Yahima smiled shyly but said nothing in response as she placed the food on the table in front of them. Then she disappeared into the kitchen.

Breakfast at the Hemmingtons' was a simple affair, consisting of hearty bread and cheese, and something called cornmeal mush. At hearing the name, both Jax and Beau were hesitant to try it, but found it to be quite tasty, served with butter and some kind of fruit syrup. Their drink was a strong cider, also made from tropical fruit.

They ate while discussing their hopes about building a boat. But without a place to work, and with the lack of working drawings or designs, they soon exhausted the subject. With the lull in their conversation, Jax decided to attempt to satisfy some of his own interests.

"Yahima," Jax called out. There was a soft shuffling sound in the kitchen, and the native girl reappeared at the table.

"Yes, sir?" she replied.

"I'm sorry to interrupt your work," he said, "but I'm a student of history. And one of the things I'm especially interested in is the history of the relationship between white people and natives. Can you tell me anything about your people, and your experience with the colonists?"

She glanced nervously toward the front door, then back to the table, never actually meeting Jax's eyes. "No, sir. I am sorry, I cannot." Then she turned and went back into the kitchen, leaving Jax looking after her with furrowed brows.

"You always were really smooth with the ladies," Beau said.

"Did I say something wrong?" Jax asked quietly.

Beau shrugged and shook his head. "I don't know, man. Didn't sound wrong to me, but who knows what's happening inside a four hundred year old brain?"

Jax was disappointed by the curtailed conversation and turned back to his food.

They realized with some surprise that they quickly began to feel satisfied by the seemingly scant breakfast. They finished eating in silence, after which they gathered up the few dishes they had used and carried them into the kitchen. Yahima was sweeping the floor and seemed nervous when they came in, watching as they put their dishes on the work table.

"I'm sorry," Jax said softly to her. "I didn't mean to upset you."

"No sir, thou didst not upset me," she replied shyly, then tentatively looked up at Jax. "Many thanks to thee."

"Thank you," he responded.

"Thanks," Beau echoed. Yahima nodded silently as the men took their leave.

§

Brit and Allie had also put on clothing that had been left for them, though they had also opted for fewer layers. The blouses and skirts were more form-fitting than the baggy pants and T-shirt that Allie usually wore, so despite the length of the skirt, Jax found that he liked her new, feminine look.

It was nearly 9:00 when the four of them met at the Constabulary. Payne was not there. In fact, the Constabulary was eerily empty. They were about to leave when a door opened and a young man emerged into the main area. He was startled, apparently surprised to see them.

He looked at them through squinted eyes, and then his face lit up with an expression of recognition. "Oh, hello!" he said enthusiastically. "Of course! Thou art the Americans! I hath been hearing about thee. Welcome!"

"Thank you," said Jax, somewhat taken aback by the man's fervor. Then gesturing toward the empty room, he asked, "Where is everyone?"

The man looked blankly at him for a moment, then looked around and apparently realized that they had not come just to see him. "Oh, there was some sort of incident involving the Indians and they hath gone forth to remedy the situation."

"What kind of incident?" Beau asked.

"Of that, I am afraid I do not know, sir."

"Do you know when Governor Payne will be back?" Jax asked.

"No sir, I do not."

"Morning? Afternoon?" Beau probed.

"I am sorry, sir. I simply do not know."

"Okay, thanks," Jax sighed.

"Thou art so very welcome sir," the man enthused as they went back outside.

"Well, he was a big, steaming pile of help," Beau said.

Brit looked up at the others. "An incident with the Indians," she said. "That sounds ominous."

"Yeah, and that *looks* ominous," Jax said, pointing up at the battlement above the gate.

"Yeah, I noticed that too," said Beau. The guard posted all along the top of the wall seemed to be about double what it was when the Americans had arrived two nights ago.

"Well, I guess we're on our own for now," said Allie. "Want to look around?"

They wandered through the village, being greeted as celebrities by the villagers, seeing much of what they had seen yesterday, though to Brit, it was all new. They visited shops and again felt as if they were in some kind of theme park.

As the sun rose higher in the sky, and the temperature and humidity rose with it, they found one particular spot to be their favorite. A river, plunging down from the central mountain, flowed into the fortress on the west side, then split into two branches and flowed out the east side and into the sea, providing fresh drinking water on the way.

At the point where the river split and formed two branches, they found a small grassy grove of trees and rocks, and the area offered a welcoming bit of nature within the compound.

"Okay, I think I'll stay here for the rest of the day," Beau said with a sigh. He threw himself down onto the grass in the shade of one of the trees and wiped the sweat from his forehead.

"I agree," said Brit, sitting down next to him. "This is nice."

"Yeah, it *is* nice," said Jax as he settled down on the grass. "But I had hoped that we might be closer to getting started on a way out of here."

"I know, man," said Beau. "It'll happen."

"I can't help wondering what's happening out there, with the natives," Allie said. She looked to the west, though she couldn't see the wall from here.

"I don't know," Beau said grimly, "but I wouldn't mind having an 'incident with the Indians' myself, for what they did to Ron." Brit put her hand on his, and they were all quiet for a few moments, thinking about the friend they had lost two nights before.

Beau turned his hand under Brit's, palm to palm, and their fingers interlocked. He looked up at her face and there were tears in her eyes, but she offered a quivering smile. He gently pulled her hand, resulting in Brit leaning against him, his arm around her back.

"I feel so bad," Allie said. "I teased him so much. Mercilessly, sometimes."

"We all did, Allie" said Beau. "But you know what? He never seemed to mind. In fact he usually laughed along with us."

"Yeah," Brit agreed, "if he actually realized that it was a joke."

"He really was *so* good-natured," Jax said. "Even tempered, calm. In fact, that's what caught my attention about him from the very beginning."

"I know what you mean," said Beau with a smile. "Remember when we first saw him, in that electronics lab at MIT?"

"Yeah, that's what I was thinking about," Jax replied with a nod. He turned to Allie and continued. "I took Beau with me to the campus when I first started looking for an IT specialist. My plan was to question some of my professors and get their recommendations about who might be a good candidate for the position.

"Ron was working on a group project when we got there. Some kind of machine surrounded by all these computer nerds. I don't know anything about the piece of equipment they were building, what it was supposed to do or anything like that, but something went wrong. It started smoking and sparking, and everyone started to panic."

"Imagine, if you will," Beau interjected in a Rod Serling imitation, "a room full of electrical smoke and hysterical computer geeks. There was the smell of burning plastic and hot metal. And this deep, loud, ominous-sounding hum."

"But there in the midst of all that pandemonium was Ron, his arms buried to the elbows in the machine, calmly working on the errant circuit board and ultimately fixing it by himself."

"I was kind of hoping for a dramatic explosion or something," Beau said, "so the anticlimax was a little bit of a disappointment."

"But Ron was the man," Jax continued. "His cool-headedness saved their project. And I decided that I didn't need to question any of the faculty. I had found the man for the job."

Again, they were quiet for a few minutes, relaxing on the grass, listening to the sound of the river tumbling over the rocks. Though they could see parts of some of the buildings in front of them, they relished the relative seclusion that was afforded them by the trees and other natural growth in what they came to call "the oasis." Though grouped together as two couples, they were each still sequestered in their private thoughts, mostly about Ron.

"I need to walk," Allie said abruptly and she stood up. Jax saw that she had tears in her eyes and, casting a quick look toward Beau and Brit, he stood up and followed her.

He caught up with her at a little stone footbridge that crossed the southern branch of the river. She had stopped at the apex, looking at the water.

"Are you okay, Allie?" he asked, putting his hand gently on her shoulder.

"I will be," she said with a forced smile, but her eyes were still brimming with tears. Jax took her in his arms and held her tightly, and he could feel the silent sobs that began racking her body.

Finally, she pulled away and shook her head with frustration.

"It's stupid," she said. "I don't know why I'm being so emotional."

"You watched a friend die, suddenly and violently," Jax said trying to comfort her. "That doesn't happen every day, and it's naturally a distressing thing when it does."

"But it's not like I was even that close to Ron. I hadn't known him for very long, certainly not as long as you and Beau knew him."

"I know, but he was a good man, a good friend. He was a sweet guy, and he was taken away from us way too soon."

"I just keep seeing him lying there in the sand with that arrow sticking out of his body."

"I know honey. It's okay."

Allie pulled away a little and took off her glasses, hanging them by the earpiece on the tie-belt of her skirt, and she wiped her eyes. Jax watched her, his hands still on her waist, and she looked up at him and smiled through the tears.

"Thanks," she said. He didn't reply but placed one hand on her cheek, and she leaned into it. Then he slipped his hand around the back of her neck and pulled her closer until their lips met and, heightened by the emotions of the moment, they kissed each other, soft and tentatively at first, then hard and hungrily.

As his arms wrapped around her, he could feel her body pressing tightly against his. Allie's arms around his neck, her blouse raised up a bit and he felt the bare skin of her back and suddenly wished they were in a more private place. They separated only enough to catch their breath, their eyes locked on each other.

"I was wondering if I had a chance with you," she whispered.

"A pretty good one, I'd say," Jax replied.

§

The afternoon had come and gone, but the four of them, relaxing in their newly discovered romances, barely noticed. In the back of his mind, Jax was still wishing he could get started building a boat, and was chafing at their lack of progress. But with Allie lounging against him under a tree, he was not complaining.

They had rejoined Beau and Brit and had passed the afternoon talking about various subjects, from Ron to their current surroundings. The soft gurgling sound of the river nearby and the songs and squawks of tropical birds provided a gentle, relaxing soundtrack.

"You know," said Brit, "if I was given a choice, instead of being forced into it, I could see myself living here. For a while, anyway."

"I know what you mean," Jax agreed. "There really is something appealing about this place. And I think it's more than just the historian in me talking."

"I don't know," said Beau. "I don't think I could do it. I mean it's nice, the people are all friendly and hospitable, and it's a beautiful and intriguing environment, but –"

"Yeah, I see your point," Jax interrupted sarcastically. "With all that against it, who would want to live here?"

"I just think it would get old really quickly," Beau continued in a slightly belligerent tone of voice. "I know everybody talks about the good old days, simpler times and all that. But like you and I were talking about last night, there's something to be said about modern conveniences."

"I agree," said Allie. "Yes, this *is* kind of a romanticized era in an idyllic setting, but I think that, coming from our backgrounds, we would get tired of it pretty fast. We'd start missing the things we gave up. Wondering what our Facebook friends are up to, or who's winning on *American Idol*."

"You had me up until *American Idol*," Beau said. "I *do* miss *Stranger Things*, though. And just knowing what's happening in the world news."

"Yeah, maybe," said Jax. "Don't worry, I'm not saying I want to stay." He looked at his watch. "Although you could never tell by the way we pissed away the whole day."

"My God," Beau said as he looked at his watch. "It's after 4:00."

"We should get back to the Constabulary and see if Payne is there." They all stood up and started making their way back toward the north.

"I didn't realize how hungry I was until you mentioned the time," said Brit.

Several people smiled and greeted them as they walked. Some stopped to introduce themselves and to welcome them. As they neared the Constabulary, they could see that there was still a heavier guard on the battlement around the wall, but little activity. They opened the door and went inside. Payne and a few other men looked up from various papers on the tables.

"Ah, thou hast returned," Payne said. "Didst thou pass a pleasant day?"

"Yes, we did," said Allie, and she realized that she was still holding Jax's hand, though she was unaware of the semi-permanent smile on her face. "It was nice."

"Splendid!"

"So, what was going on this morning?" asked Beau.

"This morning?" Payne echoed. "What dost thou mean?"

"Some incident with the Indians, is what we heard," Brit said.

"Oh, 'twas nothing," Payne said, waving his hand, with a completely unconcerned expression on his face. "They shake their bows at us on occasion and we respond by waving our guns at them. We show them our strength and they back down. Nothing to worry thyselves about."

"Saber rattling?" Jax replied. "The whole thing was just a display of power?"

"Aye, I suppose it could be described in such a fashion."

"The Cold War continues," said Beau.

"Well," Jax said, "I don't know when you got back, but we were wondering if you had a chance to line up any space for us to work on a boat."

"A boat!" Payne said. "Of course. I fear I had forgotten about that with the activities of the day. My deepest apologies. I shall do that tomorrow, I promise thee."

"Okay," said Jax, trying not to look or sound too discouraged or unappreciative. "Thanks."

"For now, go back to thy places of lodging, have some supper, get some rest, and perhaps on the morrow or the next day, I shall deliver some good news to thee."

They agreed and said good night as they left the Constabulary, disappointed, but hoping for better news tomorrow. Jax gave Allie a kiss and a hug outside Susan Wilkinson's home. As he was lingering over holding Allie in his arms, he noticed that Beau was doing the same with Brit. After saying good night, the girls went into Susan's house and closed the door behind them, and Jax and Beau continued toward the Hemmingtons' home.

"I hope, sir," Jax said affecting an English accent, "that thy intentions with regard to my good sister are honorable ones."

"Aye, sir," Beau replied with a humble head bow, his accent only a little worse than Jax's. "Verily, sir, thou canst be most assured that my intentions toward her art indeed of the noblest and most honorablest nature, sir."

With a smile, they opened the door to the Hemmingtons' home and went inside.

§

Jax awoke with a start as John Hemmington was kneeling beside the mattress and nudging him.

"Please forgive me, Mr. Malone, but it is time to rise," he said.

"Time to –" Jax looked at his watch in the dim light and saw that it was a little before 6:00 a.m. "Time to rise?"

"Yes, sir. It is Sunday. We must prepare to go to church."

Beau was waking up and heard what John said. "Church?" he mumbled.

"Yes, sir."

"I was hoping we could get started on building a boat today," Jax said.

"Oh, no sir. Not today. Please hurry. Breakfast will be ready soon." With that, John left their room.

"We're going to church?" Beau asked.

"Doesn't sound like we'll be able to start working on a boat," Jax said. "They must have a major blue law in effect here. I guess they don't work on Sundays."

"But we're going to church?"

"Come on. We can get to know some of the people there. Besides, if that's where all the people go, that's where the carpenters will be. Church is probably just about all there is to do around here on Sunday anyway."

"Church?" Beau whined, trying to bury his head in his pillow.

"Get up, you big baby. It won't last that long. It might even do you some good."

The parish priest, Stephen Mylton, was a portly man with a booming voice, a voice that reached into the farthest corners of the large but plain meeting house and echoed back.

His voice was scolding when speaking of the various sins and vices that his sermon touched upon, and angry when speaking of the devil and his minions. Interestingly, though, he was able to lend some warmth to his thunderous voice when the message called for it.

"The Lord sayeth, 'For I was an hungred, and ye gave me meat. I was thirsty, and ye gave me drink. I was a stranger, and ye took me in. Naked, and ye clothed me. I was sick, and ye visited me. I was in prison, and ye came unto me.' Aye, brothers, these things are done unto the Lord, e'en though we see him not. How so?

"He continueth, 'Inasmuch as ye have done it unto one of the least of these my brethren, ye have done it unto me.' In the spirit of this counsel, Roonock is indeed pleased to welcome its newest residents, Jaxon and Britannia Malone, Beau Bannister and Allison Worthington, cast upon our shores by an accident of fate. And by the devilry of the Indians, they lost their friend, Ronald Rushby, at the hand of those wicked, godless savages." His voice rose in volume and his jowls trembled as he called down evil on the natives, and the audience responded with many audible sounds of disfavor.

Then turning to look at the four Americans in the audience, his voice warmed again as he said, "We welcome thee, friends." The statement was met with thunderous applause.

He continued the sermon for a few more minutes. Then, following the final hymn and prayer, the four were indeed welcomed by many.

The Americans had started moving toward the door but were soon surrounded by parishioners shaking their hands, patting their backs, and expressing condolences over Ron's death. After more than ten minutes had passed, they were still no closer to the door.

"I don't remember when I've ever shaken so many hands," Beau said.

"I know," Jax responded. "My face is starting to hurt from smiling so much. These people are amazing."

"We are none but common folk, Mr. Malone," said Mylton, the preacher, who was now next to them and had apparently overheard their exchange. "Some of the parishioners hath put together a dinner, as be our custom on Sundays." He leaned closer so that Jax could hear him over the noise of the churchgoers. "It is our hope that thou and thy friends wilt join us."

"Thank you, that's very kind of you," Jax said. Looking at his companions and seeing their positive reaction, he nodded toward Mylton. "We'd be happy to. Thank you again."

The dinner lasted for a couple of hours, and the mood was joyous and celebratory. Even though there were over a hundred people gathered in the vast dining hall, there was no shortage of food.

The feast was followed by what seemed to be an impromptu music concert, as various colonists displayed their talents on musical instruments of the past.

"I always did like Renaissance Festivals," Beau said. The others just smiled in response as the music continued.

§

Monday morning dawned much like other days in the colony, warm with gentle ocean breezes filtering softly through the forest. Jax and his crew had been disappointed that morning when Payne had informed them that he had not yet located a carpenter whose space they could utilize for their boat-building venture, but he had heartily assured them that he would keep at it.

They spent the day much like they had a couple of days before, looking around the colony, meeting more people, and finally spending time lounging around at the oasis, basking not only in each other's company, but also in the warm memories of the previous day. It was nearly 4:00 when they went back to their respective lodging places.

"Ah, good e'en gentlemen," said Mary as Jax and Beau entered the Hemmingtons' home. "Thou hast arrived early, for supper is not yet ready. But please, make thyselves comfortable." She went into the kitchen and Jax and Beau looked around at what they thought of as the living room.

"I think I'd be a little more comfortable in some cushy, overstuffed furniture," Beau said quietly, "but I guess we'll have to make do with wooden straight-backed chairs."

As soon as they had sat down, the kitchen door opened and Yahima came out bearing two steins. She handed the steins to them with her head bowed.

"Thank you, Yahima," Jax said, and she looked at him briefly, her face expressing a mild conflict that she seemed to feel. She nodded, then turned and went back into the kitchen.

"Not bad," said Beau, sipping the ale in his stein. "Not quite as cold as I like, but it tastes good." Jax absently sipped some of his, his mind a jumble of thoughts, from Yahima's confused reaction to his desire to build a boat. He decided to focus on what he had any control over.

"We should start working on plans for our new boat," he said.

"Are you sure you aren't setting your aspirations a little too high?" Beau asked.

"What do you mean?"

"Well, have you ever built a boat before?"

"No, of course not."

"I didn't think so. And neither have I. So, do you think maybe a raft might be more in keeping with our abilities?"

"Maybe so," Jax said, "but considering the distance we have to go, and the obstacles that exist between here and there, I want to be able to have more control over it than we could with just a raft." He looked at the cell phone on his belt. He had turned it off a couple of days ago to conserve the battery, but he still carried it. "God, I wish we could just call someone."

"I know," Beau agreed. "I wonder how far we'd have to go to get outside this EMF interference zone. And to get to where we'd have cell phone service. I don't suppose Verizon covers the open sea."

Jax shook his head and sighed, feeling almost helpless. He drained his stein and placed it on the table in front of him. Almost immediately Yahima came back into the room to take their empty steins. She took Beau's from him and picked up Jax's stein from the table. As she did so, she looked directly at Jax, and he was surprised by the expression of fear in her eyes.

"Please help me," she said in just the breath of a whisper. Before she could say anything else, the front door opened and John came in. Yahima shook her head slightly toward Jax, then silently turned and disappeared into the kitchen.

§

Phil Chesterfield looked at the GPS, scratching the side of his large belly, a common reaction for him when he was confused. After spending the whole day in his cruiser, he and his friend Jerry Sanders had reached the last location from which Jax had called several days before. From there, they headed south, the direction that he knew Jax was going in examining the grid that Phil had proposed.

There was no sign of Jax or the *Camilla*. He had attempted radio contact but had received no answer. In fact, aside from static, there seemed to be nothing coming in on the radio, on *any* channel.

The swollen sun was dipping into the ocean in the west, and Phil was preparing to drop anchor for the night when he noticed that the GPS was also acting up.

Cannot find satellite.

"What's the matter?" Jerry asked, seeing the puzzled look on Phil's face, and recognizing his telltale belly scratching.

"The damn GPS is fucked up," Phil answered. "It can't find the satellite. That kind of message is fairly common if you're driving through a tunnel, or in an underground parking garage. On the open sea, it shouldn't be a problem."

"Maybe this far out, we're just out of range of the satellite."

"No," Phil answered impatiently, shaking his head. "The Global Positioning System has at least thirty satellites in various orbits around the globe. There are always a few satellites within view. Each GPS receiver actually uses multiple satellites to plot your location. At least three, usually four or more are always in line of sight."

"Hmm. Well, it's going to be too dark pretty soon to keep looking. Do you know how to fix the GPS?"

"Hell, no," Phil growled, frustrated. "I'm no electronics engineer. If it can't locate the satellites by morning, we may just have to plot our course visually. I know we're at the approximate starting point of the grid. We'll just have to continue southward and see if we can see any sign of them."

P lease help me," Yahima had said last night. As the four of them walked to the Constabulary, Jax kept seeing the fear in her eyes as she quietly stated her plea. He remembered her unusual reactions when they had contact with her at breakfast a couple of days before. And the way she instantly turned and disappeared when John came in the front door last night, she obviously didn't want the Hemmingtons to know. Was she afraid of them, or of something else?

She had spoken quietly, directly in front of Jax, so Beau hadn't seen or heard it and wasn't able to offer any explanations. And they hadn't seen Yahima again as she was either kept busy in the kitchen last night, or else went to her room in the basement. And she was not around this morning either. Mary was there and had served them their breakfast.

But Jax just couldn't get Yahima's fear-filled eyes or her uneasy, frightened plea out of his head. "Please help me."

"Ah, good morrow my friends," said Payne as they entered the Constabulary. "I am happy to see thee. I believe thou may be pleased with my good news."

"Really? What's that?" asked Beau.

"I hath succeeded in locating a carpenter who hath offered thee the use of his tools and his workshop. Thou canst begin working on thy boat whenever thou art ready."

"That's wonderful!" Jax said enthusiastically. "Thank you so much."

"Not at all. If thou wouldst like, I could take thee there now."

"Yes, please."

The shop was on the western side of the compound, near the smaller western gate of the colony, not far from the oasis that they had discovered the other day. The shop itself was fairly small, but there was a sort of courtyard in front of it which would serve their purposes very well.

Jax had not yet figured out the logistics of building a boat, or of getting it to the water. But the carpenter, Henry Hewet, was exceedingly helpful and accommodating, and offered to assist them in their endeavor. He was a pleasant man, around thirty years old, with dark hair and eyes, and skin browned from daily working in the sun. He was also, as it turned out, Thomas Dare's son-in-law.

The majority of the morning was spent with Hewet sketching out plans, with all four of the Americans offering suggestions. Hewet had been one of the men that Justin Wilkinson had referred to a few days before as having built a small boat for fishing, so his basic knowledge in the craft was helpful. They just had to scale it up, and modify the transom to accommodate the outboard motor that they had salvaged from the shredded Zodiac.

A wooden boat would be heavier and more unwieldy than the Zodiac, so it could not be so big that the motor would have little effect. Jax had his old pleasure cruiser in mind as they were drawing and modifying the plans. Eventually the drawing ended up being much sleeker than the design that Hewet had originally made, a design that surprised the colonist, but he immediately saw the benefit of the new slender and narrower lines.

"Well," said Hewet, "it is mid-day, my friends. We hath done some fine work. If thou art satisfied with the progress that we hath made with these plans, perhaps we can begin construction preparations for thy boat this afternoon."

"That would be great, Mr. Hewet," Jax replied. "We all really appreciate your help in this."

"I assure thee," Hewet smiled, "it is my pleasure. Dost thou have plans for dinner? For thou art welcome to join me at my home."

"We're going to the Hemmingtons' home for dinner," Jax replied. "But thank you very much for your hospitality." Hewet waved it off with a smile and a nod and they parted ways.

"Are you sure about this Yahima?" Brit asked. Jax had told them this morning when they were on their way to the Constabulary about her odd behavior the night before, and that he had accepted Mary's offer for dinner thinking that it may provide an opportunity to find out more.

"To be completely honest," he said, "I don't know anything, really. I just know that she seemed really afraid."

"How do you think you can get any more information from her if she's afraid of the Hemmingtons and they're there?" asked Allie.

"I'm not sure I can. I'm just hoping that if there are four of us there, there might be more distractions for John and Mary, and maybe an opportunity will present itself. I'm just going to play it by ear."

It didn't take them long to reach the Hemmingtons' house, and the atmosphere was delightfully pleasant. Yahima was there and she helped to serve the food, but there was little opportunity for actual contact, though Brit tried.

"May I help in the kitchen?" she asked.

"Nonsense," Mary replied. "Thou art our guests."

Jax sincerely enjoyed the pleasantries, as John and Mary were, as before, personable and welcoming. But below the surface, he was irritated, and he chafed at his inability to follow up on Yahima's contact from the previous evening. That is until they were finished and preparing to go back to Hewet's shop.

John was taking his leave to return to his job at the metalsmith shop, and Mary was outside bidding them all goodbye.

"Oh, excuse me," Jax said. "I left something inside. I'll be right back." Mary seemed as if she were about to offer to get whatever it was for him, but fortunately the others picked up on what Jax was doing and kept her involved in conversation.

He closed the door behind him and went first to the side table where he had purposely left a sketch for their boat, as an excuse to come back in. Then he went toward the kitchen door and quietly called to Yahima. She came warily out of the kitchen, looking around, presumably, for John or Mary.

"What's wrong, Yahima?" he quickly asked. "What can I do?"

"I do not know," she said with a glance toward the door. She cast her eyes about, as if she were thinking quickly.

"Obviously," Jax said, "we can't talk long now. When can we meet?"

"Mrs. Hemmington will probably send me for water early tomorrow morning," she finally said. "Canst thou meet me at the Watering Hole in the northern stream ere breakfast?"

Jax remembered this pool from their previous wanderings through the colony, where the people apparently went to collect the water that they would need for the day. He remembered the "Ye Watering Hole" sign.

"Of course. I'll be there." With tears in her eyes, Yahima threw her arms around him, then ran back to the kitchen.

§

They had not gone very far when they noticed that something was happening. People were running past them, back toward the north gate.

"What's going on?" Beau asked when he was able to make eye contact with one of them.

"More visitors cometh!" he said excitedly. "Another boat!"

With a quick glance at each other, all four of them turned around and started running too, mixing with the crowd. The gate was just closing when they arrived at the northern end of the compound. Accompanied by an armed escort were two men, a large, many-chinned man with grey hair, and his tall, thin companion.

"Professor Chesterfield?" Jax said when they got close enough to recognize the two men in the crowd. Phil looked up at the sound of his name.

"Jax!" Phil bellowed as he ran toward him. "You're alright!"

"I'm fine," he said. "But I lost my boat."

"We saw what was left of the Zodiac on the beach. But you lost the *Camilla*? That's fucked up. Why didn't you call me?"

"Electronics are screwed up out here. We've decided that it's EMF interference from some kind of weird tectonics situation. I don't know. It's just a theory. But Allie could explain it better."

"I thought it was just my equipment that was fucked up."

"No, it's area-wide."

Phil remembered his friend just behind him. "I'm sorry," he said. "This is my friend Jerry Sanders." Jerry and Jax shook hands.

"Nice to meet you, Jerry," Jax said quickly, as a formality, then he urgently turned back to Phil. "Phil, where's your boat?"

"It's anchored off-shore, near the beach where you came ashore."

"We need to get it now!" Beau insisted.

"He's right," Jax said. "I'll go talk to Payne." He headed toward the Constabulary, through the noisy confusion and crowd of welcoming people, and arrived just as the door opened and Payne came out. "Governor Payne, we need to go back and get their boat right away!"

"Go back?" Payne said. "But that is a dangerous trek through the forest."

"Well your men should have thought of that before they brought Phil and Jerry here."

"Dost thou know these men?" Payne asked, looking up at them in surprise.

"Yes I do. Please, Mr. Payne."

"I am very sorry. We are not accustomed to such activity so the thought did not occur to my men. But thou art quite right. I shall assemble a fresh troop to accompany thee back. Hopefully the Indians hath not already inflicted their evil damage."

§

It was a sullen group of people who made their way back to the fortress an hour and a half later. Their trip to the beach had turned out much like the one just a few days before.

"Damn it!" Beau exclaimed as they came through the gate. They were greeted by Allie and Brit who had not accompanied them. "We were too late!"

Phil did not say anything. He seemed to be in shock, and was breathing heavily as he mopped the sweat from his forehead.

"What the hell is with those natives?" Jax asked rhetorically. The crestfallen looks on Brit and Allie's faces reflected his own mood. Payne came out to meet them when they arrived. He saw the disappointment on their faces, and he conducted them into the Constabulary.

"I am so awfully sorry," he said as they sat down, wiping the sweat from their faces. His expression was one of extreme sympathy. Most of the men who had escorted them disappeared into the "break room" at the back, but a few minutes later, three of them came out bearing mugs and placed them in front of the six Americans.

"Thank you," said Jax, and they all gratefully drank the cool beer.

"I cannot fully express the sorrow I feel over thy unsuccessful quest," Payne said, his countenance reinforcing his words. "And in accordance with thy suggestion earlier, I have instructed my men that, in the event that we receive any new visitors, they shall immediately insist that the people return to their boat posthaste."

"Great," Beau said grumpily. "Doesn't help us much now."

"I well know," Payne said, sympathetically nodding his agreement. He put his hands together and placed his fingertips under his chin in his characteristic gesture. "But please rest assured, my friends, that thou art most welcome here among us indefinitely." Turning toward Jax, he continued. "Hast thou begun thy work on a boat?"

"We've gotten the plans drawn up," answered Jax. "We were going to start working on it this afternoon." He glanced at his watch. "I guess it'll have to wait till tomorrow now."

"A boat?" Phil asked, breaking his silence.

"Yes," Jax explained, "Governor Payne has arranged for us to work with one of the local carpenters to build a boat. He has been really helpful and accommodating." He looked up at Payne who smiled sympathetically and nodded his acknowledgment.

"I want to help," Phil said, and Jerry agreed.

"Absolutely!" Beau said. "The more help we get, the sooner we can leave!"

§

The next morning, Jax rose early and quietly crept out of the house. He was at the "Watering Hole" before the sun was up. He moved a short distance away into a grove of trees, and he watched for Yahima from his concealed location.

She never arrived.

Instead, he saw John Hemmington come and dip two pails into the water and then head back toward the house. Disappointed, Jax went back himself, making up a story about wanting to get out for an early morning walk.

When possible, Brit was spending her time in the colony's archives, learning all she could about the history of Roanoke and the survivors. At times when none of the colonists were available to supervise, or when they had not pulled anything new for her to see, she helped out with the boat construction, as did Allie.

The construction of their boat, Jax realized, was going to take much longer than he had anticipated. He had not thought about the necessity of first making the lumber. The grueling process started with actually cutting down trees. The five men went outside the walls, and while three of them chopped trees, two stood guard with muskets, and they switched off periodically.

Once the trees were felled, the men had to spend time hacking off the limbs, leaving only a bare trunk. The trunks then had to be dragged back into the fortress to Hewet's work area, at which time they cut, split and planed them by hand.

Fortunately Henry Hewet had an ox, so dragging the trees to his carpentry shop was not quite as difficult as it could have been. But overall, the procedure was backbreaking and maddeningly time-consuming. In the process, the Americans were developing a fine collection of blisters.

"It's going to take us forever to get this done," Phil growled bitterly.

"I know," Jax replied. "We're still getting accustomed to this slower pace ourselves."

"Well, don't get *too* accustomed to it," Phil replied. "We have to get out of this backwards, God-forsaken place!"

"Please excuse me, sir," said Hewet who had overheard Phil's comment. "We are not at all God-forsaken, for he is here with us and blesseth us in all our endeavors."

"Yeah, well," Phil said, his bluster turned down a bit, "it was just a figure of speech. I didn't mean to start a theological discussion."

Hewet, though appearing somewhat baffled at Phil's angry outburst, seemed relatively satisfied with his response and went back to work.

Phil lowered his voice and continued to Jax and Beau. "Really, though, this place is driving me crazy, and I've only been here a day. I don't know how you guys have lasted as long as you have."

"It's really not that bad," Jax said. Phil scoffed at that with a disgusted look on his face. "I mean, don't get me wrong," Jax continued, "we definitely want to get home, but the people are wonderful. They're so helpful and hospitable. And the history of this place is amazing!"

"Yeah, well I'm not a historian," Phil said, "so you'll forgive me if I think this place is a shit hole." Jax glanced with some embarrassment toward Hewet, as Phil's voice had already risen again.

"Come on, Phil," Jerry said quietly, trying to placate him. "I know this work is slow and difficult, but at least we're still alive. We could have been killed like their friend."

"I know, I know!" Phil replied with irritation, his chins shaking back and forth. "That's a glowing endorsement. 'Being here is better than being dead.' I'm glad we're alive. I'm just really fucking pissed! I wish I was alive on my boat. I wish I could lob a missile or two onto this island and blow the whole fucking thing away."

Their work for the rest of the day was strained, as Hewet seemed uncomfortable after Phil's outburst.

§

Jax had attempted to make contact with Yahima again that day, but there always seemed to be obstacles. So the next morning, he repeated his actions of the previous day, rising early and going to the Watering Hole.

He kept watch once again from behind a tree. This time, he saw her coming towards his hiding place, bearing two buckets in her hands.

She saw him as he stepped out from behind the tree and, looking behind her to make sure she was not being observed, she ran toward him into the cover of the trees.

"I am so happy to see thee, Mr. Malone," she said as they stepped back into the small grove of trees for concealment. "My apologies for not coming yesterday morn. Mrs. Hemmington gave me an assignment which lasted longer than either of us expected so Mr. Hemmington fetched the water in my stead."

"That's okay, Yahima," Jax replied. "You said 'help me.' What is it you need my help with?"

"I need thy help in getting home," she said with tears forming in her eyes.

"I'm not sure I understand what you mean. I can't even get *myself* home."

"But is not thy home a long distance from here?"

"Yes, it is," Jax said, his eyebrows furrowed, as he became increasingly confused about their exchange.

"My home is not far."

"I still don't understand, Yahima. Where is your home?"

"My village is just on the other side of this island."

"Well, why do you need my help? I'm sure you know this island much better than I do."

They heard footsteps approaching and he stopped talking. Jax grasped Yahima's shoulders and pulled her up against him so they could both fit behind the trunk of the tree and remain unseen. Holding her against him with his arm around her back, Jax leaned around the edge of their hiding place. Carefully peering out through the trees, Jax saw a colonist drawing water. After a minute, he was gone and Jax looked back at Yahima.

Her face was inches away from his, and he was struck by her beauty as she held his gaze, despite the tears in her eyes. He hadn't realized until then that her arms were around him as well. Nervously, Jax let go of Yahima and she stepped back, reluctantly, it seemed. He tried to get his attention back to their conversation.

"I just don't see how I can provide any assistance," he said, shaking his head.

"Alright," she said as she started to back away, wiping her eyes. "I am sorry to have bothered thee." She started to turn away from him, but Jax stopped her.

"Wait," he said, holding her upper arm again. She seemed to cower from him then, but she stood still, her eyes down.

"Yahima, are you afraid of me," Jax asked, puckering his eyebrows again. His voice softened. "I'm not going to hurt you." She looked back up at him, her eyes glistening in the dim light of morning.

"No," she replied. "I sensed that thou wouldst not. Thou dost seem much different from the other white people here. Thy confidence and strength, and thy compassion, made me think that thou couldst help me in my time of need."

"I don't get it. How can I help?"

"Help me get back to my home. My village."

"But I thought *this* was your home," he said, glancing around toward the colony.

"Few of us live here of our own free will," she said bitterly.

"I still don't understand. All of the colonists that we've spoken with talk as if they love it here."

"I am not speaking of the colonists, Mr. Malone. I refer rather to the Indians. The natives. We are here only to serve the white people."

Abruptly, a dark feeling began growing in Jax's gut as Yahima spoke. He looked at her through narrowed eyes, fearing to ask the question.

"Wait a minute. Are you telling me that the white colonists are keeping you here as slaves?" he finally asked.

"Yes, Mr. Malone. We are slaves." Jax was silent for quite some time as he processed what she said.

"Call me Jax," he said absently. He nervously pushed his hands through his hair, feeling overwhelmed by the weight of what Yahima had said. "You're not just talking about John and Mary Hemmington, are you? It's not just them. You're talking about the whole colony, right?"

"Yes."

"Oh my God!" he said under his breath. Jax searched his mind for a plan of action, none of which seemed to have any hope of success.

Talking to the Hemmingtons about it would serve no purpose since, as Yahima said, it was a colony-wide situation. Talking to Governor Payne about it would likely serve no purpose either. The knowledge that Jax had of the apparent mindset of slave owners in the past gave him little hope of talking any sense into him.

"I still don't know what I can do," he finally said, "but I do want to help. Let me talk to my friends and see if we can come up with any kind of plan."

Yahima smiled, sending the tears rolling down her cheeks, and she wrapped her arms around him, holding him tightly. Jax put his arms around her in response, barely thinking, as his mind was awash in his feelings of dread and outrage. Finally, he gently pushed her away from him so he could look her in the eyes.

"Go ahead and draw your water," he said, "and then get back to work as if nothing has happened. We don't want to arouse any suspicions until we're in a position to do something about it." Yahima nodded, still smiling.

"My thanks to thee, sir," she said as she stood up on her toes and gave Jax a quick kiss. She picked up the buckets and, with another look at Jax's face, she stepped out of the grove of trees and walked toward the pool.

§

"Oh, come on, I don't believe it," Brit said, looking at Jax through narrowed eyes. "You're serious, aren't you? Slavery?"

"That's right. She said that few of the natives live here voluntarily. We didn't have very long to talk, so I don't know any details about how it's implemented, but she was totally serious about it."

They were talking with the girls outside, near their respective lodging places, before they separated for the day. Brit was going to go to the Constabulary's archives, to study more of the history, while Jax and Beau were going to resume their work on the boat. Allie had decided to go with them, to help out around the workshop.

In relating to them about his meeting with Yahima that morning, Jax had left out the parts about the physical contact. He wasn't sure what to think about it himself.

They all seemed reluctant to believe the story.

"Are you sure she's not just some disgruntled employee, wanting to get back at a boss she doesn't like?" asked Beau.

"She doesn't want to get back at them. She just wants to go home."

"So what are we going to do?" Allie asked.

"I don't know," Jax replied. "I just wanted to get it out there so we can all be thinking about it. I figure that, with a little brainstorming, we can come up with some kind of plan."

After discussing it for a few minutes more, they agreed to meet again before dinner to pool any ideas they might have had. Then they went their separate ways.

Even though they were a little later to arrive at Henry Hewet's shop, Jerry was just arriving himself when they got there.

"Phil's disappeared," he said without preamble.

"Disappeared?" Allie asked. "What do you mean?"

"Just like yesterday morning, after breakfast, I was waiting outside the Archards' house where he was staying, but he never came out. I finally knocked on their door and Mrs. Archard answered. I asked her about Phil and she said that he was gone. She didn't know any more than that."

"I know he hated this place," Jax said, "but I didn't think he'd make a run for it."

"I'm not saying that. He wouldn't have just left us here," Jerry said.

"He knows we need a boat," said Beau. "There's no other way off this island. And now there are fewer of us to work on it."

"I told you he wouldn't just leave us here," Jerry said more indignantly.

"Well, where do you think he went, Jerry?" Allie asked softly, trying to calm him down.

"I don't know. I saw him go into the Archards' house last night after we left here," he recounted, as if trying to retrace his steps. "But I was exhausted after working here all day yesterday, and I just went to bed right after dinner. I didn't see him again." He looked at them in distress. "He knows I don't like it here either. If he had a plan to get out of here, he would have at least included me."

"Okay," said Jax with a calming voice. "We'll get it figured out." He thought for a moment, then sighed. "I hate to slow down our progress here, but I'll go talk to Payne. Maybe he knows something, or maybe he can help us find Phil."

"No, you stay here, Jax," Allie said. "You'll be a lot more help here than I will. I'll go talk to Payne. And I'll let you know what I find out."

"Okay, good idea," Jax said. He gave her a quick kiss and she turned and left, while the rest of them went in to get started on the day's work.

§

Brit settled into the chair as she looked at the latest selection of historic documents that had been provided for her study.

As her apparent respect for the fragility of the old papers had been observed, along with her reverence for their inherent historical significance, Governor Payne and Lieutenant Governor Dare had begun allowing her greater privacy as she perused them. Doubtless they had responsibilities of their own and did not have time to stand over her, supervising her as she read them.

This morning, she had other things on her mind, and she was too distracted to pay much attention to the documents she had been given.

She still found it difficult to believe that these sweet, humble and devout people were keeping the natives as slaves, as personal property. Brit knew the people were from a different era, but still it was difficult to reconcile slavery with the year 2017.

She hoped that, as she continued spending time in the archives, she might be able to dig up something that would either refute or corroborate the statement of the native girl. It also might be helpful to talk to Ruth, Susan Wilkinson's cook, but she doubted that she would have an opportunity to do so without Susan around.

She glanced quickly through the documents that had been provided for her and saw that they were rather mundane pages, providing a picture of everyday life four hundred years ago. Normally she would be enthralled by such things, but not today. In light of this latest revelation, it seemed dull and uninteresting to her.

One thing she did notice, though, was the subtle but now observable slant against the natives that the writings had come to display. Having heard the native girl's accusation, this prejudice seemed to be more apparent now.

Brit looked around the room, noting the dark wood paneling. It had seemed cozy and welcoming before, like an old, comfortable library. But now she felt claustrophobic, as if the dark room was closing in around her.

She rose from her chair, stretching her reluctant muscles as she did so, and looked around the room, opening cabinet doors, pulling out drawers, looking at what was inside.

Her heart was pounding as she poked around, and frequently looked over her shoulder, knowing that, while it had never been expressly stated to her that she was not allowed to look at everything they had filed here, it was likely frowned upon, in fact probably implicitly forbidden. But she kept on.

As Brit continued her inspection, she quickly discovered a pattern to their filing system. She found several large drawers that contained technical drawings of structures and devices that were in use in various places around the compound. The style was quite old-fashioned, of course, line drawings that reminded her of some of the drawings of Leonardo da Vinci that she had seen.

Some drawers contained bills of sale, receipts, official constabulary documents and reports, etc. The problem was that, without knowing the context of the documents, Brit often found it difficult to determine which documents, if any, might have any real significance to them.

But as a thought occurred to her, she started looking through the receipts and bills of sale. Most of the receipts seemed to be for supplies and equipment, and some things that she couldn't decipher. Then she found a bill of sale which proved to be quite a different matter.

> 7 Julye, 1647
> Sold by John Tayler
> Younge adult male Indian, in goode health and well-built.
> Sold for six chickens to Paul Dorrell.
> Witnessed by Charles Brooke.

Leafing through the documents, Brit found several more. Surely, though, it was just a historical characteristic of the colony, just like in America. Closing that drawer, she opened others and glanced through them until she found what seemed to be the most recent one.

14 April, 2017

Sold by Roger Viccars

Indian woman, about 17 years of age, in goode health and pleasant shape. Believed to be of goode childe-bearing stock.

Sold for one pig to Charles Bishop.

Witnessed by William Payne.

Brit slowly slipped the document back in place in the drawer and closed it, her mind deluged with the horror of the situation in which they now found themselves. She went back to the chair where the documents that they had selected for her were still scattered on the table.

Pondering what to do, she remembered one of the documents she had seen earlier. She got up and went back to the large drawers where she had started her investigation. One of the technical drawings she had seen suggested a possibility, and she studied it more closely.

Then she closed it up and left, hoping to be able to talk to Jax before lunch, or dinner as the colonists called the mid-day meal.

At almost the same moment that she exited the archive, she saw Allie leaving Payne's area. Her face bore a frustrated expression.

"What's up?" Brit asked as they went outside and started hurrying toward Hewet's shop.

"Phil's gone," she said.

"Gone? You mean he left?"

"Who knows? Nobody's seen him."

"Why would he just leave the rest of us here? And where would he go?"

"I don't know. Nobody seems to know anything. Following a wild goose chase that lasted most of the morning, I finally tracked Payne back to the Constabulary where I started. God, what I wouldn't give to have access to a working telephone system!"

"So what did you find out?"

"Nothing!" Allie said, throwing up her hands, the annoyance audible in her voice. "He doesn't know anything either. But I do know that Phil could not just walk out of this guarded fortress without someone seeing him."

"Well actually, there might be a way. I'm going to talk to Jax about it now."

§

Jax and Beau were stacking lumber against the far wall of the courtyard, while Jerry assisted Henry Hewet in planing other boards. Jax and Beau seemed tense, possibly even angry. When Jax saw Allie and Brit, he met them at the gate into the courtyard, and he wiped the perspiration from his forehead.

"What did you find out about Phil?" he asked Allie.

"Nothing," she said, the frustration still plainly discernible in her voice. "Nobody knows anything about him."

Jax sighed and shook his head, looking off into the distance. After a few moments, he seemed to notice Brit's presence.

"What are you doing here? Are you finished with your history lessons already?"

"I did a little unauthorized snooping," she replied, ignoring the sarcasm in his voice. "I found several bills of sale, for natives sold as slaves, dating back several centuries, and some as recent as just a month or two ago. Those recent ones were witnessed and signed by William Payne."

Jax stared hard at Brit, and finally, not knowing how to respond, he looked away and forced a disgusted exhalation.

"Slavery, in the twenty-first century, among so-called civilized people!" He said it quietly, for fear of being overheard by Hewet, as Beau joined them. "Well, I guess it goes without saying that Yahima can't just walk out the gate and go home," Jax finished.

"It seems none of us can," Allie said. "During my discussion with Payne, I asked if he thought there might be any chance that Phil had walked out by one of the gates and nobody remembered or noticed. Payne's response was that *nobody* is allowed out of the gates, at least not without some form of official business."

"What do you mean, nobody is allowed out?"

"I mean just that. They don't let people leave. Supposedly for their own protection."

"So we're prisoners here too?" Beau asked.

"Well, there's more," Allie continued. "Payne said he was going to tell you, but since I was there, he told me so I could pass it on to you."

"What?" Jax said in a dull tone, as if he was already fearing more bad news.

"The outboard motor from the Zodiac is probably not usable now."

"What the bloody hell are you talking about?" Beau asked.

"He was all contrite and apologetic, as usual. He had the motor put in storage for safekeeping, leaned up against a corner as we last saw it. But he said that sometime during the night, it must have fallen over and broke. Obviously he doesn't know anything about motors, so he couldn't tell me what was actually wrong with it aside from the fact that it's in at least two pieces."

"Just from tipping over, it's in multiple pieces now?" Jax asked angrily.

"He wanted me to stress to you that he is so very sorry and embarrassed."

"I'm getting so sick of his passive-aggressive bullshit," Beau said.

Brit placed a hand on his as she saw Hewet look up curiously at Beau's outburst.

"Any chance we could get out of here with a rowboat?" Brit asked.

"I'm getting discouraged about getting any kind of boat built at all," Jax said looking at Beau, and trying to keep his own emotions in check. "Have you noticed how Hewet is beginning to criticize our plans and our work?"

"Have I noticed?" Beau echoed. "Are you kidding? I was there. I haven't done anything right all morning."

Turning to the girls, Jax continued.

"Yeah, it's like there's something wrong with everything we do, at least as far as *he's* concerned."

"Hmm," Beau grunted in agreement. "And something else I've been noticing: Every time we mention to someone that we're building a boat to get off this island, they always act surprised, even shocked that we would want to do that, and they always talk about how 'treacherous' the sea is."

"Yeah, I've heard that too," said Allie.

"They always use the same word, as if it's a practiced comment," Beau said. "I get the feeling that they don't want us to build a boat. I think they just want to keep us busy and out of the way. And discouraged," he added, glancing toward Hewet.

"And I find it hard to believe that they don't have a lumber mill here," Jax continued.

"I know," said Beau. "I thought of that too. There's a river flowing through the colony and nobody is using it for power?"

"I'm sure someone is," Jax said quietly. "We're just not being given access to it." He sighed. "I don't know. I don't mean to sound paranoid. I'm beginning to sound like a conspiracy theorist. Maybe Phil's negativity has rubbed off on me."

"Well, who can blame you," said Beau. "After everything that's happened to us in the last few days, all the obstacles we've encountered, and now the outboard motor's destroyed? It all just seems too coincidental."

"Well, back on the subject of the river," Brit said, "I discovered something interesting this morning. I found some technical drawings that show the spot in the western wall where the river flows into the compound."

"Oh, right near the oasis," Beau said.

"Right. They used some kind of cement material and built a tunnel under the wall. The river flows in through that tunnel, but in the area directly under the wall is a large metal grate secured on this side with three hand screws."

"Which would prevent enemies from being able to enter the colony by way of the river," said Jax.

"Exactly. But it *would* allow someone from inside to get out unseen if they could get that grate opened and swim the length of the tunnel."

"How long is the tunnel?"

"According to the plans, it looked like it was about a hundred feet long."

"That's not too bad," Jax said, encouraged. "I was able to go about four hundred feet deep when I was freediving."

"Yeah, but here you'd be going against the current," Allie said with a worried tone, "and you'll have to get the grate opened while you're under there."

"On the plus side," continued Brit, "according to the specs, it did look like it was built in sections with beveled edges, fitted together. You may be able to find some hand holds in there. But there's also another grate at the other end of the tunnel, with a similar hand screw arrangement."

"Well, they couldn't make it *too* easy, could they?" Jax said with a sardonic grin.

Beau nudged Jax as Hewet approached.

"Ah, good day, ladies," he said, doffing his hat. Turning to the men, he said, "I shall see thee after dinner."

"See you later," said Beau.

§

"So what's gonna happen, Cap'n?" Beau asked as they walked slowly toward the Hemmingtons' house for their noon meal.

"I don't know," Jax admitted. "Not much of a choice. Live inside this compound with slave owners, as prisoners ourselves, or go outside and be at the mercy of hostile natives."

"I assume Yahima could convince them that we're okay people," Brit said.

"Maybe, but who knows what they might do before she has a chance. Remember how quickly they killed Ron."

The four of them were subdued at dinner, though the Hemmingtons tried to engage them in conversation. What added to their distraction was the bruise on the side of Yahima's face, her split lip, and the way she moved as if she were in pain.

Though they tried to make a show of enjoying their time there, and participating in the conversation, Jax spent almost the whole meal assembling a plan in his head. If only he could manage a couple of minutes alone with Yahima.

With a few well-timed looks and subtle gestures, he was able to make Beau and Brit understand what he needed.

Like before, John was the first to take his leave to head back to his job at the metalsmith shop. Brit asked Mary something about the flowers in front of her house, which she was only too happy to expound upon. After she and Beau had gotten her outside to look at them, Jax quickly went into the kitchen, followed by Allie.

"Yahima, what happened?" he asked, indicating her injuries.

"I fear I took too long fetching the water this morn," she replied. "I did not have a ready excuse and received a beating for the offense."

"Oh, you poor thing," Allie said.

"I'm sorry, Yahima," Jax said, but as he glanced toward the door, he decided they needed to stay on topic. "I'm sure we don't have much time. Can you meet us tomorrow morning, at the same place and time?"

"If I am not detained, I will be there without fail," Yahima said.

"Good. If we help you get out of here, will we be safe from harm from your people?"

Yahima's eyes opened wider as the reason for this meeting became clear.

"I will lead you there," she said as she threw herself into his arms. "I will tell them that thou art good and excellent people, deserving of their trust and care."

"We'll see you then," Jax said, pushing her away, and he and Allie quickly went out the front door. Beau had a look of relief on his face, as if they had just about exhausted their discussion of Mary Hemmington's flowers.

As they walked back toward Hewet's shop, Jax briefly explained the plan. Nearing the village square where they were about to turn west, they were at the small grove of trees near the Watering Hole, where Jax had hidden while waiting for Yahima. Suddenly, there was a sound from the trees that caught their attention.

"Psst. Hey mister," said a young voice. Jax looked into the trees and saw several young, dirty faces peering at them. One boy, perhaps twelve years old, seemed to be taking the lead and motioned for the Americans to follow them into the grove.

The children were dressed similarly to the others in the colony, but were quite dirty. There were seven of them, boys and girls, ranging in ages from about eight to twelve. They all seemed nervous, and often cast glances out from among the trees. Some were muttering among themselves, but the leader quieted them.

"I'm Micah," he said, and put his hand out. Jax smiled and shook his hand.

"Nice to meet you, Micah," he said, and he introduced the others.

"Some of my friends didn't think we should talk to thee," he said, hooking a thumb over his shoulder toward them without introducing them. "But I thought ye looked alright."

"I'm glad you did," said Jax, still smiling. The term 'street urchin' came to mind. He thought they looked like a scene out of a tropical version of *Oliver Twist*.

"Thing is," Micah continued, "thy friend didn't leave." He looked at Allie. "We overheard thee talkin' 'bout him with Payne. He didn't walk out of here. He never left."

Jax and Allie knelt down to be on their level as they realized that this was not just a random meeting with a bunch of little rascals.

"What are you talking about, Micah?" Allie asked.

"And we think Payne lied to thee, too," he said, ignoring her question. "He knoweth about it."

"Payne knows about what, Micah?" Jax asked. "What did he lie about?"

"About thy friend. He didn't leave. He's still here, but he's chained up."

"You're talking about Phil Chesterfield?"

"Aye, the big fellow," and Micah put his hands out as if resting them on a large belly. "He's in a cell in the jail."

"The jail?" asked Beau. "Where's that?"

"Right over there," Micah said, pointing toward the village square, "next to Payne's office."

"And you saw Phil in there? Our friend, the big man?" asked Jax.

"Aye. We know all the hiding places." Micah's face expressed a certain smugness, or pride at having figured out the colonists' secrets.

"Hiding places?" Jax asked with a frown. "I don't understand. Can you take us to see him?"

"Sure thing, mister," Micah said. The other kids started fidgeting and a couple of them poked him with their fingers. He made a show of shrugging them off as he continued talking. "But ye must make us a promise first."

The four adults exchanged glances and Jax looked back at the boy. "What promise?" he asked.

"There be many of us who don't like it here and don't want to be here," Micah said. "When thou escapeth, take us with thee."

"What about your parents?" Jax asked, feeling uncomfortable. He didn't want to be involved in a mass kidnapping.

"We got no parents," Micah said matter-of-factly. "They was taken away."

"What do you mean, they were taken away?"

"They didn't like it here and didn't want to stay. But nobody can go against the colony's wishes, so they was taken away. Some of us managed to get away from them, though, and we banded together. We keep an eye on things and protect each other."

"Where do they take them?" Jax asked, trying not to be impatient.

"To the jail, to start with," Micah said, pointing again toward the square. "After that, they kill 'em."

"How do you know this?" Beau asked as they all began to feel a mounting dread.

"We seen it a couple o' times," the boy said without emotion. "But most o' the times, the people just disappear."

"Micah," Jax said quietly, struggling to remain calm, "*we* don't want to stay here. Are you telling us that we will be killed?"

"Aye, eventually, if thou dost not change thy minds. Or at least act like it. Like I said, many of us don't want to be here, but we learnt to blend in. Those that don't, disappear."

"Okay," said Beau, looking at his watch, "this shit's getting a little too heavy. Jax, we're going to be missed if we don't get back to Hewet's place."

"I know," Jax replied, "but we can't stay here, knowing that our lives will be in danger, and we can't leave Phil."

"I know that, too," Beau said. "Here's what I propose: the three of you go back to Hewet's and work as if nothing has happened. Make some excuse for me. Because I'll go with the kids and find Phil and see if we can work out a way to get him out. It will likely be easier for one of us to see him than for all of us to go tramping through those hiding places they mentioned."

"That's actually a good idea," said Brit, "except that I'll go back to the Constabulary. I'll rummage around and see if I can find anything else that might help us to make an escape."

Jax was hesitating, but saw the wisdom in what they were suggesting. "Alright," he finally said. He turned back toward the kids. "Will you take Beau to see Phil? Can you do that safely?"

"Of course, mister. We'll show 'im. If ye promise."

Jax looked up at the others, then back to Micah and nodded. "We promise."

The kids nodded and Jax turned to Beau. "Okay, you go with them. We'll go back to Hewet's place. But I'm thinking we may not stay. I'll see if I can figure a way to get to the river. I've got some preparing to do."

With that, they went their separate ways.

Rather than walking through the square, the kids walked around it, using "side streets," and Beau followed carefully. Having heard their tales of people being killed, which he still wasn't sure he believed, he felt self-conscious following this group of little outlaws. But nobody paid them any attention. Wearing the colonists' "uniform," they looked like everyone else now.

Filing around the back of a row of old, and apparently little-used buildings, they came into what seemed to be an abandoned alley, almost hidden from the street, scattered with debris and filth. Walking around a stack of wooden crates, Micah reached down and grabbed a hidden mechanism at the bottom of the wall, and a section of it swung out on some sort of concealed hinge. Behind it was a small dark doorway. The kids disappeared into it, down a steep, narrow staircase, and Micah motioned for Beau to follow them.

"What the hell am I getting myself into?" he muttered to himself, then he entered the cramped passageway and started down.

The stairway quickly became dark and damp. But they did not go very deep. Having gone down only about two and a half flights, they reached the bottom where the sandy floor was wet, having apparently reached the water table. At the bottom of the stairs was a pit with a small fire burning in it, and several torches soaked in pitch were arranged in front of it. Micah picked up a torch and touched the end in the fire. Then he took off down the passageway which opened up a bit so that Beau did not feel so cramped, though he did still have to stoop over.

A few times, they seemed to come to the end of a tunnel, but by using some hidden mechanism, a doorway opened up. They closed the door behind them to likely confuse any who might find the entrance to the tunnel, but stopping them from being able to go any farther. The tunnel turned and branched off so many times that Beau quickly lost his bearings and stopped trying to keep track.

Eventually, they came to a large, cavernous room, perhaps a hundred feet long, with stone columns supporting a gothic style rib-vaulted ceiling its entire length. Here, there were other torches, lanterns and candles in various places, dimly illuminating the large subterranean room, and Beau could see that there were other people here too.

There were several adults, and a number of children and adolescents. One or two of them looked up, but nobody paid them any real attention. Many of them seemed almost unhappy, even listless, but apparently they preferred being here to being above ground with the other colonists.

The other kids separated from their group here and went in different directions, and Micah motioned for Beau to follow him. They walked about halfway down the length of the hall and Micah went behind one of the stone columns and into yet another passage. They climbed a flight of stairs, continued down a hallway, then up another flight.

"We must be very quiet now," Micah whispered. "We're coming near the jail and we can't make any noise."

Beau nodded and continued following. The hallway grew narrow, with the wall on the right being solid rock, slanting away from them as it rose from the floor, so that the passage was wider at the top than at the floor. Beau recognized that it was likely the mound of rock against which Payne's office and a few other structures were built including, apparently, the jail.

Micah placed the torch in a sconce built into the wall, then they turned a corner and proceeded on another twenty feet, walking silently.

Eventually, they came to a somewhat brighter point in the now dark hallway, and Beau could see a dim light shining through a hole in the wall on their left. The hole was down low and he had to kneel down to look through it, but when he did, he saw a metal vent cover on the inside. Through the slots, he could see a cell, little better than an old, medieval dungeon. Sitting on a bare cot, perhaps six feet away from him, was Phil.

Beau took a moment to look around the cell, taking note that the heavy wooden door was closed, and that there was nobody else in the cell.

"Phil," he whispered. "It's Beau." Phil looked with surprise toward the vent. His face was bruised, his eyes blackened, one of them swollen shut.

"Beau," he whispered through his split lips. "What the hell's going on here?"

"It's a long story. We're going to try to get you out of here."

"Better make it soon, buddy. I don't like the way they've been talking. I think these bastards actually plan on killing me!" Beau heard the panic as his voice rose from the original whisper.

"Take it easy," he said. "Try to stay calm." Then he turned to Micah. "Is there any way into that cell besides the door?"

"I'm not sure," Micah whispered. "I shall have to ask around."

Turning back to the vent, Beau whispered, "Okay, Phil, we'll figure out something. Just stay calm. We'll get you out of there."

"Alright," Phil whispered, and he nodded, the resignation on his face now supplanted by a bit of hope.

§

"Do you people actually live down here?" Beau asked.

"No," said Bethany, one of the adults in the group. She had the voice of a young woman, but her face, though not unattractive, seemed prematurely lined. It was said that, as the oldest of their group, she had the most cumulative knowledge of the underground passages.

"Or rather," she continued, "I should say, *most* of us do not. There are a few here who are considered outlaws or otherwise undesirable up above. I'm afraid they have little choice but to remain down here all the time. But there would be greater problems if all of us were to try to live down here, problems which, I fear, we have not the design and implementation skills to overcome.

"For instance, while there are cisterns that gather fresh water, we have no way of growing food down here, or disposing of waste. Many of us simply come down here to get away from the other colonists when we have the opportunity. Otherwise, we must always try to blend in, support ourselves, etcetera."

"What do you people do down here?"

"Not much, really," Bethany said. It seemed almost as if she was embarrassed to say it. "We just find it easier to be down here with people of like minds than to try to fit in up above. More than anything, I think it's simply a matter of comradeship."

"I would think, if there were enough of you, you could organize into a force to be reckoned with."

Bethany smiled ruefully. "I fear we lack the expertise to organize ourselves into such a force."

"Who built this place?" Beau asked looking around with wonder at the subterranean architecture.

"We don't know for certain. Some say it was the early governors of the colony. Others say it was folks like us who needed to escape from them. At any rate, these passages and rooms have been here for hundreds of years, almost as long as the colony itself."

Something about the way Bethany spoke struck Beau as different. She had an English accent like the others, but her grammar and sentence structure seemed a bit more familiar, more modern.

"Your accent doesn't sound quite as pronounced as the others," he said.

"That's because I'm not from here. I was born in New Jersey."

Beau was shocked at this unexpected revelation.

"Wait a minute," he said. "New Jersey? As in the United States of America? Bruce Springsteen, Bon Jovi and the Sopranos?"

"I'm sorry?" Bethany replied.

"Nothing. Go ahead."

Bethany looked flustered for a moment, but then continued with her explanation.

"My family was sailing on vacation when I was six years old. We came upon this island and came ashore to investigate. We were surprised to find this fortress here and were welcomed by the inhabitants.

"When it came time to leave, however, we were told that the Indians had sunk our boat, and indeed, we saw no further trace of it.

"My parents remained, for a time, hopeful of a rescue, but eventually accepted that it was not to be. They were very unhappy here and never managed to fit in.

"A short time later, they disappeared. I never saw them again. I was raised by a couple in the colony, and in the thirty-three years I've been here, I suppose I acquired the accent."

Beau sat silent for a few moments, allowing the information to sink in.

"I had no idea," he finally said. "Payne told us that *we* were the first ones that they had managed to rescue from the Indians."

"Payne's a bloody liar," Bethany said bitterly. "There are several outlanders here. Some of them who had certain skills or knowledge even contributed to the culture."

"What do you mean?" Beau asked.

"They supposedly 'invented' things which made life here a bit easier, made the people at least a bit less backwards. Of course, their inventions were things that were already in existence on the outside, but here, they were brand new."

"Like repeating rifles?" Beau asked, remembering the brief discussion with Justin Wilkinson about their firearms a few days before.

"Oh, yes. Mr. Endicott," Bethany said with a nod. "He's not down here with us, though. He has managed to fit in better and stays above, in the colony."

"You mean he's still around?" Beau asked, stunned again. "I didn't realize that the repeating rifle was such a recent development."

"Oh, these people are quite stubborn and resistant to change. There are few things which would convince them to relinquish their hold on their dear old-fashioned ways. Although I admit that they do seem to be quite a bit more interested in advancing their weaponry."

"Well, what about the jail? Is there any way that we can get our friend out of there?"

"We think so," she said. "If they interrogate him again. We don't have a way into the individual cells, but we can get into a room between the cells, where they conduct interrogations."

"That sounds tricky," Beau said. "We'll have to confront the jailers to get him?"

"Most likely, unless they leave him alone in the interrogation hall. That does happen sometimes, though not often. But if they follow their usual procedure, he will likely be interrogated at least one more time tonight or tomorrow morning."

"What is the purpose of the interrogations?"

"They just try to find whatever they can use," Bethany replied. "In the case of your friend, one of our people heard an earlier interrogation of him this morning. Apparently he had been overheard saying something about propelling a missile from his boat onto the island. His interrogators said that Payne wants to know more about that capability, what kind of bombs he has, and how to adapt it to the defense of the fortress."

"That's ridiculous!" Beau sputtered. "I was there. I heard Phil say that yesterday. He was just angry. He didn't say he was going to do it, or that he even could, just that he *wished* that he could. Besides, his boat is gone now too."

He realized that this also confirmed that Hewet could not be trusted. He's the only one who could have reported Phil's statement.

"Logic, I am afraid, does not enter much into the daily affairs in the colony."

"Alright," Beau sighed, "well, I need to get my friends and see if we can get Phil out of there."

"Oh, I'm afraid that's not possible," she said. "You saw the cramped passages. The fewer people involved, the better. You may come, if you like, but leave the rest of them out."

Bethany's eyes brightened a bit as a thought occurred to her.

"In fact, you told me earlier, when we met, that you and your friends were going to help an Indian slave escape early tomorrow morning. Since those plans are already in place, they should proceed with them, as the timing makes perfect sense. After we make good your friend's escape from the jail, you and he may join them."

"Remember thy promise," said Micah, who was still sitting nearby.

"Don't worry, little man," said Beau with a nod. "If we manage to get off this island, I assure you we will definitely make sure that anybody who wants to leave can do so."

§

"Thou still wisheth to build a boat?" Hewet asked incredulously. "But thy motor hath broken."

"Yes, I'm aware of that," Jax said with some irritation. "And yes, I still wisheth to build a boat." Allie put a hand on his arm as she heard the impatience in his voice.

Hewet seemed a bit surprised, unaccustomed to hearing anger and sarcasm from Jax, but he nodded in response. Jerry, listening from behind, seemed surprised too. "And where is Mr. Bannister?" Hewet asked.

"He's thinking about new designs for a boat that won't need a motor. He thinks best when he's alone." Jax sighed. He pushed his hands through his hair and paused in a characteristic posture with his hands resting on top of his head as he looked away, thinking. He decided at this point that he had gone far enough with his ruse.

"In fact, you know what?" he said, as he looked back at Hewet. "Maybe we *should* just call it a day. I've got some ideas to work on myself. I'm kind of discouraged and don't feel like I'd get much done here."

"Very well," Hewet replied, a bit perplexed at first. "Indeed, that idea appeareth to be a sound one. I shall be here on the morrow. Perhaps we may start fresh then."

Jax nodded and turned away, followed by Allie and Jerry. Sensing his mood, neither of them said anything, walking quietly behind him. Hoping for some privacy, Jax led them to the river, into the trees, and they walked upstream until they came to the source, the mouth of the tunnel.

At this point, the river just seemed to appear from underground, as if bubbling up from a spring, but now they knew its source. They were upstream from where they had spent their blissful days just a few days ago, before they knew the awful truth about this place.

The area was surrounded by trees, which Jax was happy to see, considering its proximity to the wall and the sentries. It would provide some privacy. Stopping here, Jax related to Jerry their plan to escape early tomorrow morning, as well as the possibility that Phil may still be there, and Beau's hopes for a rescue.

"You two keep an eye out," he concluded. "I want to check out the grate that Brit described, and see if I can make any advance preparations." With that, he stripped down to his underwear, took a quick look around, and slipped into the water.

He could feel the current, coming from the west. He submerged and swam against it, and he soon found the tunnel which carried the river under the wall. Entering it, he discovered that the current was particularly strong inside, but with some strong kicks and strokes, he was able to make some forward motion despite the opposing force.

He quickly arrived at the metal grate that Brit had described, but he was surprised by its size. It was a huge metal grill eight feet in diameter with a large corroded hinge on the left side and three hand wheels, one each in the three, six and twelve o'clock positions.

He stuck his leg through one of the openings in the grill to brace himself and tried turning the top wheel. It was old and corroded, and Jax struggled a bit. After straining against it with all his might, it broke loose and began to give, and finally turned. He unscrewed it completely, then repeated his efforts on the bottom wheel. By the time he got the third one unscrewed and the grill creaked open with the current, his oxygen was nearly gone.

He pulled his leg out of the grill and let go, allowing the river to carry him out of the tunnel. He surfaced slowly, just in case anybody had joined Allie and Jerry on the shore. They were alone and eager to hear his report.

"It's just like Brit described," he said between breaths. "Piece of cake. This one's open and ready to go."

"Great!" Allie said. "What's next?"

"I'm thinking I might as well try to make it to the outside one and see if I can get it open. The more I can do in advance, the less I'll have to do tomorrow and the better our chances." With that, he filled his lungs to capacity and slipped under again.

By now, he was starting to feel tired from his previous exertions with the first grill, so he searched for, and found, the joints that Brit had mentioned, about every three or four feet. They provided enough of a fingerhold that he could pull himself forward rather than just swimming against the current.

The tunnel was not entirely straight. It curved just a bit so that he could not see one end from the other, and it soon got dark in the middle, before the end of the tunnel finally came into view.

The outer grill was the same. Each hand wheel was corroded to some extent, and it took a great deal of exertion to loosen them. He was only able to loosen one wheel before he had to go back for air. But repeating the steps two more times, he finally got the grate open. After releasing the last wheel, rather than go right back, he carefully surfaced on the outside, to have a look around.

Jax found himself in a small lake, surrounded by trees, and with the tunnel about ten feet below the surface. The fortress was not visible through the trees, which was good, because it meant that they would not be visible when making their escape.

Treading water, he looked around him and saw lush, verdant jungle completely surrounding the lake, pulsating with the sound of tropical birds and insects. The clear blue sky overhead looked the same as it did from inside the fortress, but to Jax, it was somehow different.

I never thought the open jungle on an uncharted island would ever look so good, he thought. *Everything looks different when seen with the eyes of a prisoner. Or a slave.*

Not wanting Allie or Jerry to worry about him, he submerged again toward the tunnel and, like the drain in a bathtub, allowed the current to pull him back to the other side. Coming up out of the water, he regretted spending as much time as he had when he saw the fear on Allie's face, followed by the intense relief.

"I'm okay," he said. "I've been outside. Our escape route is wide open now."

§

Brit had spent some time looking at more documents but had not found anything that seemed important to them in the context of their current knowledge of the place, or of their impending escape. Not wanting to waste her time here, she pumped up her courage and tried a door that she had never seen open. It was unlocked and, as nobody had been in to check on her in a while, she ventured in.

The room was much smaller than the cavernous room she left, and as it was getting late, and there were no windows in this room, it was difficult to see what was in it. However, she could see, on a countertop just beside the door, a glass lamp with a box of matches beside it. She lit the lamp, feeling a twinge of incongruity, thinking that she remembered friction matches being invented sometime in the nineteenth century.

She decided that she must have just remembered wrong.

As the room became flooded with a warm glow, Brit saw a number of items on display in shelves and cubbyholes. The items were old – not just old-fashioned like everything in the colony, but some apparently actually hundreds of years old. She saw candles and oil lamps, cutlery and other utensils, pewter mugs and china dishes, pieces of crockery and various everyday items from centuries past, all with the patina of age. There were hand-written labels on the shelves, many of them faded with time, the paper yellowed, the ink rust-colored.

Brit gently picked up a delicate plate, a small chip on the edge and a spider web of hairline cracks all across the surface of the glaze, but otherwise in good condition. The label on its shelf said, "Dinner Plate, Eleanor Dare." She realized that she was holding her breath and she slowly let it out. But she continued looking at the relic, carefully turning it over in her hands. It was nearly 450 years old, brought from England by a young, pregnant woman, looking forward to a better life in a new world.

How many dinners had she or her husband, Ananias, eaten from this very plate, before their young lives ended prematurely on this wild, untamed island? Brit carefully put the plate back in its place and breathed a little more freely as she continued looking around.

There was a pewter candle holder with a greasy looking, dust-covered stub of a candle in it. Its label said, "Candlesticke, Nicholas Johnson." Brit wasn't familiar with the name, as she was with Eleanor Dare, but she liked the simple aesthetic design of the piece. Sticking her finger through the hole in the holder, it felt completely natural, and she smiled at the feeling of comfort that the ancient item engendered. She could imagine Nicholas Johnson, whoever he was, lighting his way with this candlestick in his hand.

This counter ended at the wall at the back of the room, and she turned to see what was on the corresponding counter on the opposite wall.

There were several items scattered on the countertop, and some labels recently lettered, the ink still black. There was a somewhat newer looking, though still old-fashioned hammer, the handle a deep, rich brown, possibly fashioned from a local tropical hardwood.

She found fragments of glass, pottery and other mundane items, along with a couple of pieces of jewelry, apparently still being cleaned and studied. There was a generous dusting of dirt and deposits on the countertop around them, and various brushes and other delicate tools likely being used by local historians to clean the relics.

Next to these things, she found the metal parts of an old musket, recently burnished to a bright shine. Something about it seemed familiar. Picking it up, she turned it over and there, right where she expected to see it on the breech, was an ornate engraving of the letters "AD" amid the leaf design.

She remembered the thrill of discovery when she had removed the encrustation from around the piece just a few days before and found the arquebus inside. She remembered her interest being piqued by the puzzle of what "AD" meant.

The mystery was now solved as Brit saw the hand-lettered card next to it on the table, "Arquebus, Ananias Dare."

However, one puzzle remained: This relic, a vintage musket belonging to Ananias Dare, was last seen at

Brit's work station on the *Camilla*, now resting on the ocean floor after being sunk by the natives. So how did it end up here?

"It appeareth that our trust in thee was sadly misplaced," said Lieutenant Governor Thomas Dare's voice from the doorway. Brit quickly put the arquebus down and turned toward him, the question still puzzling her mind.

"How did you get this?" she asked.

"I fear that, at this time, there be more dire issues to be dealt with," he answered, and as his right hand moved, Brit saw the pistol rise to point at her.

§

Beau, having been told that Jax, Allie and Jerry had left Hewet's place, was walking toward the river. He passed the oasis where the four of them had spent a couple of days together, and he continued upriver. It was getting late in the day and he didn't know if Jax would still be there.

As he made his way closer to the mouth of the river, he could see the three of them lounging on the grass, talking.

"Did you see Phil?" Jerry asked immediately.

"I saw him," Beau replied, "and we have a plan to get him out. In fact, I'm going back down in case we can get him tonight."

"Down?" asked Allie.

"I'll tell you all about it later. Thing is, we don't know yet if we'll be able get him tonight, or if it will be tomorrow morning. So we may not be going with you when you leave in the morning, but we *will* be close behind. Anyway, I'm going back there now."

"Okay," Jax said after a brief hesitation. "I'll try to make up a believable story about you for the Hemmingtons tonight."

"Thanks." Beau noticed that Jax's hair was damp. "So how does it look?" he asked, nodding toward the river.

"Looks good. We're all set to go. I really don't like the idea of leaving you and Phil here, though."

"May not have a choice," Beau replied. "You guys have to go early or else Yahima will be missed and they'll set out looking for her."

"I know. I just don't want to leave anyone behind."

"I understand. But you won't be leaving us for long. Like I said, we'll be right behind you." Jax nodded. "Well, I better get back," Beau said. "There's a possibility that we can get Phil tonight."

Jax, Allie and Jerry went to their respective homes while Beau headed back toward the village square. He hadn't taken long in this errand, but it was late, and long shadows were being cast by the descending sun. He didn't want to try to find his way back to the alley in the dark.

As he was retracing the steps that he had taken with the kids a few hours before, he suddenly had the feeling that he was being followed. He looked behind but didn't see anyone. Continuing on, where he would have made a left turn, he decided to turn right instead and waited. A few seconds later, a man quickly rounded the corner and, obviously startled, came face to face with Beau.

"W'sup?" said Beau.

"Oh! Do forgive me, sir," the man said in a flustered tone, apologizing for almost running into him. He went around Beau as if he were just continuing on his way, though he did cast a suspicious glance at Beau over his shoulder.

Beau stood and watched him for a few moments, then he went on, except that he went straight ahead instead of turning left. He still felt an irritating tingling sensation on the back of his neck, the nagging impression that something was not quite right. He rounded a corner and came to the village square where he decided to sit on the low stone wall that surrounded the area.

Most people were in their homes now, having their supper, so there were few to be seen. Those that Beau did see did not seem interested in him and passed by on their way without paying him any notice.

After a few minutes, deciding that he was imagining it, he stood up and went on, though he still threw in a few misleading turns, just in case.

He finally arrived at the alley and turned, going back into the shadows where Micah was waiting for him. After opening the hidden door, Micah held it open for him and, just before he went inside, he looked behind one more time, around the stack of wooden crates, but there was still nobody there.

It was early, the sun not quite up yet. The dark blue sky, laced with high, wispy clouds, was streaked with shades of orange and magenta from the beginning of the day just starting to show from the eastern horizon.

From inside the fortress, though, Jax couldn't see the horizon. He was pumped, ready to make their escape, though he was still concerned about what kind of reception the Indians would give them. And about how they would ever get off the island.

He had left the Hemmington's home early, as on previous days, and had stopped at Hewet's shop on his way to the river. It was still early and Hewet was not there yet, so Jax went into the courtyard and got the long coil of rope that he had seen there. Standing on the bank of the river now, he draped the rope over his shoulder and dove in. He submerged and swam into the tunnel, past the first grate, still standing open as he had left it. The bulk of coiled rope over his shoulder created more drag in the water, so he made his way against the current by pulling himself along using the joints in the concrete sections.

He tied one end of the rope securely to the second grate and let go of the rope, watching as it uncoiled and stretched out with the current into the darkness of the long, curved tunnel. Then he allowed the current to carry him back. Knowing that most of the others could not swim as strongly or hold their breath for as long a time as he, he was happy to see that the rope was just long enough, terminating just barely outside the tunnel, but not long enough that it would float along the surface of the river, drawing attention to it.

Carefully, Jax emerged from the water, looking around carefully to make sure there was nobody there.

Coming up on shore and brushing his wet hair out of his face, Jax followed the river downstream, eventually coming to the area near the Watering Hole where they were to meet, and he saw that Yahima was already there. She looked nervous but smiled when she saw him. They had just said their greetings when he saw Beau approaching.

"We didn't get a chance to get Phil last night," he said, "so I'll be sticking around."

"Alright," Jax sighed. "I still don't like it, but I know it's the only way. Just be careful. Once people notice that we're gone, you may have a harder time getting away."

Beau nodded, as they heard footsteps. Jerry was coming towards them and he smiled, and just a few seconds later, Allie came running. She did not seem as happy.

"Brit never came home last night!" she gasped between breaths.

"What?" Jax asked. "Where is she?"

"I don't know." Her voice was strained, her tone worried. "The last time I saw her was before we split up yesterday after lunch. She was going to the Constabulary to see if she could find anything else that could be helpful. She never returned."

Jax felt his throat tighten in fear, and he tried to think clearly. It wasn't working. He felt the old anxiety and protectiveness for his sister return.

"Okay," he started with a sigh, "I'll head over to the Constabulary."

"Forget it," Beau replied firmly.

"I have to find her!"

"Don't be stupid. You have to get these people out of here before anybody's missed. I have to stay here anyway. I'll find her."

"I can't leave her, Beau. She's my little sister." The desperation in his voice touched Beau, who put his hand on Jax's shoulder.

"I know buddy," he said. "I love her too. I'll find her." Their eyes locked for a few moments before Beau gave Jax's shoulder a push. "Now go on, you damn hippie, get out of here."

Jax exhaled and nodded. "Be careful."

Yahima placed a hand on Beau's arm. "I will instruct my people to post scouts nearby in anticipation of thy escape," she said. "They will lead thee to my village."

"Thanks," he nodded.

Allie squeezed Jax's arm and the four of them turned and hurried upstream, toward the west. Beau stayed long enough to wave when Jax looked back over his shoulder. Then he spun around and headed back toward the village.

§

The four of them stood on the bank of the river, looking into the water with varying expressions of anticipation. Yahima was eager, her face reflecting the long-awaited happiness of freedom. Jerry's face was calm but still looking forward to a relative freedom elsewhere on the island, though he didn't know how they would ever get home.

Allie was grim, wanting her freedom as well, but dreading the swim through the long, dark tunnel. She was the one that Jax was most concerned about, given her 'claustroscubia.' But as he stood in front of her, his hands on her shoulders, Jax looked inquiringly into her eyes. She took a deep breath, took off her glasses and hooked them through her bra inside her blouse, and gave him a strained smile and a nod.

Jax went first. Kicking and pulling himself on the rope, he surfaced on the other side, took a few breaths, then submerged again, giving the rope a couple of tugs. After that, he could feel the rope go taut and, hooking his leg through the grate, began pulling the rope hand over hand.

It was a tiring procedure, with the current pushing back against Allie. Jax kept pulling as quickly as he could, wanting to get her out of the tunnel as fast as possible. After nearly a minute, he could see the panic on Allie's face as she came into view.

She held the rope in a death grip and looked as if she was straining to see, but she almost smiled as she saw Jax. As she came alongside him, he put an arm around her shoulders, convincing her to let go of the rope. She grabbed onto him tightly, and he maneuvered her around to hold onto his back, so he could use both arms. He pulled her through the mouth of the tunnel and up to the surface of the lake, and he guided her to the shore.

He waited a moment as she sat down on the ground, gulping deep breaths. She sat with her head back, looking up at the sky. After a few moments, she looked at Jax, moved by the worry on his face, and she nodded, reassuring him that she was alright. He filled his lungs and submerged again.

He repeated his previous actions, pulling the rope hand over hand as it went taut. Eventually he could see Yahima emerging from the darkness.

When she reached him, he did the same thing he did with Allie, having Yahima hold onto his back. He pulled her through the opening and up to the surface of the lake where she took a deep breath and looked around. He helped her to the shore where Allie stood waiting. Yahima hugged him tightly and kissed him on the cheek.

"I cannot fully express my thanks to thee," she said, and despite the water on her face, Jax could see that there were tears in her eyes.

"It's okay," Jax said with some embarrassment, looking toward Allie. Pulling away from her, he stepped back into the water and started preparing to dive again, when Jerry came up from the water, having pulled himself over.

"That was easier than I expected," he said.

"Well, we're not out of the woods yet," Jax said, helping him ashore. "We need to put some distance between us and this colony." They inadvertently looked in the direction of the fortress, though they could not see it through the dense forest. Jax turned back and was surprised to see Yahima getting undressed.

"I will go first," the Indian girl said, with her wet linen blouse and camisole now on the ground at her feet.

The other three were not sure what to think as she slipped her skirt off. Jax tried to pry his eyes away, but Yahima was beautiful, with a slim, supple figure, which she was now baring in complete innocence.

Jax glanced nervously at Allie as Yahima finally stood naked except for a short petticoat-style undergarment. "My people will not attack us if they see me leading thee," she continued unashamed, as she started walking toward the west.

Jax looked again at Allie who had her head tilted to the side as she was wringing the water from her dark hair. He noticed that the color was returning to her face again.

"Think we should adopt the new dress code?" he asked, and she smiled wryly at him.

"Let's go, lover boy," she said. He smiled and fell into step, though he glanced behind him with regret at leaving his sister behind.

§

Brit was locked in a dark room somewhere behind the Constabulary. The room contained a chair, a small table and a cot, similar to the ones in the dorm area, but with no bedding. A large clay pot stood in the corner where she was able to relieve herself. The room was dimly lit by one sputtering candle, similar to two others which lay beside it on the table.

With no ventilation, the greasy wax smoke of the candle combined with the stench from the pot made breathing difficult.

The room was paneled with dark hardwood planking. Having pounded her fists against the timbers, she felt no give and heard very little sound, so she knew the timbers were quite thick.

She had been alone for a few hours now, and had only gotten fitful sleep. There were no windows in the room, so she had no idea what time it was when she heard the heavy door opening. It was Thomas Dare, returning with a plate of food. She stood up to face him when he entered.

"I brought some food for thee," he said.

"Why are you keeping me here?" Brit demanded, ignoring his statement.

"Thou hast become a danger to us," he replied. "Thou hast forced us to take these steps."

"How am I a danger? I've been looking at these historical items for days now. You've allowed me to do that."

"Aye, but thou hast, until this time, respected our privacy and our trust. Thou hast now violated our private collections, things which were meant to remain unseen by outsiders."

"Outsiders? I thought we were welcome to remain here," Brit said angrily. "You and Payne were welcoming us as your friends and neighbors. In fact, the whole colony did too, just a couple of days ago, at church and the Sunday feast."

"Thy words are true, but thou and thine hast declined our hospitality."

"How have we done that?" she asked, the tears welling up in her eyes.

"Where art thy friends?" Dare asked, ignoring her question.

"How the hell would I know?" she spat at him, the tears spilling down her cheeks. "You've had me locked up in here all night!"

"Thy foul language will do thee no favors, young lady," he said softly.

"What are you going to do to me?"

"Normally, we would dispose of someone so rebellious," he said, then his voice became quieter and took on a chilling tone. "But thou art pleasing to look upon." A shiver went down her spine as the old man's eyes travelled down the length of her body. "I heard some of the men speaking of the state of thy wardrobe on the eve of thy arrival. Apparently thou art proud of thy shape." He placed the plate of food on the table and came closer to her. "But pride, my dear, goeth before a fall."

With that, a small dagger in his hand, he reached out and in a single savage movement, ripped her blouse apart as she screamed in surprise.

"Even now," he continued in a voice shaking with a pious rage, "I see that thou doth wear only a minimum of clothing. A blouse but no chemise." Brit turned away from him. Though she was still wearing her bikini top and her skirt, she felt violated, and she was attempting to cover her breasts, and seething with hatred for the man.

But then he just as quickly cut her skirt off of her from behind.

"And a skirt but no petticoat."

Clothed now only in her bikini, she was gritting her teeth, breathing hard from embarrassment and contempt. Under normal circumstances, Brit would have been perfectly comfortable in just her bikini, feeling no embarrassment.

But not so under this old man's perverted gaze.

The man seemed glued in place, unable to pull his eyes away from Brit's body. Her slashed and ripped clothing hanging from his left hand, he pressed his right fist, still gripping the dagger, to his mouth, as if he were attempting to suppress a ravenous hunger. His eyes continued feeding it, but still, it seemed to remain unsatisfied.

Finally, he looked up at the side of her face, glaring at him over her shoulder, and without another word, he turned quickly and left, locking the door.

Sitting down on the cot, three things occurred to Brit. First was that Dare had asked her where her friends are. That meant that they must have made their escape, and she felt a mixture of happiness that they had succeeded, and disappointment that she was not with them.

The second thing that she thought of was that her time here was going to be a living nightmare. 'Thou art pleasing to look upon,' Dare had said before ripping her clothing off of her body.

Even worse than slavery, she thought, was she being kept as Thomas Dare's personal plaything? The sex toy of a slobbering old deviant who, on the outside, portrayed himself as a good and pious, God-fearing Christian?

The third thing that came to mind was that she had to find a way to get out of there, or die trying. She leaned over, placing her head down on her knees, and she cried.

§

Beau was glad that, as backward as these people were, they, or their ancestors, had at least put some thought into ventilation. The walls of the building were not built against the stone cliff, and the gap between them provided air circulation in the jail. As it turned out, the vents were also what gave Beau access to the interrogation room where Phil now sat, with one other man at the table and one man standing at the door.

Beau was accompanied by two young men, brothers, named John and Eric. Each had worked as guards and soldiers above ground in the past. Beau was happy to have people with at least some form of combat experience with him. Bethany felt that, given the cramped areas that they had to navigate, the fewer people involved in the operation the better, and having already been in there himself, Beau tended to agree.

The three of them, completely silent, having made their way through the dark and narrow tunnels, now waited outside a ventilation grill which looked barely large enough for Beau to fit through.

He had serious doubts about Phil.

The grill was only about a foot above their walkway, but perhaps as much as eight feet off the floor of the interrogation room, which further fueled his doubts about being able to get Phil out that way.

The interrogation seemed lackluster, almost superfluous, as if it was just a final formality to be dealt with. Phil seemed exhausted and in pain after the more aggressive interrogations he had endured the day before.

After a few minutes of half-hearted questioning, the man sitting at the table with Phil, sounding almost bored with the procedure, heaved a sigh. "So thou still contendeth that thou hast no missiles?" he asked, not even looking up at him.

"Yes," Phil growled back at him. "I still contendeth that I have no missiles. Are you satisfied, you son of a bitch? Where the hell do you suppose I would keep them?" he asked, as he patted his pockets sarcastically.

Beau grimaced. He could see how Phil's anger and antagonism could get him killed.

The interrogator looked at the other man, shook his head and stood up. They left the room, closing the door behind them, and Eric nudged Beau's shoulder.

The vent had, at some earlier time, been altered by the "Roanoke Underground" as Beau had begun referring to them. He fingered a latch, pushed on the vent, heard a dull click, and it swung inward toward the room.

Phil looked up at the sound and was visibly relieved to see Beau slipping down feet-first through the hole in the wall. He did fit after all, but was still thinking that Phil might be a problem.

Bethany had told Beau that, if the men *did* leave Phil, they would likely be gone for only two or three minutes.

"They will go to report their findings to Payne or some other official," she had said, "to open up another room nearby where they execute prisoners, and to fire the furnace where they dispose of the bodies. At least, that seems to be the way it usually works." Beau still found that story difficult to believe, but he did not want to give them time to prove it.

"Help me move this table," he said quietly but urgently to Phil. It was a heavy wooden table, but despite Phil's condition, the two of them were able to move it under the vent without scraping it on the stone floor. "Up you go," he said.

"I don't know," Phil said, expressing his own doubts as he looked at the vent opening, but he laboriously climbed up on the table anyway. Beau climbed up too and, bracing his back against the wall, interlocked his fingers to provide a boost, while John and Eric each reached an arm through the opening.

Phil placed a foot in Beau's hands and Beau strained under the weight, tilting his head to the side to avoid the press of Phil's belly. He got him high enough that John and Eric were able to grab his hands. Together, the three of them got his upper torso through the vent. His belly, as expected, was the main problem, but with the two young men pulling him, his body stretched just enough for Phil to squeeze through the opening.

Once Phil was through, Beau got down from the table and picked it up, straining under the weight of it as he managed to set it back in its original position. He felt something warm on his upper arm and, looking down, saw blood on his shirt. He realized that he must have popped a stitch.

He would deal with it later.

He went back to the wall and jumped up toward the vent, grabbing onto the lower edge, and John and Eric helped him up.

He pulled the vent cover back, heard the dull click as the mechanism took hold and he locked it in place, and they started making their way back down the dark corridor. They had just rounded the corner to where they had left the torch in the sconce on the wall, when the two men returned to the room.

Looking around, they saw the room exactly as they had left it, except that the fat man was gone. They saw the vent, but seeing how high it was and remembering the man's girth, it did not even register in their minds as a consideration. One of the men approached the table and saw a few drops of blood on its surface in the center. He looked up toward the stone ceiling above it but saw nothing.

They looked at each other with a mixture of anger over having lost a prisoner, and superstitious fear.

§

Jax, Allie and Jerry filed through the forest behind Yahima along the trail that she was following. The sun was fully up now, but was still low in the east and unable to cut through the dense foliage around them.

In spite of the early hour, though, the temperature was warm and a mist was already wafting around them. The pungent smell of tropical vegetation and composting undergrowth was strong, and the calls of birds and insects could be heard, but was slightly muffled by the mist.

Yahima had instructed them to not talk, and in fact to walk as quietly as possible, so that she could better hear the sounds around her. She did not tell them that she had a small measure of fear that her people could attack the Americans. She wanted to be better able to hear them and to intercede before they had a chance.

They had been walking for about an hour when she motioned that they stop. Keeping her hand up to keep them quiet, she listened carefully, turning her head slightly in different directions. Watching Yahima listening so closely to the forest, Jax realized that it had become quiet – the insect and bird sounds were more distant now.

"Get thee behind these trees," she whispered, motioning off the trail, and the Americans were quick to do so. Turning back in the direction she had been looking, she spoke up and said something in a language unfamiliar to the Americans.

After a pause, there was a response from ahead of them. Yahima replied, beginning a short conversation with the disembodied voice. Then, apparently satisfied, she motioned for her new friends to join her again on the trail. They cautiously came out of the trees and moved close behind Yahima.

As they slowly started forward, they began to see people emerging from the forest around them, and Jax was chilled to see how easily they could disappear into their surroundings. The natives were fierce-looking men, many with tattoos on their bodies and faces. They were armed with bows and arrows, and each one of them had an arrow fitted to his bowstring.

Jax heard Yahima catch her breath, then she darted forward, ending up in the arms of one of the warriors. He held her briefly, keeping his eyes on the white people, then he gently pushed her away, standing her in front of him so he could see her. She looked up at his face and smiled, then turned to face the Americans.

"This is Arasibo, my brother," she said. Then she turned back to Arasibo and the others, and said something in their language. The other natives were quite close now, curious about the foreigners, but still cautious, glancing at them frequently as they listened to Yahima. As she continued speaking, Arasibo looked at Jax and gradually his fierce expression seemed to soften.

"I hath told them," she said, "that thou art friends, and that it is because of thee that I am able to rejoin them." The natives still seemed unsure, distrustful, but Jax noticed that they relaxed their hold on their bowstrings.

"Friends," Arasibo said, though it sounded more like a question. His face was still cautious, his eyebrows pressed together.

"Yes, friends," Jax said, smiling nervously. Allie and Jerry, not sure of what else to do, also echoed the word "friends" and nodded.

Arasibo looked at the three of them, then back at Yahima, seemingly mulling over a strange and difficult concept in his mind. Friendship with the white people was apparently a foreign idea to him. He looked at the other natives with him, and he seemed to consult primarily with one man who was older. Finally, he nodded.

"Friends," he said. "Come." Then he and the older man turned and began walking up the trail. Yahima smiled at Jax and nodded, and they all started following, with the other natives falling into step behind them.

Though they had either tattoos or paint on their faces, being closer to them now, Jax could see that they had fine features.

Their thick, black hair hung long in the back, but was cut shorter in front. They were well-muscled and held themselves upright and proud, as they walked easily through the wild and forbidding forest, as familiar to them as the islands of Boston Harbor were to himself. He decided that, despite the fear that they initially instilled in them, particularly on their first meeting when Ron was killed, they were a beautiful people.

"We are near my village," Yahima said, and Jax suddenly realized how odd it was for this wild, nearly naked native girl, surrounded by other primitive natives, to be speaking to him in old English with a British accent, in the wild jungles of this uncharted Caribbean island.

Walking beside her, Jax asked, "Are there others of your people who speak English?"

"Oh, yes," she said. "Many of us do. In fact, many of *these* do," she said motioning to the warriors marching around them. "English is a second language which a great many of us learn while growing up." Jax looked around him, at the men who were closest to him, and one of the warriors met his eyes and nodded, as if in agreement with Yahima's words.

"You speak English so fluently," said Allie who was walking alongside Yahima on the other side. "I think you speak it better than me." Yahima smiled.

"I thank thee for the compliment," she said.

Within a few minutes more, they emerged into an expansive clearing where quite a large village appeared in front of them. Hundreds of round grey thatched-roofed huts were scattered around a central area in which a large communal fire was burning. There were perhaps as many as a hundred native people in this clearing, busy with various tasks, but they had suddenly gone silent as the strange parade filed into the village.

Many of the brown faces seemed fearful, or at least confused, when they saw the white people among their warriors, and the natives gathered their children close to them. Hearing the sudden silence in the village, others came out of the huts to see what was happening, so that at least two hundred curious natives now confronted them.

These people were clothed like Yahima and the warriors around them, with only a simple skirt or loincloth, with many of the young children completely naked. Several had tattoos and piercings, though the ones in the village were not wearing face paint as some of the warriors accompanying them were.

The group marched toward one hut that stood a little apart from the others. While the other huts were round, this one was the only square hut in the village, and an elderly man, pushing aside a woven grass curtain, emerged from its doorway as they approached.

The man who seemed to be in charge of the warriors motioned to Arasibo, and together, they came near the old man with an apparent attitude of deference. A conversation in the native language ensued, which the Americans did not understand, but they eagerly watched the expressions of those speaking.

Before their conversation was over, as natives continued gathering around them, one woman wove her way through the crowd and approached Yahima, and with tears in her eyes, embraced her. The three men stopped their quiet conversation to observe the reunion. Yahima was crying now too, as she put her forehead against the forehead of the older woman.

Realizing that they were now the center of attention, Yahima turned to Jax and, smiling, said, "This is Casiguaya, my mother."

"I heard what my son told the Cacique," she said, in nearly perfect English.

"The chief," Yahima translated.

"Yes," Casiguaya nodded. "Thou art welcome in my home."

As if taking his cue from her, the chief nodded to the two men, and Arasibo turned and approached them. Jax held his breath, not quite knowing what to expect, though after witnessing Yahima's reunion with her mother, he was guardedly optimistic.

Arasibo stood in front of Jax and held out his hand.

"Welcome, friends," he said.

ow can Brit just vanish without a trace?" Beau asked as John applied a fresh bandage to his arm. A few feet away, Eric was dabbing away the dried blood from Phil's face. They were sitting with Bethany in the large gothic underground room that Beau had come to think of as the Cathedral.

"I'm awfully sorry," Bethany said. "Our networks do not give us access to every portion of the colony. It is entirely possible that she could be in some area that we cannot see."

"But why, though? I don't understand what purpose they would have in detaining her."

"Art thou quite certain that she did not go someplace of her own accord?" asked Eric. "Thou said that some of thy friends did like it here."

"That was before we learned about the slavery," Beau replied, "and that we were prisoners here. And even when she *did* like it, she still wanted to go home. She was planning on escaping with us this morning. She wouldn't have just wandered off. They have to be keeping her someplace in the colony, against her will. But where?"

"I'm sorry, but I do not have that answer," Bethany said.

"If they were holding her as a prisoner, wouldn't they keep her in the jail, like they did Phil?"

"It would seem likely, but I'm afraid we cannot explain all of their actions."

"I do not wish to alarm thee," John added, "but if she did gain the disfavor of someone in the colony, the possibility does exist that they could have already done away with her without our yet becoming aware of it."

"No!" Beau said, shaking his head. "I refuse to believe that. Brit's alive."

Bethany nodded, understanding immediately. "Of course. I assure you that we will remain vigilant in our search for her." That seemed to placate Beau.

"Thanks," he said with a sigh. John finished with the bandage and packed up his kit, patting Beau on the back.

"Thanks from me too," Phil said to Bethany. "I understand you're the brains of this outfit." She gave a subtle smile and shook her head.

"We all work together, Mr. Chesterfield," she said humbly. "I've just been down here longer than some of my colleagues."

"Well, I appreciate it just the same."

She nodded toward him as Micah brought a clean shirt for Beau, which he put on.

"I don't think I can just sit around down here," Beau said. "I've got to do something. I have to find Brit."

"I do understand your feelings," Bethany said. "However, it would seem that there is little that you can do. Your friends have made their escape by now, and from what some of the children have reported, the people above are at a loss, and seem to be quite busy searching for them, and for you."

Beau put his head back and sighed. "I hate waiting!"

§

Three white twenty-first century Americans sat in the middle of a large primitive village in the jungle on a tropical island. Though surrounded by hundreds of nearly naked savages speaking to them in old, Elizabethan English, with something similar to an English accent, they felt welcome and happy.

When Yahima had said that they had not had anything to eat yet, many of the natives were quick to sit them down in a large circle and to place an abundance of food in front of them. Jax thought it tasted good, but was afraid to ask what some of it was, having seen what looked like iguana skins stretched and drying nearby.

"A few days ago," Yahima said to Jax, "inside the fortress, thou asked me about the history of the white people and the Indians."

"Yes, I remember," said Jax as he stuffed some more mystery meat in his mouth.

"I am sorry that I refused to answer thee at the time."

Jax waved it off and shook his head. "You didn't know me. And there were so many larger issues at the time."

Yahima smiled and nodded. "We are the Taíno people. We have lived in these scattered islands of the sea for centuries. However we did not occupy this particular island until after Cristóbal Colón came to our home."

"Cristóbal Colón?" Jerry asked.

"Christopher Columbus," Jax explained. "Cristóbal Colón was his name in Spanish."

"Oh," Jerry nodded, putting another piece of fruit in his mouth.

"According to our history," Yahima continued, "Cristóbal Colón was at first good and decent to us. But when he returned about a year later, he started treating us badly, requiring us to pay him a tribute in gold or cotton. If anyone was unable to pay, their hands were cut off and they were left to bleed to death."

"Oh, my God! Is this true?" Allie asked, horrified.

"I'm afraid so," Jax replied. "That's just one of the many reasons Columbus isn't very popular with Native Americans."

"Many of the Taíno people tried to repel the white people, but were not strong enough to do so. In time, the white people began forcing our people to work for them, taking them as slaves. To escape the white tyranny, many fled to neighboring islands, and that is how we came to be here."

"We lived in peace for a few generations," said Arasibo, Yahima's brother. "Then the white people arrived here too, when their ship was sunk in a storm."

"They built their home on the eastern side of the island," Yahima continued, "and though we were wary and kept our eye on them, we left them alone, as we wanted to be left alone ourselves."

"But they didn't leave you alone?" asked Jerry.

"For a while, they did. They cowered fearfully inside their fortress and stayed on their side of the island.

"But eventually, they became more confident and began making advances outside their fortress. They still left us alone, but they were coming closer. Watching us, curious about us.

"As their confidence increased, they began wielding greater power over the Indians who had come with them, attempting to force them into a position of servitude. Their power turned into mistreatment and distrust. Finally, most of the Indians abandoned the white people and sought a life with us.

"At first, our people were cautious. But we allowed them into our village and after a while, we and they became one people."

"And I suppose that made the whites angry," Jax said.

"Indeed," Yahima replied. "They greatly resented the Taínos and wanted to get 'their Indians' back. So they assembled a force to fight against us, with their loud and deadly weapons. Our people had never fought against such weapons and, though they killed many white people, many of our people were killed as well."

"We managed to repel the white people that time," Arasibo contributed, "but we quickly learned that we were no match for them in sustained battle. Their muskets killed with great accuracy over a long distance. What developed after that was a strained and cautious hostility between our two peoples."

"Meanwhile," Yahima said, "inside their fortress, they were developing an arsenal, as they built a forge with which they were able to manufacture more of their guns. Some of the white people did not agree with their program and spoke out against going to war with us. This, of course, drew the ire of many of their own number."

"How do you know this?" Jax inquired.

"Because some of them finally came and joined us as well."

Allie glanced at Jax in surprise. "Payne never told us anything about that."

"No, he didn't. White people came and lived with your people?" Jax asked.

"Aye, that is correct. An outspoken young white girl named Virginia Dare was one of the foremost ones among them. An Indian woman who had been a close companion of hers as she was growing up had left and was living with us.

"This Virginia Dare was sympathetic toward the Indians, and by extension us, the Taíno people, and she did not want to see her friend or others of us killed or mistreated. So she and some friends gathered together others of her mind and they made their escape from the colony under cover of night."

"Virginia Dare came to live with you people?" Jax asked in amazement.

"Yes. Do you know of her?" Yahima asked.

"Just a little. Back where we come from, she's kind of the stuff of legend nowadays."

"Well, there was, as thou might imagine, quite a lot of tension between them at the outset, but ultimately the Indians who had lived among them intervened and spoke in favor of allowing them to stay. Which is, in fact, what happened."

"Are there still white people living among you now?" asked Allie.

"No, the white people and the Taíno – or Indians, as they now refer to all of us – became one people many generations ago. Thy legendary Virginia Dare, for example, married a young Taíno chief and bore him five children, who eventually married other Taíno people or Indians."

"So the white people were gradually absorbed into your tribe," Jax said, "thus creating a new 'race' hundreds of years ago."

"Our chief, Baracoa," Yahima said, motioning toward the old man they met upon entering the village, now sitting opposite them in the circle, "is descended from Virginia Dare's firstborn son."

Jax smiled at the old man and wished that Brit were here to hear this. He knew that she would be fascinated by the history.

"He is very wise and communes with the spirits," Yahima continued. "He is also our Bohique – our priest. Usually, the positions of Cacique and Bohique are occupied by two different people. But Baracoa is a special man. He knoweth things before they happen."

"What kind of things?" Allie asked.

"Usually things related to the weather or other natural events."

"Oh, so he's a weather man," Jerry said with a grin.

"More than just weather," Yahima said seriously.

"He hath been saying that the gods will make the ground tremble very soon," Arasibo said. Yahima looked at him.

"I had not heard this prediction."

"He can predict earthquakes?" Allie asked, her brows puckered as she thought about the tectonic phenomena they had been discussing a few days before onboard the *Camilla*.

"Aye," Yahima responded, visibly troubled. "He knoweth about them many days in advance."

"What about now, though?" asked Jax. Skeptical about the paranormal direction they had taken, he wanted to get the conversation back to its original topic. "After all this time, you and the white people are still enemies?"

"They are bounders," Arasibo said bitterly. "We try to have little to do with them. But they know that we are not their match in battle, so they still come from time to time and take some of us as slaves."

"They come here to your village and take you by force?" Jax asked.

"They came only a few days ago. They killed two of our warriors and took two boys and a girl back with them." Yahima looked at Arasibo when he said that, but he did not meet her eyes. Looking at Jax, he continued. "My eldest son is now one of the white devils' slaves."

"Oh no," Yahima said. "They took Nibagua?" He nodded curtly, glancing at her only briefly.

"They now have my wife and my son."

"I guess that was the 'incident with the Indians' we were told about," Allie said to Jax.

"Haven't you ever tried to get your people back?" Jerry asked.

"Long ago, we tried," Yahima replied. "But as Arasibo said, we cannot match the power of their weapons, and we lost many of our people to their muskets and their cannons."

"We still try to fight them off when they come," Arasibo said, "but there are too many of them, and we are not able to overpower them. They almost always go back from their raids with some of our young people as their prize, and leaving many of our warriors dead."

"This is just so difficult for us to comprehend," Jax said, shaking his head.

"From whence thou comest, white people do not own slaves?" Arasibo asked.

"No, not for almost a century and a half," Allie said.

"I'm afraid white people don't have a very good historical record in dealing well with those who are different from them," Jax said. "But we're slowly getting better. Throughout history, white people as a group have inflicted a lot of damage, and have done much to be ashamed of. But some of us try to do right by others."

"Thou hast undoubtedly made some enemies of thine own people today," Yahima said, "but thou hast indeed gained many new friends in our village." Many in their group smiled and nodded their affirmation.

§

Drawing on his Navy SEAL training, even though Beau was a man of action, he remembered that patiently waiting for the right time was an important part of any operation. It was especially vital when someone he cared about was involved. So he spent time gathering intelligence, learning all he could about the network of tunnels and passageways under the colony, and about what the Underground knew of the colony's defenses.

He had spent hours questioning people in the Cathedral, trying to acquire any knowledge that could prove useful. Eventually many of them had filtered out, returning to their homes above ground, but Beau's ears were always tuned for the occasional return of young scouts who might carry information about Brit. Beau was especially curious about the location of their armaments, but unfortunately, nobody down below had any definitive knowledge of that.

After a while, his activity turned into aimless pacing, and he was feeling aggravated by his inability to do anything, and itching to get outside, above ground again, into the light of day.

Phil didn't help, being the impatient type himself, though he had dialed it down after seeing that it had almost gotten him killed. Bethany *did* help, though, for she was always calm and proved to be a good influence on him.

Having gathered all the intelligence he thought he could, he sat down next to Bethany, to wait.

§

How long had it been since Dare had left? He had returned a few minutes after ripping Brit's clothing off, but only to leave her a mug and a container of water. He had not even looked at her then, just meekly leaving them on the table, next to the as yet untouched plate of food. Then he left, locking the heavy door behind him.

She had drunk some of the water, and had changed the candle when it nearly reached the pewter candle holder. She knew that it must have been hours. Was it afternoon? Evening?

She paced the room, her arms instinctively pulled across her body, even though there was nobody there to see her. She had already examined the room minutely, searching for any weaknesses in the timbers, but had found none.

She thought about using the plate or mug to tap on the wall, but decided against that too. Knowing that slavery was a way of life here, and not knowing who might be on the other side of whichever wall she tapped on, she was afraid she might only make her situation worse.

Brit was chafing, not only from her imprisonment, but even more from not knowing what was going on. She heard the old inner voices in her head, dark voices she had not heard since the death of her parents. She had cried for a while, but the tears had stopped now. She forced herself to think about Jax, about how he had cared for her for so long, despite having to battle his own demons at the same time.

She knew what the plan had been for this morning, and she knew from what Dare had said that apparently the plan had been carried out. Jax and the others had escaped. She had the feeling in the back of her mind that Jax would not leave her, but apparently he had. He had to, for the safety of the others.

She understood that, but she felt so alone. It would be up to her to get herself out of here, but she could not for the life of her think how to do it.

§

New scouts had been sent out nearly an hour before, and now the previous shift returned to the village. Jax watched them anxiously, and when one of them noticed him looking in their direction, he shook his head.

"Where could they be?" Jax asked. Pushing his fingers through his hair, he left his hands resting on top of his head as he began pacing nervously. Allie was beside him and placed a hand on his arm.

"Beau will get her," she said. "If anybody can get her out of there, it's Beau." Jax looked down at Allie, his eyes showing the anxiety he felt, and he took her in his arms and held her tightly, silently.

"I shouldn't have left her," he said after a few moments. "You know I almost killed myself several years ago? But it was knowing that I still had to take care of Brit that stopped me." Allie pulled away to look up at his face.

"You know that our parents were killed in the World Trade Center on 9/11." Allie nodded. "I felt responsible in a way. Not for their deaths, but because I didn't die myself. I know it's irrational, not at all logical. The psychiatrist called it 'survivor's guilt.' I was supposed to be there too, but I didn't go. So they died and I didn't.

"I hadn't really had much to do with my parents for a while. One of their business ventures a couple of years before they died involved a proposed dredging operation, kind of like underwater strip-mining, near a protected area. I didn't agree with it and Dad and I had some words, and I left after calling him some not-too-savory names.

"I went on with my life and they went on with theirs, but they did try to reconnect with me. They would invite me over for dinner, or just call on the phone to talk things out, but I never listened. I was too focused on my own righteous principles and didn't want to hear their side of anything.

"We didn't have any further blow-ups, but we didn't really have any contact to speak of either.

"When they invited me to the meeting they were going to on 9/11, it wasn't entirely because of any expertise of mine. I found out later that the meeting was with an environmental action group aimed at making offshore oil rigs safer for the environment. In wanting me there, I think they were reaching out to me, trying to heal the breach between us. And I just blew them off."

"And you felt even more guilty," Allie said.

"Yeah. I had kind of been in shock for a while after the attack, but when we were notified that they were definitely among the victims, that's when the depression really hit. I had moved back into their house, to be with Brit.

"I stayed inside, often sitting in Dad's office, usually in the dark, and I started listening to the guilty voices. And after a while, I couldn't listen any longer, but I didn't feel like I could turn them off."

Jax paused and took a deep breath, as if calling up the courage to continue.

"Dad kept a revolver in his desk," he said quietly. "I hated guns – still do. But one day, I just felt like I couldn't take the pain and guilt any longer. So I took the gun out of the drawer and cradled it in my hand, studying it, almost caressing the cold, black metal. I was trying to develop some kind of affinity with it, so I could do what I felt like I had to do. I remember wondering if I would feel anything when I pulled the trigger, or would it be over before I even had time to feel anything?

"I was thinking about this when I heard Brit call me from the next room, and I could tell that she'd been crying. I thought about what it would do to her, being the one to find my body so soon after the loss of our parents. I could picture her standing over me, her tears falling on me. I even saw her take the gun out of my hand and put it to her own head and pull the trigger." He closed his eyes against the tears. "So I put the gun back in the drawer and went to her.

"After that, we both started seeing the psychiatrist regularly," he continued with a sigh. "It was a long haul, and we both shed a lot of tears, alone and together. And there were times when we both felt like we weren't going to make it through, but eventually we did. Eventually, we sent the dark voices packing." He paused for a few moments. "But we couldn't have done it without each other."

Allie leaned against him and Jax held her tightly, and she felt his body shake a couple of times as if he were stifling back sobs.

§

Brit heard a key rattle in the lock and was up in a second. She quietly crossed the room on her bare feet and snatched up the heavy ceramic mug from the table. She had not been able to come up with any plan beyond getting out of this room, but it was a start. The heavy door creaked open and the moment she saw Dare's head, she swung the mug.

She winced when she heard the dull 'thunk' against his skull, but she didn't waste any time thinking about it. Dropping the mug, she took off out the door, and into the office that this room was attached to. She had the impression it was Dare's office, but she didn't bother to find out.

She left the office, trying to remember the route they had taken from the archives area where he had found her the night before. They had not gone outside, but instead had followed a branching hallway, past several closed doors, and she had thought that she could find her way back. Now, she was not so sure. She was getting confused.

Where she thought she had to turn left, she could only go right, and the configuration of doors in the hallway did not look familiar. Should she keep going and see where she ended up? Should she go back and risk running into Dare again? She realized belatedly that she should have locked him in the cell before leaving, but she had acted quickly, instinctively. Too late now.

Before this, she had had no idea that this building was so large, and she stood impatiently at another branch in the hallway, wondering which way she should go. Considering the Constabulary and the historical archives, she assumed the structure was a government administration building. As such, there was the chance that she could run into any number of officials. The fact that she didn't implied that it must be night time.

Unable to apply any logic to the twists and turns of the hallway, she decided on a direction at random. Then a thought occurred to her. She wondered if, perhaps, she could get out through one of the offices, if it happened to have a window. She started carefully, quietly trying door handles, but they were all locked.

By now, though she was nearly naked, she was sweating, partly from the exertion and partly from the still, close, warm atmosphere in the hallway. Perspiration was dripping in her eyes, stinging them, and she impatiently wiped her eyes with the back of her sweaty hands, but it didn't seem to help. And she realized that the sweat was running down her body, dripping off of her, leaving a trail behind her.

Brit decided to stop, despite the feeling of urgency and panic, and tried to calmly retrace her steps in her mind, comparing the memory of her route last night to the route she had taken now. She took a deep breath and closed her eyes, visualizing the twisting and turning hallways.

She thought she remembered where she went wrong in her flight. In spite of the feeling that she should not go back toward Dare, she decided to backtrack, following the drops of her perspiration on the floor glistening in the sparse light of the lanterns hanging in the hallway.

She arrived at the point where she thought she had made a wrong turn and saw Dare stumbling toward her, his hand on his left temple where a crimson trickle of blood seeped out between his fingers. Before he could reach her, she dashed down the corridor to the left and ran, slipping on the old polished wood floor. She realized that this was the way – it felt right.

Just around the next corner was a door, and Brit knew it was the door to the archives. She padded quickly ahead, rounded the corner and ran into a man who seemed as startled as she was. Knocked almost off balance, he grasped her by the upper arms, then instantly let go when he realized that it was a sweaty, almost naked young woman who had run into him.

"I do apologize, miss," he stammered, attempting to look away. She was about to go around and run past him when she heard Dare's footsteps coming closer from behind.

"Detain that woman!" he shouted. In response, the man reached out and grabbed her, his hands slipping on her skin until he was able to get an arm around her neck from behind, though he seemed to be taking great care with where he placed his other hand.

Brit, now in a state of panic, attempted to get free of his hold, and in doing so, managed a savage blow to his diaphragm with her elbow, and the young man immediately let go of her, gasping for breath. Regaining her balance, she was about to turn and run when Dare, now right behind her, swung the ceramic mug, glancing it against the back of her head, dropping her to the floor.

"Get thee up, man, and help me," he hissed at the man who was picking himself up. Dare went around the corner into the Constabulary dorm where he got a blanket, then went back into the hallway. Brit was stirring but was dazed, unable to pull herself up. Dare threw the blanket over her head and, together with the other man, got her to her feet and walked her out of the hallway and to another exit, thus avoiding the Constabulary.

It was dark and they kept to the shadows. Even so, nobody was out to see these two men guiding a blanket-covered figure through the town. She was dizzy and stumbling but, with each man taking an arm, they eventually arrived at the town square and into the jail, pushing her into an empty cell.

"Go back to thy duties," Dare said to the man, "and tell nobody of what thou hast seen." The man nodded, then turned and left.

Snatching the blanket off of Brit, Dare's face twisted into a sadistic sneer, he looked at her, waiting for her eyes to find him. He forced himself to look at her body, allowing the revulsion to grow.

How could he have found this devil to be attractive? This harlot who used her body to capture the hearts of unsuspecting men?

As she slowly regained her senses, she looked around her new cell, then saw the old man, the figure she had come to despise in the last twenty-four hours, standing in the doorway.

"I was wrong," he said at last, quietly, his voice quivering with emotion. "I find thee to be horrible. Thy form may be exceedingly pleasant to the eye, but it containeth a devilish being that corrupteth the soul of its unlucky victims, and thou shalt not be allowed to contaminate the minds and hearts of our men any longer."

Slamming the door behind himself, he turned the key and left as Brit, still reeling from the blow to her head, lay down on the cot.

§

It was night, after 9:00, and Beau, still frustrated after a day of inactivity and a maddening lack of information, was lying down on a padded bench, attempting to get some rest. A few others had stayed underground as well.

Phil, even less patient than Beau, had begun complaining again. He was irritated that they had to stay in the dark, musty Cathedral, and his fuse was pretty short. He was also experiencing some pain from his cuts and bruises, so that was adding to his irritable nature.

Having already broken up an argument between Phil and one of the Underground people that afternoon, Beau opened his eyes and sighed when he heard him starting in on someone else.

Beau had been toying with an idea for a while, and with Phil making trouble again, it now crystallized in his mind. He sat up and sighed, then rose to his feet.

"Phil?" he said as he walked over to where the fat man was railing against a young Underground resident. Beau didn't hear what the problem was, and he didn't want to know, but he was careful to keep his voice calm. "I was wondering if you could help me with something."

Phil, his train of thought suddenly derailed, seemed disoriented for a moment, but then he went to meet Beau.

"What do you need, Beau?" he asked.

"I wonder if you would be willing to take a message to Jax."

"Outside the wall? Sure!"

"We were supposed to leave right behind Jax, but that was before Brit disappeared. I know Jax is worried about Brit, but I don't want him coming back before we get her. The fewer of our people we have in here, the better."

"I understand. Just tell me how."

"Well, that's the tricky part," Beau said. "You'll have to go out through the river tunnel like Jax did. But Jax left the grates open and the rope in place, so you can pull yourself through. Think you can do that?"

"Sure," Phil said confidently. "I think I can do that. I managed to pull myself up through a little air vent out of the jail."

With three other men pushing and pulling your fat ass, Beau thought.

"Good man," he said. "Get some sleep. I'll wake you early in the morning, before the colony is up."

The night passed quickly for Beau as he got some sleep, but less so for Phil who was excited to get out of the fortress and away from the colony. He didn't know what awaited him out there, but it had to be better than this.

He was already awake and heard the alarm on Beau's watch at 4:00 in the morning.

"Why so early?" Phil asked.

"Everybody gets an early start here. I want to get you out of here unseen and be able to get back before anybody is up and about."

"Gotcha," Phil replied. He eased himself up, aching from the beatings he had received, and groaned as he rested his head in his hands for a moment.

The route to the river was familiar to Beau by now, though it was trickier in the dark, so he took it slowly. Still, it only took them a few minutes to reach the spot where the river appeared, bubbling up from the tunnel underground.

"I'll go first," Beau said, "and make sure everything is still as Jax left it. When I'm ready, I'll give the rope a tug, you take as deep a breath as you can manage and I'll start pulling you over. If you can pull yourself along the rope, that will make it go even faster." Phil nodded, feeling a little nervous now.

They both went into the water, and Beau found the end of the rope, waving about just below the surface of the river. Filling his lungs, he submerged and pulled himself across as Jax had the previous morning. Coming up out of the water in the lake on the other side of the wall, he took a deep breath and went back down, tugging on the rope.

Phil felt the tug and he took all the air into his lungs that he could manage, then started pulling himself on the rope, surprised at how difficult it was to move against the current. His aches and pains didn't help either.

The tunnel was pitch black, but he could feel Beau pulling him across and decided that keeping his eyes closed was better. Then he couldn't see how dark it was.

He was certain that he must be almost all the way through when his lungs started to complain. He kept going hand over hand, and he sneaked a peek but still could see nothing. It was so dark, but he thought he must be close to the end of the tunnel by now.

Why could he not see any light at all from the abundant stars and the crescent moon that had lit their way to the river?

When his chest started to burn, he began to panic. He tried to pull himself faster, but his left hand missed the rope. He struggled to hold on with his right hand, but when the current bounced him against the ceiling of the tunnel, it knocked some of the air out of him. His grip loosened and he slid back a few feet before he got both hands on the rope again.

The fear was overwhelming now, as he knew he had to take a breath but knew there was no air to be had. He could no longer pull himself, but just struggled to maintain his hold on the rope.

Beau could feel the erratic movements of the rope and he kept pulling as fast as he could. Phil's size was working against them both as the water had a much larger area to push against.

As Phil came closer to the end of the tunnel, Beau could just barely make out the lighter form ahead of him, when the rope went slack and he knew that Phil had lost his grip. Beau pulled his leg out of the grate and swam with the current, trying to keep his eyes on Phil. He managed to grab his arm before he lost sight of him completely in the dark.

He hooked his left arm under Phil's armpit so he could hold the rope with his left hand, while pulling with his right. Fighting the current, Beau finally managed to get Phil out of the tunnel and up to the surface of the lake.

At least a minute had already passed, so as soon as he had taken a couple of much-needed breaths himself, he immediately started giving mouth-to-mouth while kicking toward the shore. He felt the ground rise up beneath his feet and he gave a mighty push, propelling Phil up on the shore.

He placed his ear on Phil's chest. After quickly moving around a couple of times, he found a heartbeat, so he resumed mouth-to-mouth, and soon he felt the big man start to stir. Suddenly Phil coughed, spewing water from his mouth, and Beau quickly struggled to roll him on his side.

Phil endured a spasm of coughing as he gradually cleared the water from his lungs, hacking and gasping, and both men lay quietly for a minute, regaining their breath.

Phil sat up and looked at Beau, and was about to say something, when Beau heard the slightest shadow of a sound and put his hand up. He wasn't sure he had heard anything for certain, but he kept listening and again heard what might have been a silent footstep in the dense undergrowth.

"Is somebody there?" he asked quietly.

"Art thou Mr. Bannister?" whispered an almost inaudible voice from the darkness.

"Who wants to know?"

"I am Yuquibo," said the voice. "I am a Taino, placed here with orders to wait for thee, to guide thee to our village."

Beau sighed in relief, feeling the tension leave his body. "I'm Beau Bannister."

The stars were fading, but the sky was beginning to lighten slightly from the east. Beau could see a dark and stealthy form approaching quietly, carrying a bow, barely illuminated by the available light. Phil saw the ominous figure and seemed afraid. He started to scramble from his place, but Beau put a hand on his shoulder.

"It's okay, Phil," he said calmly. "Yahima said that she would have scouts waiting for us. This man is a friend."

The native approached stealthily and knelt beside them. "Art thou well?" he asked.

"We're fine," Beau replied. "It was a long swim, and Phil here almost didn't make it, but we're alright now."

Beau stood and held his hand out to Phil, struggling to help him to his feet. "Are you okay?" he asked, trying to see Phil's face. Phil was breathing a little more easily now and he nodded. "Good," Beau said.

He turned toward the Indian. "I'm staying here," he said. "I have somebody else to get out of there, so I have to go back. I won't be going with you, but Phil will." The warrior seemed a little surprised at this, but nodded.

"Remember the message you're taking to Jax?" he asked, turning back to Phil.

"Beau's going to get Brit," he said, nodding again, reciting what Beau had told him. "You stay here and don't go back into the colony."

"That's right," Beau said. "The fewer people I have to keep track of the better."

"Got it. Thanks, Beau," Phil said, then looked at the native.

"Come with me," Yuquibo said, and Phil fell in step behind him.

Beau watched them walk away toward the west. "Sorry, Jax," he said quietly. "He's all yours now."

Jax woke up when he heard the sounds of the natives arising early in the morning and starting their daily routine. Apparently ascertaining that Jax and Allie were a couple, Arasibo had arranged for both of them to sleep in a hut that was now vacant after the colonists' last raid. He wasn't certain, but Jax thought that he had detected a flicker of displeasure on Yahima's face when Arasibo was telling them of the arrangements.

Jax and Allie were a little hesitant at first, their relationship being so new, but the hut contained two beds, mats made of woven palm fronds stuffed with grass, and they decided that rather than being too particular, they would share the hut, on separate mats.

It had been difficult at first, when they entered the hut and saw various items that had been owned by the previous tenants. The young man had been killed a few days before, trying to defend his village from the colonists. His wife had been taken by them several months before that. Jax and Allie felt a little melancholy as they looked at the furnishings, knowing that the young couple would never inhabit this hut again.

As Jax looked around the village this morning, he saw that Allie was already up and gone from the hut, her sleeping mat empty. He yawned and stretched, then sat up. Unaccustomed to sleeping on the harder surface, he felt a little sore on a few pressure points, but aside from that, he felt more relaxed than he had all week.

He stretched some more, twisting his body in different directions, to ease the discomfort. Pushing aside the mat hanging in the doorway, he went outside and smiled, marveling at the setting in which he now found himself.

The sky overhead was blue and bright, though the sun was not yet visible above the deep green jungle surrounding the village. He could smell the nearby ocean, combined with a mixture of scents from the forest, and the food being prepared by the natives.

Some of the natives worked on various duties in front of their huts, while others were engaged in activities in a common work area. Some men were arriving from different directions in the forest, carrying fish and other fresh catches, which the women took from them and began preparing.

Among all the naked brown people, Allie was easy to find with her light skin and her light colored linen, helping some native women in the common area. She looked up at him and smiled, and Jax felt an unfamiliar feeling of warmth and happiness, to a degree that he had never experienced in any of his previous relationships. He smiled back at her, then at others who looked at him, and without exception, they all smiled back.

The natives, while being fierce warriors and hunters, had also turned out to be a sweet and loyal people. They were intelligent, with a refreshing, well-developed sense of humor. They were not above playing jokes on each other, and in the day that Jax had spent with them, he had seen that even the one who was the object of the joke joined in the good-natured laughter.

The natives took great care, both of the children and of the older ones in their midst, being particularly considerate and respectful of their elders. They gave no indication, Jax noticed, of being cannibals, as Payne had alluded to early on. Once the natives were convinced that Jax, Allie and Jerry meant them no harm, they welcomed the Americans into their village and treated them as if they were family, and included them in various activities, as Allie was currently helping them in the food preparation.

Jerry emerged yawning and stretching a couple of huts down, and also smiled at him. Jax turned back toward Allie, and as he started to walk over toward her, he noticed that people's heads were turning toward the east. A few moments later, he saw a commotion in that direction.

Yuquibo, a young native man that Jax had met the day before, was entering the village after his overnight watch. Directly behind him was Phil, his round face looking irritated and red. Drenched in perspiration, he was huffing from his trek through the forest from the colony.

Jax strained to see behind him, but could not see Beau or Brit, and he felt the anxiety rising again. Jax saw that Yuquibo's face was stern, and that didn't help. As Jax made his way toward them, Phil saw him and smiled with relief.

"Oh my god, Jax," he said. "I thought we'd never get through this fucking jungle! The bugs and humidity are driving me crazy. This goddamn island is a pain in the ass!" Yuquibo, looking quite unhappy, rolled his eyes and shook his head, sighing as he turned to join his fellow villagers, and Jax understood immediately what the problem was.

Although the swelling had gone down, the flesh around Phil's eyes was still black, and multiple cuts and contusions covered his face. Jax was sure he must be in pain.

"Are you alright, Phil?" he asked.

"No, I'm not alright!" Phil snapped at him. "Do I look alright? I've had my boat sunk by a bunch of savages, I've been kidnapped and beaten by colonial assholes, and I'm stuck on this shit hole of an island with no way off of it."

"Where are Beau and Brit?" Jax asked, ignoring his complaints.

"Beau sent me here to let you know that he's going to get her, but that he doesn't want you to be anxious and go back. He figures the fewer people he has to worry about in there the better."

Jax felt a hand on his back and turned to see Allie joining him. He put his arm around her shoulders and turned back to Phil. "Is that all?" he asked. "Has he located her yet?"

"No, not by the time we left, but he was confident that he would."

"How am I supposed to not be anxious?" he asked rhetorically. "Could he project any kind of timetable? Anything at all?"

"Sorry, Jax." Phil looked around the village and put his head back a little, sniffing the air. "Is there anything to eat? I'm starving!"

Jax inadvertently glanced down at Phil's belly, then hoped that Phil hadn't noticed.

§

Beau had been careful again once he got back inside the stockade as he made his way back to the alley entrance to the Roanoke Underground. It was still early and, while he didn't see anyone, he again had the feeling that someone was watching or following him. By now, he was convinced that he was just being paranoid, but he didn't want to take the chance of discovery, so he again made several false turns and double-backs instead of going directly to the hidden door in the alley.

Once back inside the Cathedral, he found his padded bench again and tried to get a little more rest until the others who had spent the night were up and about. The atmosphere was definitely more comfortable with Phil gone. It seemed as if Beau had just closed his eyes when Micah ran over to him and shook his shoulder. He was instantly up.

"What is it, Micah?"

"We hath found her," the boy said breathlessly. "Thy lady, Brit. She is in a jail cell now, placed there only in the past hour or so." Bethany had overheard and approached them, along with a few others who had heard as well.

"Is she alright?" Beau asked anxiously.

"Methinks that she is, though I was not the one to find her. Reginald, one of the other boys, saw her in his explorations and reported the find. She is in the cell right next to where the fat man was."

Beau looked around and saw John and Eric among the people gathered around.

"Okay, John, Eric, we made a good team before. Let's go get her." John and Eric looked to Bethany who pondered for only a moment, then nodded toward them.

They took the same route as the previous morning, arriving without a sound at the small vent into the cell where Brit lay on a cot facing the wall, sleeping fitfully. From behind her, Beau saw that she was wearing only her bikini. He also saw a little tangle of blood in the hair on the back of her head, but was happy to see that she was breathing.

Studying the cell through the vent, as he had at Phil's cell, he made certain that she was alone. He was just about to speak her name when he heard a key rattling in the cell door. Brit jumped, startled from her sleep, as the heavy wooden door swung open and Thomas Dare stood in the doorway, looking sternly toward her.

"Come along, harlot!" he growled.

Brit looked up at him from the cot, again attempting to keep herself covered. "Where are we going?" she asked.

"Thou shalt meet the lord and answer for thy sinful practices."

"What are you talking about?" she demanded.

"Enough questions, woman!" Dare bellowed. "Come with me now!" and he grabbed her wrist, yanking her from the cot and dragging her out of the cell.

Beau didn't wait to see or hear more. He rushed ahead to the larger vent in the interrogation room. There was nobody in the room, but he wouldn't have cared if there had been. He just hoped the door out of the room was not locked.

He released the latch and pushed the vent cover open as he had when he rescued Phil the day before and swung himself down into the room, ran across the floor and turned the heavy handle on the door.

It opened and Beau quickly but carefully stuck his head out, listening and looking for Dare and Brit. He was aware of John and Eric moving through the passageway, up to the vent behind him. But he saw nobody outside the door and went out into the dim hallway, doubling back in the direction that Brit's cell would be.

Beau heard what sounded like keys jingling behind him, back in the direction from which he had come, and he paused, thinking that he had misjudged the direction that Dare had taken Brit. But as he was standing in front of her now empty cell, he heard shuffling feet ahead, then he heard Brit's voice.

"Let go of me, you bastard!" This was followed by a slap and the dull sound of somebody falling onto the stone floor. Beau continued forward until he reached another open door, and it was from this room that the sounds were emanating.

The room was exceedingly warm, and mostly dark, unlit except for the fire blazing through the opening in one of the stone walls. Brit was on the floor in front of the immense stone hearth, with Dare standing over her, holding a sword.

In the split second that Beau stood in the doorway, he saw Brit holding her face, likely where she had been slapped to the floor. He also saw Dare, a demonic sneer on his face, as he lifted a sword, ready to plunge it into Brit's body.

"Dare!" Beau shouted. The man turned around, looking toward him with surprise as Beau ran into him, knocking him off balance. The older man fell against the stone wall, hitting his head, and ended up in a pile at Beau's feet. Beau took the sword out of his limp hand and turned back to Brit.

"Are you okay honey?" he asked, as she looked at him in a daze. He helped her up and held her in his arms. Brit seemed weak, but was able to stand. Beau put the sword down and took off his shirt, giving it to her. As she slipped it on, they heard a gunshot outside the room they were in.

He motioned for her to stay where she was as he snatched up the sword again and looked out in the hallway. Brit nodded, wrapping the shirt around her, and she regarded with disdain the old man lying on the floor.

Beau headed back the way he had come and when he reached the interrogation room, he saw John struggling hand-to-hand with a man that Beau recognized as Phil's interrogator from yesterday morning, the pistol still in his hand. A quick glance and he noticed Eric's feet on the floor, the rest of his body hidden by the heavy table in the middle of the room.

The interrogator was trying to point the muzzle of the gun at John, and as he was a bit taller and stronger, he was about to succeed. Beau readied the sword in his hand and took a step forward to help. At that moment, though, John savagely pushed the interrogator away and let go with his right hand just long enough to, in one swift motion, snatch his knife from its sheath and plunge it upward into the man's abdomen, just below his sternum.

The man fell back across the table with a jangling sound, the ring of keys hanging from his belt clattering against the table top. Beau rushed around the table toward Eric and knelt down beside him. Seeing the bullet wound in his chest, Beau felt his neck for a pulse. John watched with fear and anger etched into his face, panting to catch his breath, as Beau looked up and shook his head.

"I'm sorry, John. Your brother's dead." Tears glistened on John's lower eyelids as his gaze never left his brother's face. Beau stood up, placing a hand on his shoulder, and left him to have a moment alone with his brother.

Back in the room Beau had left, Brit was sitting on the hearth, but to the side, away from the heat of the flames, keeping an eye on Dare who was still unconscious. Beau could not see the intensity of her stare, but he did see the tenseness of her body. When she heard him approach and saw him standing in the doorway, she stood and ran to his arms.

"Are you okay, baby?" he asked, as he held her face in his hands, looking into her eyes. She seemed more alert now, her eyes clear, though they were filling with tears of relief.

"I'm fine," she nodded. A look of confusion crossed her face. "I thought you escaped."

"I stayed to find you and Phil." He sighed. "Oh honey, I was afraid I'd lost you," he said, holding her in a long embrace.

They heard a quiet rustling sound and turned to see Thomas Dare stirring. Beau went to him and pulled him roughly up onto the hearth and, seeing the dagger on his belt, took it from him, then searched for other weapons. "Must be getting rusty," he said. "Back in the day, that would have been the first thing I did."

Dare was looking wobbly and feeble, his eyes unfocused. His head was bloody in two places, dry and crusty on the temple where Brit had hit him earlier with the heavy ceramic mug, and now in the back where he had hit it against the wall when Beau pushed him.

"We need to get out of here," Beau said to Brit.

"What are we going to do with him?" Brit asked.

"Let's lock him in a cell. Someone will find him when they come in later." Brit was silently watching Dare, and Beau couldn't interpret the expression on her face. "Brit? Are you alright?"

She looked up at him almost as if he had broken a trance.

"Yeah, I'm fine," she nodded. "Let's do it."

§

"It's almost like there's another colony underground," Phil was saying. "I mean, they don't all live down there – a few do, who have gained the disfavor of the colony. But most of them go down there during the day, and they just spend their time taking turns at patrolling the colony from inside those hidden tunnels."

"And you said the girl who is in charge of them is from New Jersey?" Jax asked.

"Yeah, Bethany," Phil said, some crumbs of food falling from his mouth. "Well she says she's not really in charge, but everybody does seem to look to her for guidance."

Like the previous morning, they were sitting in a large circle in the central, common area of the village, finishing a breakfast of more mystery meat, fruit, and some kind of flat bread that tasted vaguely of coconut.

While Jax was a little disgusted by Phil's gastronomic athleticism, the natives seemed amused by it. They used large leaves or thin split slabs of wood as plates, and Phil had already managed to polish off three helpings.

"Wouldst thou like some more, Mr. Chesterfield?" asked a native woman. Phil helped himself to some more food.

"It sure is weird hearing these Indians talking like that," he said quietly to Jax. Jax noticed that food seemed to be the only thing that could interrupt Phil's train of thought.

"I know," Jax agreed. "Many of them learn it early, along with their native tongue. It's been passed down through the centuries from the original white people who settled with them."

Phil's ingestion seemed to be slowing down now, and he got back to talking about the Roanoke Underground, and the jail that he had been kept in.

"I guess anybody who has gained the disfavor of the colonists are killed and incinerated. Apparently that's what *I* narrowly escaped."

"That's not making me feel any better," Jax said. "My sister is still in there."

"It really is unbelievable," Phil continued as if he hadn't heard Jax, and he reached for another piece of flat bread. "It's almost as bad as Nazi Germany in there. Only on a much smaller, more amateurish scale."

"What about the Underground?" Allie asked, trying to change the subject.

"Oh, it's amazing," he said. "Tunnels branching out all around the colony. Drove me crazy spending much time in there, though. Nothing but candle or torchlight. It's great to be back in the sunlight!" He was about to put another bite of meat in his mouth when he stopped and looked at it. Leaning over toward Jax, he whispered.

"You know, somebody told me the Indians might be cannibals."

"We were not told the truth about the natives," Jax replied.

"Hmm," Phil said, and popped the meat into his mouth. He chewed and swallowed it. He picked up a piece of fruit, and before he could put it in his mouth, another thought occurred to him. "What about our boats? Do you suppose the colonists lied about that, too?"

Jax looked over at him, surprised that he himself had not thought to ask. "That's an excellent question," Jax said and turned toward the natives. "Yahima, do your people sink the boats of visitors to the island?" The look of confused surprise on her face told him the answer before she even said anything.

"No, of course not," she said. "Why would we do anything such as this?" Arasibo and others nearby looked up at Jax, all displaying a similar confused expression.

"William Payne told us that it was the practice of the natives to sink the boats of anybody who comes to the island. When we went back to where we came ashore, our boat was gone."

"We are not brutes," Arasibo said indignantly. "We do not do such things."

"Excuse me," Jax said, trying to keep his voice from sounding too accusing, "but your people destroyed our inflatable boat, killed our friend and were threatening to kill my sister."

"Nibagua," Arasibo nodded. "His family was killed by white people. He argued from the beginning that whites should be killed on sight. Others of us were not so willing to incite the wrath of the white people. They already made it difficult enough for us. We thought it wise to not provoke them beyond what was necessary.

"Nibagua was the first one to see thy boat that day. Later, he brought me and another to see it, though we could not. Nibagua was of the opinion that, should more white people come to our island, they should be killed before they had an opportunity to offer further threat.

"I argued against taking such rash actions. We finally decided to wait, hoping that the boat would not come to our island and that no action would be necessary.

"He and a few others acted on their own that night. And he is dead now." Arasibo looked down at his hands for a moment, then back up at Jax. "We did nothing to thy boat, but I am sorry about thy friend."

"Thank you, Arasibo," Allie said. "I'm sorry about your friend too. And I am very sorry about how the colonists have treated your people. But I assure you, we are not like that."

"We know that now," Yahima said. "Thou art good and kind folk, not at all like the white people in the colony."

"Well that's great," said Phil, seemingly unmoved by the apologies. "This little love-fest is really heartwarming. But still, our boats are gone. If you didn't sink them, who the hell did? The colonists?"

"Art thou certain that thy boats hath been sunk?" asked Arasibo.

"My boat was gone the next morning," Jax said.

"And mine was gone only a few hours after we landed," said Phil.

"Aye, but that doth not necessarily mean that they were sunk. We hath seen where they hide them."

Beau, having taken the ring of keys from the dead man's belt, turned a key in the lock of one of the cell doors. Brit stood beside him, holding the dagger that Beau had taken from Dare, and John stood close behind, his face grim, but having seemingly regained his composure after the death of his brother. He was holding tightly to Dare. When the door opened, Beau saw a man inside, looking out at him fearfully.

"Who are you?" Beau asked.

"My name is Ambrose Tomkins," the man replied shakily, cowering on his bare cot, pressing himself against the wall.

"Why are you here?"

"I was placed here by that man, in point of fact," he said, pointing at Dare. "I hath taken a rebellious stand among my people, stating that the Indians should not be forced into servitude. I fear that I was too outspoken on the subject."

"No such thing," Brit said grimly.

"Come on out," said Beau. "Lieutenant Governor Dare's going to take your place in there."

Tomkins was wary, but he stood and slipped out the cell door, after which Beau pushed Dare inside and onto the cot. He closed and locked the door, then he turned and looked at Tomkins.

"How long were you in there?"

"I am not certain, sir," he replied. "A few days at least. I was rounded up with a few others who shared my defiant and treasonous beliefs."

"You mean there are more of you in here?" asked Brit.

"Aye, miss, at least ten of us, if they hath not yet been killed. There are always some of us who do not agree with slavery or other policies of our colony, and if we are found out, we are always dealt with harshly. Some of us, I fear, do not hide our displeasure very well."

"Yeah, and I'm afraid I'm one of them," Beau said coldly.

They heard a door opening and closing behind them, and John took a few steps toward the front of the building.

"Someone approacheth," he said as he turned back to them. Beau followed him toward the front door where there was a small lobby area, and they saw the man who had entered the building.

"Who art thou?" he asked as Beau and John ran toward him. Then his confusion was replaced with an expression of recognition. "Oh, I know thee," he said, pointing at Beau. "Thou art one of the newcomers, the Americans. We hath been looking for thee and thy friends."

"Yeah, we decided we were tired of the spotlight," Beau replied. He raised the sword and John raised the pistol. "Come on in. Who are you?"

"Joseph Warner," he said timorously, putting his hands up in front of him. "I am a jail keeper, here to begin my shift."

"Well, Joey, I think you're going to have an easy shift," Beau said. "You'll be able to relax for a while."

A quick search revealed a dagger and a pistol, both of which Beau confiscated. As John escorted him toward the cells, Beau found the key for the front door and locked it, then rejoined the others.

He opened the door to the cell next to Dare's and found it occupied by another rebel, who was replaced by the jail keeper, Joseph Warner. As they opened one cell after another, their number eventually grew to fourteen.

The last door that Beau opened turned out to not be a cell. It had rows of rifles, pistols, ammunition, and swords, all arranged in racks running along each wall.

"Looks like we found a small armory," Beau said appreciatively. "Let's take them."

"Are you sure that's a good idea?" Brit asked.

"We've killed one of the colonists, we've jailed two more, and we've released their prisoners. Considering we're all outlaws now, I think it might be a good idea to arm ourselves for protection." He and John placed their pistols in their belts and entered the room, taking the guns down and handing them to the former prisoners.

"Get these weapons to the interrogation room," Beau said to Tompkins.

"It is providential for us that the other jailer, the only person who saw how we got in here is dead,"

John said quietly. "I hope that our location can remain a secret to the other colonists."

In only a few minutes time, the armory was emptied of its weapons which were being handed up through the vent in the interrogation room. After all the people were helped up into the passageway, Beau went back to the front door and unlocked it, hoping that this would help to protect the secret of their entry and exit.

§

"You're telling me my boat is still around?" Jax asked.

"I know not if it is still afloat," Arasibo said, "but we did not sink it. We hath seen it not since we left thee on the beach that night."

Jax was stunned. Having resigned himself to the idea of his boat being destroyed, the thought that it could still be seaworthy, and possibly within reach left him nearly speechless.

"You said you've seen where they hide them," Allie said. "Where is that?"

"There is a large sea cave on the eastern side of the island," Arasibo said, "south of their fortress. A few of us hath seen it, and a few years ago, two even ventured near the entrance of the cavern, where they saw many boats. Some of the boats were quite old and wrecked. It looked as if the colonists were taking them apart, but there were some newer boats which were still floating."

"What do they do with them?" Jerry asked.

"We do not know. Those who went up to the cave did so after the white people had taken a boat. It was three summers ago. There were many white people on the boat, inspecting it, as if they were looking for something. Whether they found what they were looking for, we know not."

"Can you take me there?" Jax asked.

"I can, but it is guarded by white men with guns. It will be a dangerous venture."

"They're not going to keep us here against our will," Jax said firmly. Arasibo smiled grimly and nodded in response.

"You told us yesterday," Allie said, "that your people came here long ago from another place. Have none of your people tried to leave this island, to go someplace else away from the white people?"

"Some hath tried over the years," Yahima replied. "I do not know if they were successful or not. But most of us hath friends or family members in the fortress, kept as slaves. Those of us who hath stayed do so out of loyalty to them. We do not want to abandon them, or give up hope of seeing them again."

"I can understand that," Jax said quietly. "I'm not leaving here without Beau and Brit." Allie sympathetically placed her hand on his shoulder.

"Canst thou help us get *our* people back?" Arasibo asked. Jax was taken by surprise again.

Phil made a scoffing sound, but Jax held up his hand toward him and spoke up before Phil had a chance to say anything rude or embarrassing.

"I'm not sure what I can do. I have no weapons. *You're* armed against them better than I am."

"But thou knowest the white people," Arasibo persisted. "Thou knowest how they think, and how they plan."

"I'm afraid that's not entirely true," Jax said. "The world we come from is about four hundred years beyond where they are. Things are different now. *People* are different." Arasibo and Yahima, as well as other natives within earshot, looked downcast.

"But thou didst get *me* out," Yahima said.

"Yes, and you can bet that their security is going to be much higher after that. They're going to hold on to their slaves a lot tighter from now on. Getting even *one* more out of there will be a lot more difficult, let alone all of them."

"I don't even know how long our escape route will remain open," Allie said. "It's possible that they do inspections of the compound with some frequency and will probably find how we got out of there."

"But I promise you this," Jax said to Arasibo and Yahima, "when we get out of here, we will let everyone know about the colony and about what they are doing, how they're treating your people. Slavery has not been tolerated by either England or America for a very long time and I'm certain that powerful people will be moved to help you."

Yahima looked at her brother, who seemed to be pondering what Jax said. Then he nodded.

"Then we must get thee to thy boat."

§

Nicholas Harvie leaned back in his chair and sighed as he looked around the cavern. Reflections from the surface of the water rippled across the uneven rocky ceiling high overhead. Even though the cave was quite large, Nicholas usually experienced a feeling of distress or uneasiness at high tide, when the opening was closed up as it was now, isolating him from the outside.

The tide was going out now, though, so he knew that the cave would be open again soon, and his replacement would arrive to take over guard duty. He could hear the recurring sucking sound of the waves continually slapping against the upper part of the opening as the surface of the water lowered.

The cave on the southeastern side of the island was quite deep which prevented the lagoon from draining completely, so the interior stayed flooded even at low tide. But there was also high ground inside the cave around the central lagoon, so there was always at least one guard inside, as well as two or three outside.

A floating dock structure rose and fell with the tides, and almost completely encircled the interior lagoon. Currently there were four boats floating at the docks, now nearly level with Nicholas at high tide, while other older ones were in various stages of dismantling.

Nicholas sighed again, feeling an uneasiness that was becoming more and more familiar to him. It wasn't just his assignment to guard duty in the cave. He got that assignment often enough that he had learned to tolerate the anxiety, the distress of confinement.

But like so many of the other colonists, he had met and, to some extent, gotten to know Jax and his friends over the course of the last several days, particularly last Sunday. With the possible exception of the fat one, he liked these people. They seemed to be good and decent folk who did not deserve to have their lives forcibly taken away from them.

Nicholas had been raised with the idea that their colony, their very lifestyle, had to be protected at all costs, and while he was growing up, he seldom had an opportunity to question that philosophy.

This secret cave was one of the means of protecting their colony.

The colonists' work on dismantling these boats, beyond the initial investigation after acquiring them, was not a high priority, and the disposal could take many years. Part of the reason was simply a lack of manpower. Nicholas knew that he and the other few men who were used to guard or dismantle the boats in the cave were sworn to secrecy about its existence.

Nicholas had recently started to wonder how many people really knew about it. Lieutenant Governor Dare, obviously, since their orders came through him, and Governor Payne apparently initiated the orders. Nicholas knew of only about ten men on the force who served as guards at the cave, because they were the ones who relieved him, or the ones that he either relieved or served with.

But as infrequently as his guard duty came up, he was certain there had to be more.

He could only remember one or two boats landing on the island in his whole life, and he hadn't really thought about the implications of their philosophy on the visitors. But two boats in the space of just one week – that had been enough to cause these disturbing thoughts to surface.

That, and the rumors.

Lately, he had been hearing about people being taken from their homes and never being seen again. That part was not just a rumor, for he knew a couple of people who had disappeared, friends with whom he had shared his own misgivings about what the colony had become.

The part that Nicholas found particularly disturbing was the explanation that someone had given him concerning what happened to those nonconformists. About a dark and isolated section of the jail, and a furnace, an incinerator used to dispose of the bodies of dissenters. Nicholas was not sure if he believed that, but he did know that people sometimes seemed to just disappear, never to be seen or heard from again.

He was fearful, not just for the friends who had vanished, but also for himself. He and his slave girl, Anacaona, had fallen in love, and they had spoken between themselves, in the privacy of their home, about getting married. But since she was an Indian, Nicholas knew that it would not be allowed. Some of the whites mixed with the Indians in the early days, but not now. The Indians were slaves to work for the colonists.

Or enemies to be fought.

Nicholas got up and walked around the cave, hoping to get the disquieting thoughts under control. He focused his attention on the boats. He found them fascinating. Knowing what boats and ships looked like back in the era in which his people had first arrived on the island, he knew that they were nothing like these sleek, self-powered craft.

The largest one, the *Camilla*, the one they took from Jax, was not really as slim and sleek as the others, but it appeared mighty. That one took up the greatest space in the lagoon. It stood fairly tall, with all manner of appendages sticking up from the top of it, and it had barely fit through the opening of the cave at low tide. At high tide, those appendages had nearly touched the ceiling of the cave.

They had found some interesting things on the boats, only a few of which they really understood. There was a lot of strange paraphernalia on Jax's boat, but aside from a flare gun and a shotgun, nobody knew what any of it was for.

An older one of these four boats had proven interesting too. The interior of the boat was in the process of being dismantled, but the hull was still intact and floating in the lagoon. They had taken it over ten years ago.

On that boat, they had found numerous brick-shaped packages made of some kind of thin, transparent material, containing a white powder. Their studies of that substance had caused some unusual, and at times frightening reactions among those of their people investigating.

The previous owners of the boat could not shed any light on the purpose of the powder, as they had resisted the idea of being incorporated into the colony, attempted an uprising, and were killed. In the end, Lieutenant Governor Dare oversaw the disposal of the offensive material.

Other things on the boat, and those before it, which could not be readily identified, were set aside or discarded, and there was quite a store of intriguing items stacked along the west wall of the cave.

Nicholas walked slowly around the interior of the cave, listening to the lapping of the waves as the tide continued flowing out and the mouth of the cave began to open up. His guard shift would be over in a few hours and he would be able to go back home to Anacaona.

His slave.

Nicholas heaved another sigh, feeling helpless.

§

James Morales didn't know what was going on, but he didn't like it. He stared at the calendar, trying to decide what to do. Phil and his friend Jerry had left nearly a week ago to search for those treasure hunters. The last time he had heard from Phil was on Monday afternoon, and it was now Saturday.

James sublet a closet of an office from a small fishing charter company. The office barely had room for a desk, a file cabinet and a chair. He really didn't need any more room than that, but he always made it a point to meet clients down on the dock, to give a better impression. James flew a charter floatplane out of Miami, giving aerial tours around Biscayne Bay and sometimes as far as the Everglades.

The university had missed Phil and was trying to find out where he might be. They had called James to see if he knew anything, but he didn't know much. This morning's newspaper revealed that an official investigation was now underway.

Being a former University of Miami professor, James had met him years ago. He never really liked Phil, but he was able to get along with him better than some. He knew how irascible and testy Phil could get, and he had the feeling that Phil thought that they were better friends than they actually were. The truth was that James could barely stand Phil for more than an hour or so.

But even after James had left his job at the University, they still had contact from time to time, especially when Phil wanted something. Just a few months ago, Phil had inquired about flying low over the very area currently in question, to see if there might be any visible signs of his pet shipwreck from the air, counting on the clarity of the water. He knew it was a long shot, but wanted to give it a try.

When James quoted his usual price, minus a 15% "Friend Discount," Phil had balked at it, apparently thinking that a real friend would do it for free.

It was sometime after that that Phil had evidently decided to hire a professional, using grant money that he had just acquired. James didn't hear any more about it from Phil until a week ago when he called to, again, ask about the possibility of flying out to where his people were searching for the shipwreck.

James had a full calendar at that time, though, and was not available, but Phil still had a problem with it. In the end, he had decided to take his boat, but he had checked in with James during the first part of the trip. Phil had planned to be back before now.

James thought about calling the Coast Guard, but he remembered that Phil had already done that without success. He had said that outside America's territorial waters, and with no actual evidence of any trouble, there was really nothing they could do.

With a sigh, James double-checked the appointment book open on his desk and the calendar on his wall, to confirm what he already knew. He had no charters until Monday. He was free for the rest of the weekend.

He stood up, locked the door to his dingy little office and walked down the dock toward his plane.

B eau led the others back through the tunnels toward the Cathedral. Eric's death notwithstanding, there was almost a celebratory mood among them. But each of the fourteen people was now loaded down with weapons and ammunition, and their good moods were counterbalanced by a grim foreboding of confrontations ahead.

Almost as a confirmation of that, Beau heard a muffled sound ahead and motioned for everyone to stop. He stood still, listening, and again heard the distant report of a rifle, echoing through the hallway from the direction of the Cathedral.

"Come on!" he said, and he took off running, clutching the rifles to his chest with his left hand. In his right hand was the torch, its flame sputtering as he ran, and he struggled to see ahead of him in the dim passage. In time, the tunnel opened up into a room just off the Cathedral and Beau stopped at the doorway as the others caught up with him, almost colliding with some who were running for their lives.

He tossed the torch away into the dirt, so as not to provide a target for the enemy. Squinting to see details in the dimly-lit cavern, he looked through the doorway, rapidly surveying what was happening. He saw a scene of panic as the unarmed Underground people were attempting to hide or run away from their assailants. Some who were not so lucky already lay dead in the Cathedral. With dismay, he recognized Micah among them. It looked to Beau as if there were about ten armed men.

"The guns are loaded and ready to fire," John said grimly beside him. Beau looked down at the rifles, and though they were of an unfamiliar design, the mechanisms were simple. He turned toward John, and as he did so, he saw Brit and read the expressions of fear and anger displayed on her face.

"You stay here, baby," he said. "John, you and the rest come with me." Brit wanted to protest but the fear won out and she watched with apprehension as Beau led the others into the fray.

Beau raised his musket and fired the first shot among the rebels, killing a colonist whose gun was pointing at a screaming woman. After the colonist fell, Beau realized that the woman was Bethany, and she cast her eyes about, panic-stricken, for the source of her salvation.

Other shots rang out from Beau's companions, and the attacking colonists, seeing that there was now armed resistance, attempted to take cover in their unfamiliar surroundings, but in scarcely a minute, only two of them remained.

"Cease fire," Beau shouted, and the rebels, though probably never having heard that command before, stopped and looked at him.

Beau peered through the haze of the black powder smoke toward where the two remaining colonists were hiding behind one of the massive columns supporting the vaulted ceiling.

"Drop your weapons and come out with your hands up," he called out toward them.

After a few seconds passed, he could see the two men slowly come out from their hiding place with their hands in front of them. Keeping his musket aimed toward them, Beau instructed one of his men to search them for other weapons, and they were stripped of a dagger and a pistol each.

Within a few minutes, the two men were tied up to a couple of chairs, and Beau looked them over. One looked familiar, and Beau studied his face carefully.

"You're the guy who was following me a couple of evenings ago," he said. "You almost ran into me when you came around the corner." The man stared impassively at Beau. "Why did you assholes come here? Why did you kill these unarmed people?" Still, there was no response.

Beau looked at the other man, noticing that he seemed a bit more nervous. His breathing was shallow and fast, and beads of sweat were standing out on his forehead.

"Big, brave soldiers, killing innocent women and children," Beau said. "Who sent you here? Why did you do this?" The man glanced apprehensively at his companion, then he looked back at Beau but said nothing.

Beau calmly studied the man through narrowed eyes for a few moments, then knelt down on the ground in front of him, taking a dagger from his belt. He pushed one leg of the man's breeches up above his knee and lightly placed the point of the dagger at the side of his kneecap.

"Are you familiar with the patella?" he asked the man who was visibly becoming more anxious. "Commonly called the kneecap, it's attached to the other bones of your leg by means of several sets of tendons." Beau traced the point of the dagger around the perimeter of the man's kneecap, then tapped the flat side of the blade against the bone, making him jump.

"Now, just try to imagine what it might feel like if I was to slip this blade under your kneecap and pry it up. Of course, all those pesky tendons would still be holding it in place, so I'd have to cut those too." He placed the point of the dagger against the side of the man's knee again, pressing with a little more force, and the man winced expectantly and began breathing harder. "Don't you want to talk to me?" Beau asked.

He pressed the blade a little harder, so that the point just started to break the surface of the skin, and the man nodded his head vigorously. "Aye, sir," he panted. "I shall talk to thee."

"Oh, very good," Beau said with a mock warmth in his voice. "What's your name?"

"Michael Pattenson," he said.

"Okay, Mikey. Who sent you here to kill these defenseless people?"

"Governor Payne," Pattenson said.

"Good ole Governor Payne. Why?"

"He was most anxious to find thee, sir, and thy friends."

"Hmm. I can understand his curiosity about where *we* went," Beau said. Then he motioned toward the dead bodies that were being gathered up behind him. "But why does that mean that *they* had to die?" he asked angrily. "Women and children!" He saw Micah laid out on the ground with the others, and he felt a pang as he remembered his promise that he would help the boy escape.

"They were helping thee," Pattenson said quietly. Beau looked at Pattenson's face and had the sudden urge to plunge the dagger into his heart. Instead, he stood up and looked at John.

"If they move," he said, "kill them."

John nodded grimly as Beau walked away from Pattenson, looking down at the expression of fear frozen on Micah's face.

§

Arasibo and three other natives led Jax through the forest. Phil had wanted to come too, but Jax insisted that he stay in the village. The suggestion was not well-received, and Jax finally had to make reference to Phil's girth, saying that a cave might not be the most easily accessible place for him.

The heat and humidity of the afternoon made Jax uncomfortable, and while the shade of the forest shielded him from the sun, there was little breeze to cool the perspiration soaking his linen shirt. The natives, though, seemed unconcerned as they moved quietly through the jungle.

They had been on the move for nearly an hour, heading eastward, roughly following the shore but staying concealed in the forest. Arasibo began slowing his pace, motioning for the others to do the same, and he led them toward a rocky outcropping, a cliff that stood about twenty feet up from the surf. He knelt behind the sheltering rocks and pointed down a little and to the left. Following his direction, Jax could see a shallow opening in the rocks about fifty yards away, the surf lapping at the cave.

Outside the cave, coming up out of the water on the eastern side, was a path that disappeared into the jungle on the far side of the cave, and in a small clearing off the path, a guard was leaning casually against the trunk of a tree, his musket leaning against the tree trunk. Arasibo pointed to a similar clearing on the near side of the cave where another guard was nearly hidden in the foliage.

Jax and the natives spread out a little and made themselves comfortable, continually watching the cave and clearings, as the sun slowly moved behind them. Jax tried to be as patient as the natives were, and as the hours passed and the tide went out, they discovered one other guard post.

By the time the cave was completely accessible, the mouth had grown quite large and fully open, a gaping opening in the rock.

"What do you think, Arasibo?" Jax asked. "Can we get any closer?"

"Not yet," Arasibo replied as he was watching the path, and he pointed. At that very moment, as Jax looked back down toward the cave, he saw four guards marching down the path, and in less than two minutes, the three guards outside and one inside had been replaced. "They change their guards at low tide," Arasibo explained. "They will have no reason to come back for several hours." As the previous guards went up the path and disappeared around the cave on their way back to the stockade, the new ones settled into their posts.

"Come," Arasibo said quietly.

They crept from their vantage point and started making their way toward the cave. Arasibo whispered some instructions to the other three natives in their tongue, and they spread out from there, moving slowly and quietly in three different directions, while Jax and Arasibo held back. Jax waited curiously, but in a couple of minutes' time, they heard three separate calls which to Jax's inexperienced ears sounded simply like bird calls.

"It is safe," Arasibo said, and he and Jax began making their way toward the cave. As they came through the forest, they passed the nearest of the guard posts, and Jax looked with dismay at the guard lying dead on the ground, a bloody wound in his chest.

"Arasibo," Jax said, "I don't like the idea of just slaughtering everyone."

"The white men would not have granted us permission to go into the cave if we had asked them," Arasibo said matter-of-factly.

"No, of course not but, well, won't this go badly for your village? You spoke about how you try to avoid conflict with the white people if possible."

"If our mission is successful and thou getteth back thy boat, thou canst bring powerful people to help, yes?"

"Yes, as I said."

"Then we will do as we must."

§

"I've endangered these people, just by coming here," Beau said. "And twelve of them are already dead because of me."

Beau had come into a small, musty room off the side of the Cathedral, feeling disgusted by the needless bloodshed. He wanted to get away from the two prisoners they had taken, but he couldn't escape the personal shame he felt about the dead. He was sitting on an old divan, and Brit had sat down next to him, trying to comfort him.

"It's not your fault, honey," she said, caressing his cheek. "You didn't know they would find their way to this place."

"No, but I suspected I was being followed. I led them right here."

"You did what you could to throw them off, to mislead them. But you had to come back. You couldn't have stayed out there."

"I should have," Beau said, looking regretfully toward the door, which did not quite block the quiet sound of mourning on the other side.

"If you had, you couldn't have rescued me."

Beau looked at Brit and saw a tear in her eye, sparkling in the flickering lantern light, and he took her face in his hands and kissed her. She wrapped her arms around his neck and they held each other, their lips and their tongues pressed together tightly, and Beau could feel her tears on his cheek.

"Oh God, baby," he said, "if I had gotten there only a few seconds later . . ."

Beau sighed and allowed the thought to hang there. He didn't want to imagine Brit lying on the stone floor, her body pierced by Thomas Dare's sword, and he could feel the tears in his own eyes.

"But you didn't," she said, and she kissed him again. "You got there just in time." She leaned her head against his. "You saved my life. I'm yours forever." She smiled at him.

Beau scoffed briefly at her antiquated statement, but then did a double-take, thinking that she was being serious. She saw his befuddlement and concluded with a sigh.

"I'm saying I love you, you moron."

There was a knock at the door and John stuck his head in. "So sorry to interrupt," he said, "but Michael Pattenson is asking to talk to thee."

Pattenson was still tied to his chair as when Beau had left him. The other man was too, but he was not looking as cooperative as Pattenson. He now had a welt under his left eye and was wearing an obstinate expression.

"What happened to him?" Beau asked.

"He was attempting to discourage Pattenson from talking to us," Ambrose Tomkins said, standing guard over him with a pistol. "But he hath most kindly agreed to cease interfering." Beau grunted and turned his attention to Pattenson.

"So I understand you want to talk."

"Yes, sir," Pattenson said meekly.

"What's up?"

"I beg thy pardon, sir?" Pattenson asked, his eyebrows knitted together.

"What do you want to talk about?" Beau said more impatiently.

"Oh, well sir," Pattenson began, taking a deep breath and glancing briefly at his angry companion, "I would like to throw in my lot with thee."

"Just like that?" Beau asked, looking at Pattenson suspiciously.

"I hath been unhappy with the way things are conducted here for quite a long time. I do not approve of the way New Roonock is being run, nor of many of the orders that hath been given me."

"Oh, you didn't approve of your order to kill innocent people," Beau said, growing angry, "but you still agreed to do it anyway?"

"No sir," Pattenson said, shaking his head. "I give thee assurance, I did not kill any of thy people." Beau was still looking as if he did not believe him. Then he looked behind him where their weapons had been placed.

"Is that his gun?" he asked John who was standing nearby.

"Aye," John replied and handed the rifle to Beau.

Beau looked at the revolver mechanism and opened it up. Five chambers contained unfired cartridges. The sixth one was spent.

"Something doesn't quite add up here Mike," Beau said, still looking suspicious. "Looks like you at least fired once."

Pattenson looked at his companion, then back at Beau. "Aye, sir," he said. "I killed that man there," motioning with his head toward one of the invaders lying dead on the ground. "And I freely admit that I was preparing to shoot more when thou started firing upon us."

"You shot one of your own men?" Beau asked. He looked at the body Pattenson had indicated as Tomkins stooped to examine it, finding a wound in the back. Tomkins looked a little mystified at Pattenson, then up at Beau.

"He hath been shot from behind," Tomkins said.

"Thou murderous scoundrel!" said Pattenson's companion.

Beau lost his patience with the man and turned quickly toward him. "What's your name?" he demanded. The man looked at Beau without responding, until Beau snapped the rifle closed and pointed it at him.

"Roger Rufoote," he said defiantly.

"Roger," Beau said, "I suggest you keep your pie hole shut or I'll be more than happy to shut it for you, permanently." Roger looked with murderous hatred at Beau, then at Pattenson, but said nothing more. Beau lowered the rifle and turned his attention back to Pattenson.

"Okay, Mike," he said, "what can you tell me about the folks who run this place? What's their beef with us?"

"They simply want to rule the colony without hindrance," Pattenson said. "This island is their kingdom, and they consider any who might oppose them to be a threat to their power."

"And you're telling me that you're prepared to oppose them?" Beau asked.

"It would seem so, sir," Pattenson said.

Beau pondered for a second, then nodded toward John. "Cut him loose, but keep an eye on him."

"Governor Payne will have thy head on a platter," Rufoote spat at Pattenson.

"Alright, Poindexter, I've just about had it with you," Beau said as he went behind Rufoote's chair and grabbed the back of it. He tipped it and began dragging it across the ground, and into a room like the one he and Brit had occupied earlier. He roughly tipped the chair back down and left the room, slamming the door behind him.

Walking back toward Pattenson and the other rebels, Beau rubbed his hands together. "Okay, people," he said, "let's get to work."

§

Jax and Arasibo rejoined the other three natives, and they made their way down the path toward the opening of the cave. The one closest to the opening fitted an arrow to his bowstring and carefully peered around the edge. He did not see anyone and slowly moved a little farther in. He quickly raised his bow and let go of the arrow and an instant later, Jax heard a faint thud and the sound of a musket clattering onto the rock floor inside the cave.

Jax followed the natives inside. As he rounded the entrance, he saw the boats floating on the interior lagoon. More specifically, he saw *his* boat, and he felt an overwhelming feeling of relief. There were three other boats tied up at the dock as well, one of which he recognized as Phil's cruiser.

Arasibo looked at Jax and gave a slight smile. "Thy boat is alright?" he asked.

"It looks like it," Jax replied. Trying to avoid looking at the dead guard with the arrow in his chest, Jax went down onto the floating dock, now quite low in the cave, and climbed up onto the *Camilla*. Ascending to the bridge, he performed a brief inspection and then started her up. He breathed a sigh of relief as he listened to the diesel engines running for a few moments, revving them a bit, listening for any problems. Satisfied, he shut them down.

"It's good," Jax said with a nod toward Arasibo.

Arasibo nodded in reply. His friends were inspecting the things stacked along the western wall of the cave. Jax looked toward the other natives and saw a long inventory of items, presumably from various boats the colonists had taken. Among them, Jax saw several items that resembled spray cans, scores of them, stacked along the cave wall. But he didn't take the time to check it out.

"We need to hurry," Jax said. "The tide's coming in. We don't want to be trapped in here for another twelve hours."

With that, the natives climbed into the boat, as Jax happily fired up the engines and started backing the boat out of the cave.

§

James Morales, peering out the windows of his plane, was near the area that Phil had outlined to him but so far, he saw no boats. His instruments had started acting strangely and now, without the use of his navigational equipment, he was flying entirely by sight, by the seat of his pants as the old-timers used to say. To his chagrin, he also noticed that his radio was not working, producing only occasional bursts of static.

He started doing a wide zig-zag pattern, flying south for a few miles, then making a wide turn and flying north a mile or so from his previous path. He was watching carefully out both sides for anything that might warrant closer inspection.

He was feeling irritated at burning through his fuel with nothing to show for it. He had already been doing this for hours, and had refueled a half hour ago at Cockburn Town on Grand Turk Island. Then he returned, to the best of his knowledge, to the approximate point where he had left off, and resumed his search.

He was beginning to think that this was a foolish venture and wondered if he should go back home. Finally, on his third pass toward the south, he spotted something, an island up ahead. He was surprised since he thought that this should have been all open ocean.

He flew in to get a better look and did a wide circle over the island, and as he came in lower, he saw on the western side a vast clearing with a primitive village, almost a city, made up of hundreds of thatched huts. Continuing his inspection, on the eastern side of the island, he saw an enormous settlement of some kind – a huge stockade enclosing numerous old-fashioned buildings.

Thinking that the stockade indicated a more civilized settlement, he made a wide circle as he descended, intending to come back around and set down off the beach from the stockade, but as he was lower now, he saw another beach on the southwestern side of the island. As he passed, he saw several natives gathered there, and in among them were, he was almost certain, white people waving at him.

Forgetting the stockade for a moment, he turned and came in low near the beach to get a better look, and as he did so, though he could scarcely believe it, he saw Phil and Jerry waving frantically among the natives.

James did another turn and came in for his final approach.

§

Beau had asked for volunteers for a militia, and as it turned out, there were more volunteers than guns. The killing of twelve of their number at the order of Governor Payne had incited a certain patriotism and feelings of righteous indignation in the little underground community, and they were anxious to administer retribution.

Beau had also sent out a few individuals who assured him that they could circulate above ground among many of the colonists without attracting attention. These had the simple but potentially dangerous mission of finding a few people whom they were certain that they could trust, to spread an invitation to those who were unhappy with the colony to band together.

They had taken twenty-five rifles from the jail armory, along with fifteen pistols and numerous swords. There were also several weapons taken from the invaders. Of the volunteers that stepped forward, Beau stopped counting when he reached fifty.

"I fear that we cannot arm everyone," John said quietly to Beau.

Beau thought for a moment, looking at the people standing in front of him.

"We don't need to," he said. He raised his voice for the crowd to hear. "How many people here already have experience with guns? Step forward."

From the crowd, thirty made their way toward him.

"Okay, good. John and I will begin compiling a list of your skills and experience. We have a limited supply of ammunition, so we can't waste any in teaching people to shoot.

"What I'm hoping to accomplish will not require any bloodshed, but we need to be prepared for it if necessary. We need people who already have experience handling a weapon, and especially if you have combat training, we can use you." There was an audible sound of disappointment from the remainder of the crowd. "I appreciate your desire to help, and I'm sure that before this is over, you will likely be called upon to assist us in some way."

"We also likely have very little time in which to act upon our undertaking," John added, "as this first wave of invaders will no doubt be followed by a second, when they do not return."

"Yes, good point," Beau agreed. "So form a line and tell us your experience so we know what we have to work with."

Brit was watching the proceedings with some misgivings, and as the volunteers began filing towards Beau and John, Brit approached.

"Beau," she said quietly, "can I speak with you?"

"Sure, honey," he said and left the group in John's capable hands.

"Why are you doing this?" she asked.

"Doing what?" Beau looked at her, confused.

"You're preparing for war."

"This *is* war." He leaned his head closer to hers and lowered his voice. "There's apparently a sizable percentage of the population who understandably don't like the way the colony is run. Some of them just come down here and sit around. They have no purpose, because they have nobody to organize or lead them."

"I thought we were going to escape the colony and join Jax and Allie," she said.

"I know, babe," he sighed. "And we're going to do that, but right now, I have to help these people. They're basically defenseless."

"But why is it *your* responsibility to save them?"

"Who here is in a better position to help them? I was a Navy SEAL."

"I know," she replied. When she spoke again, her voice quivered. "But I'm worried about you."

"Well, you don't need to worry. What I have in mind is a bloodless coup. There are enough people, here and above ground, that we should be able to overpower the rulers pretty easily."

"A bloodless coup is good, but as I understand it, it only works if there's no opposition. But you've seen the army they have up there."

"Yeah, and you see the army that we're building down here."

"Beau, we have about fifty guns and a few people who are marginally experienced with them. Up above, they have what amounts to a whole army of trained soldiers."

"Which is why these people need help."

"Jax is going to be worried sick about us."

"I'm sure he is, but if we escape from here and join him, then what? We'll still be stuck on this island with the threat of the colony hanging over us. And we'll also have the knowledge that we abandoned these people. And you can bet that they'll be the first ones killed by Payne and his men."

Beau gestured toward the bodies still arranged on the ground a short distance away from them and Brit, against her will, glanced at them. When she looked back at Beau, there were tears in her eyes.

"I don't want us to end up in a row of bodies," she said quietly.

"I don't want that either, honey," Beau said softly, and he took her by the shoulders. "We're going to be okay. We're going to get the job done and get out of here."

§

Nicholas Harvie walked down the path through the forest toward the cave. He had left the cave less than an hour ago, and he didn't realize until he arrived home that he had left his sword there.

When he was on duty inside the cave, it was common for him to take off the sword to be more comfortable sitting down. But with the thoughts that had been troubling him, he forgot the sword when the guard changed. The sword had been his grandfather's and he did not want to risk having it lost or stolen before his next guard duty.

And especially not now, having heard such an interesting message in the colony.

He was recalling the conversation he had had just a few minutes ago, when he rounded a large rock embankment that was the eastern side of the cave. He was instantly on guard when he saw the small clearing that was used as the eastern guard post, but the guard was not there. Looking around, he found the body concealed in the undergrowth, a knife wound in his chest.

He heard a loud sound overhead as some kind of flying machine appeared, flying low over the forest. Nicholas watched with fear and wonder as the red and white object faded into the distance toward the west.

As the roar of that machine died away, he heard a different one, a rumbling sound from inside the cave. With mounting apprehension, he looked around the edge of the entrance to see the large boat backing towards him. And there on top, on the bridge, was Jax Malone, one of the visitors who had gone missing a couple of days before. Also with him on the boat were a few Indians.

He was surprised to see Jax, surprised enough, in fact, that he forgot to hide. Jax's face registered shock and apprehension as he saw Nicholas at the cave entrance.

Jax did something with the controls of the boat and the sound quieted as the boat slowly drifted alongside him. Nicholas put his hands out in front of him, to indicate that he was not a threat, as he saw the natives coming around to his side of the boat with arrows drawn. Jax Malone quickly said something to them that Nicholas could not hear, but apparently the natives did, as they relaxed their bowstrings.

"May I come aboard, sir?" Nicholas called.

Jax looked nervously around, but seeing no other people, he looked back at Nicholas and nodded. The boat was near the end of the dock, and only about a foot away from it, and Nicholas quickly reached up and pulled himself over the starboard gunwale. The natives backed up, keeping their eyes on him.

The *Camilla* continued drifting out of the cave. Once they were far enough away that there was no danger of being dashed against the rocks, Jax came downstairs to Nicholas.

"Who are you?" Jax asked suspiciously.

"My name is Nicholas, sir. Nicholas Harvie."

"Why are you here, Nicholas? And why are you not rushing back to report us to your superiors?"

"Well, sir, I have just received an intriguing message from an old friend, one whom I have not seen in quite a long time." He looked nervously toward the natives, then continued. "It would seem that I am not the only dissatisfied one in New Roonock."

"Dissatisfied?"

"Yes, sir. I am very unhappy with what our colony has become. With the tyranny that is wielded over us."

"You mentioned a message from an old friend," Jax reminded him.

"Yes, sir. Some people that I have known have disappeared over the course of several years. I have heard disturbing things, whispered rumors about an agenda for getting rid of dissidents."

"Yeah, I'm afraid I've heard that one too."

"Well, sir, one of those people that I thought to be long dead contacted me at my door, just as I arrived home from my guard duty here. Apparently thy friend, Beau Bannister, is organizing a rebellion of some kind."

Nicholas' face shone with an almost childlike glee as he spoke.

"A few people who had gone missing over the course of many years are actually living underground, in a cavern beneath the colony. And now they, and many of their friends, are armed and are looking for others to join them."

"Did your friend happen to say anything about my sister?" Jax asked anxiously.

"No, sir, he did not. However, it has quickly become common knowledge among the Constabulary that thy sister was spirited away from the jail by Mr.

Bannister himself just this morning, after which they, and several other prisoners, simply vanished, apparently by some supernatural means."

"Oh, that's excellent news," Jax said with a sigh of relief. "So why are you trusting me with this information, Nicholas?"

Nicholas looked somewhat embarrassed, glancing at the natives, then back at Jax. "My reasons, I fear, are selfish. I hath fallen in love with my Indian slave girl, and she with me, but we are kept separate by our laws. We want a better life, one without fear of our tyrannical rulers. I wish to join thy cause, so that Anacaona and I may marry."

"Anacaona?" asked Loquillo, one of the natives. Jax turned and looked at him.

"Yes," Nicholas said softly, a hint of apprehension creeping onto his face.

"Anacaona was taken from us years ago," Arasibo explained. "She is Loquillo's sister."

These rebels must be dealt with posthaste!" Thomas Dare demanded, pounding his fist on a table in Payne's office near the jail. An inkwell and a jar of pens trembled with the shock. The redness around the wound on Dare's temple where Brit had struck him with the heavy ceramic mug was barely visible now against the scarlet of his angry face.

Payne sighed and put his pen down. Seeing that he was not going to get any work done, he closed his eyes and rubbed them with his knuckles, irritated by Dare's temper.

"I assure thee, Thomas, that nobody wanteth them dealt with more than I," Payne said in a quietly forceful voice.

"Well, then, for what art thou waiting?"

"I am not waiting, Thomas," Payne replied testily. "A team of musketeers hath already been dispatched to their hiding place, now that we know of its location."

"Aye, William," Dare said as he began pacing in front of Payne's desk, "and it is now two hours thence. I want to know that justice hath been carried out and that the offenders hath been duly effaced!"

"Thou exceedeth thy bounds, old man," Payne said, growing impatient. "Thou art not the Governor. Thou art my lieutenant and hath not the authority to make such demands, neither of me nor of those in my command. I sent men to bring the rebels to me for questioning, not to kill them."

Payne noticed that Dare twitched ever so slightly, and his eyes looked down briefly. How should he interpret that? A flicker of nervousness? Evidence of guilt for an, as yet, uncharged offense? Payne wasn't sure what to make of it, but he remembered something else that had been bothering him lately, a troubling report.

He narrowed his eyes as he looked at Dare. "Mr. Jourdan, the guard who helped thee recapture the young woman, hath told me of her condition at the time of her apprehension." Dare rolled his eyes and turned away. "Pray, how did she come to be in such a shameful state of undress?"

Payne continued to watch Dare, who seemed to fidget but made no response.

"What were thy intentions toward her? Thou hast not resumed engaging in thy old vices, hast thou Thomas?"

Dare turned back toward Payne.

"I detained the young woman so that I might make inquiries," he said with a tone that indicated that he felt his loyalty was above question. "I discovered her flagrantly disrespecting the privacy of my collections. How the creature came to discard her clothing, I cannot say."

Payne sighed and shook his head.

"Thomas, I hath, against my own better judgment, turned a blind eye to some of thy activities in the past. However, I cannot, in good conscience, condone thy mistreatment of innocent people."

"Innocent?" Dare said with a sneer. "The creature be a loose woman and a harlot!"

"No, she hath done nothing to deserve such an epithet."

Dare was about to respond when they heard a strange sound above them, like a growling animal.

They looked curiously at each other, then made their way out the door. By the time they got outside, the source of the sound had gone, but a guard from the jail saw them looking skyward.

"Some form of flying machine, sir," and pointing westward, he said, "It went down that way."

"Take two men with thee," Payne said, "and go investigate."

"Aye, sir," the guard said.

Payne sighed and went back into his office, shaking his head as he left Dare outside.

§

"My boat is there too?" Phil asked eagerly.

"Yes, it is," Jax affirmed. "It seems to be fine."

"I want to go get it."

"But the tide's coming in."

"All the more reason to go now! You said they change guards at every low tide, so we likely won't be able to get back in there after they discover their dead guards. My boat has a much lower profile than yours, so I should still be able to get it out now if we hurry."

266

Jax thought about it for a moment, looking around at the others. He had just met James Morales, the man who had flown the plane here, and they were starting to talk about a plan of action. Jax was loathe to go back to the cave, but at the same time, he didn't want to be selfish, now that he had gotten his own boat back.

"That makes sense," he said with a sigh. "Okay, let's go. It'll just take five minutes if I take you there in the *Camilla*."

Jerry offered to go too, so the three of them quickly got in the inflatable life raft that Jax had used to get himself and the natives to shore. Within minutes, they were approaching the cave, cautiously, watching for any other colonists. There was no sign of anybody else, so Jax maneuvered the boat up to the entrance dock.

Phil and Jerry climbed over the gunwale and down onto the dock. They made their way tentatively to the entrance of the cave and, seeing his boat, Phil turned and gave Jax a smile. Jax backed the *Camilla* away a short distance from the dock and the rocky cave entrance and waited.

As they made their way into the cave, Phil and Jerry moved slowly as their eyes adjusted to the dimmer light. Phil climbed up into his boat and started it up, and he cast a happy smile at Jerry.

Jerry gave Jax a "thumbs up" and a wave. Watching from the bridge of his boat, Jax was anxious to get back to the village, and the discussion about a possible rescue plan via James Morales. So when he saw that everything was alright with Phil and Jerry, he turned the *Camilla* and headed back toward the west.

Jerry turned and went inside the cave, and he saw the body of the guard with an arrow embedded in his chest. He turned toward Phil, but Phil didn't notice. His attention was held by something beyond the body. He shut down the motor and came back off the boat.

"What is it, Phil?" Jerry asked. He followed Phil's gaze and saw a number of items stacked along the cave wall.

"I just want to check this out," Phil replied, as he laboriously pulled his commodious mass up the rough-hewn steps to that level of the cave. Jerry followed him and, panting for breath, Phil squatted down in front of the rows of items that Jax had seen earlier, that resembled spray cans. He picked one of them up and turned toward Jerry. "These are incendiary grenades," he said.

"Grenades?" Jerry asked, his brows knit with confusion. "Where would these people get grenades?"

"I don't know," Phil pondered, as he turned and looked around the cavern. On the other side of the lagoon from Phil's boat was a vintage wood-hulled day cruiser. There was also an almost empty hull of a boat. At the innermost part of the dock was a large, sleek 45 foot cruiser yacht. That one drew his attention, and after stumbling back down the rocks, he went on board.

Phil was closely inspecting the interior of the yacht, not knowing if his suspicion was valid or not. He found numerous storage areas, but there was nothing in them, likely emptied by the colonists when they took the boat.

He was just about to give up when he noticed a corner of wall paneling that was sticking up, apparently warped from long exposure to the damp sea air, as the cabin door had been left open. He hooked a fingernail on the corner and pried it up enough to stick his finger under it. When he looked inside, he found a sizable compartment hidden between the inner wall and the hull, packed tightly with high-power automatic rifles.

"I think this boat belonged to a smuggler," he explained to Jerry, "a gun-runner. Those grenades were probably in one of those empty holds."

Jerry was looking on with eyes wide as Phil pulled up other similar panels and found still more weapons.

"Let's get these on my boat," Phil said. "The grenades too."

"Why, what do you have in mind?"

"I don't know yet, but with this arsenal, those colonists won't be any match for us."

They pulled out all the guns they could find in the hidden compartments and loaded them onto Phil's boat, along with the incendiary grenades.

During that time, the tide continued advancing. Phil fired up the motor again and started slowly guiding the boat out through the shrinking cave opening. They just barely cleared the mouth of the cave.

"Five more minutes and we would have been stuck in there," Phil said.

§

Three men carrying muskets crept out of the jungle onto the beach. They had seen people, mostly Indians, lingering there for a while, and they recognized among them Jax Malone and others of his party, who had mysteriously vanished from the colony. Jax and the two other white men had left in Jax's boat, and the rest of the people had gone in the direction of the Indian village.

Now all alone on the beach, the three colonists cautiously made their way toward the strange machine that had flown over their compound. It was resting on the sand, near the water's edge, the relatively still water of the bay gently lapping at the back end of the pontoons. Its skin was a smooth, shiny metal, painted red and white.

The men knew nothing about how it worked, though, and inspecting it as they were now revealed nothing useful to them.

They had each made three slow and careful circuits of the thing when they heard the throbbing drone of Jax's boat coming back. With a quick glance at each other, they retreated to the cover of the forest again to watch.

§

Less than twenty minutes after he left, Jax was back in the natives' village where a discussion was underway about James Morales' plan of action. Several of the higher-ranking natives, along with James, Jax and Allie, sat in a circle inside a sort of lodge hut. Baracoa, the old chief, had started the meeting, but now all joined in.

"If I leave now," James said, "I could make it back to civilization before nightfall. That would give me plenty of time to round up some help, and I could have an army here tomorrow."

"Where would you go?" Jax inquired.

"I'm thinking the best bet would be to head back to Cockburn Town on Grand Turk."

Jax felt a flutter of excitement at the thought of the end of their ordeal, even greater than the excitement he had felt at the beginning of their short lived boat-building venture.

"Great!" Jax said. "Now if we can just get Beau to give up his revolution and get him and Brit out of that stockade."

Allie was sitting on his right, and she leaned against him and slipped her arm through his.

"We'll get them," she said. Jax looked at her with an attempted smile, and she inclined her head against his shoulder.

Baracoa said something in the native tongue, and the natives looked at him with concerned expressions. Jax looked at Yahima, who was sitting just to his left, and who had been explaining and translating when necessary.

"Baracoa hath warned again that the gods are preparing to make the earth shake. He sayeth that it is impending, and is something of greater importance than bringing more white men to our island."

"Well," Jax said to her quietly, "please forgive my skepticism, but at the moment, I'm less concerned about psychic phenomena, and more concerned with saving my sister and my friend."

"Of course, thy concern and apprehension are completely understandable." But her face reflected her own growing uneasiness at the old man's dire prediction.

The people discussed the plans for just a few more minutes, though there was little more to be said, and then they rose. James walked out of the lodge, with Jax and the others close behind. It was a short walk to the southern beach where James enlisted the help of a few of the men to help him slide the plane back a little, into the water.

From the cover of the forest, the three colonists watched as the dark-skinned man climbed up into the machine. They glanced at each other, pondering their next move, as the machine roared to life and started moving into the bay. With a unanimous nod, they stood, raised their muskets, and started firing at the machine.

Several natives, reacting instantly, fired arrows at the men, now visible at the edge of the jungle. All three fell dead.

From the cockpit, James heard the gunshots, a few of which pierced the skin of the plane, but missed him. He instinctively opened the throttle, pouring on the speed, unaware that a few of the bullets had penetrated the engine housing. One had, in fact, grazed the fuel line, and as he pushed more fuel toward the engine, the liquid sprayed harder and faster.

The plane gained speed as it bounced over the waves, but the ride became a little smoother when the pontoons lifted off the water and James gained altitude. Banking toward the west, he continued climbing, heading toward the setting sun.

As the engine heated up, the continuous spray of fuel from the severed line ignited. The flame, in turn, traveled into the open fuel line, and the engine exploded in a magnificent fireball, sending flaming debris in all directions.

The inside of the cockpit rapidly became a blazing inferno and James screamed as his skin blistered, but only for a second. When he inhaled, the flames were sucked down into his lungs, and he was dead in moments.

No more than two minutes after the gunshots were silenced by the Indians, Jax and Allie watched in horror as the flaming airplane plummeted into the ocean like a meteor, trailing a black tail of burning fuel and oil.

§

Phil and Jerry heard the gunshots as they were approaching from the east. But when they saw the plane speed out of the bay, take off and bank toward the west, they cheered, until it erupted in flames. They watched with open mouths as the wreckage crashed into the sea, sending a column of smoke skyward, although oil and fuel on the surface of the water continued burning.

Shaking, Phil maneuvered his boat into the bay and dropped anchor. Jax and Allie were standing on the beach, apparently in a state of shock, still looking toward the burning wreckage, while natives were scattered around them.

By the time Phil and Jerry rowed the dinghy ashore, Jax had regained his composure and came over to meet them.

"What the hell happened?" Phil asked.

"Some colonists shot at his plane," Jax answered, motioning toward the three men at the edge of the clearing, their bodies perforated by numerous arrows. He looked back toward the greasy black smoke rising from the water. "They must have damaged the engine."

The shock and disappointment were still etched into Jax's face, but then he turned toward Phil.

"What took you so long?" Phil took a moment for the question to register, still lost in his stupor. Then he seemed to snap out of it and looked at Jax.

"You won't believe what I found!" he said. "Dozens of high-powered automatic rifles and incendiary grenades. We can destroy that colony and get the hell out of here!"

"We're not going to destroy the colony," Jax objected. "There are a lot of decent people in there."

"What the hell are you talking about? They're just a bunch of religiously oppressed, murderous, slave-owning, fanatics!"

"They're not all like that, Phil."

"Give them time," Phil said, his volume rising with his irritation. "They killed Ron. They killed James."

"They didn't kill Ron," Jax interrupted.

"Given the chance, they probably would have. In fact, they kill and incinerate anybody who doesn't believe the same as them."

"So *you* want to kill and incinerate *them*?"

"Yes!" Phil shouted. The blood rose to his face, turning it red where it wasn't already black or blue. "I said I wanted to blow them up, and they tortured me for it, even though I didn't even have the capability. Well, now I do. I want to wipe the bastards off this fucking island!"

Jax stood there looking at him for a moment. Already aghast at James' sudden death, Jax was trying to keep the disgust he was now feeling for Phil from showing on his face. Unsuccessful at that, with a brief shake of his head, Jax took a deep breath and turned away from him.

"We're not going to do that, Phil," he said quietly as he walked toward Allie.

§

As darkness fell inside the walls of the colony, a group of rebels filtered out, silent and unseen, from a forgotten alleyway. Keeping to the deeper shadows, they separated into pairs and spread out along the cobblestone streets. All were armed, but most of them would have seemed to any observer to be diffident and apprehensive.

By now, most of the colonists had finished their supper and were settling down with their books, mending, or other evening activities.

But a few of them were on edge, nervous. These gathered weapons, extinguished their lamps and quietly went outside, meeting up with others in the shadows.

One of these, Nicholas Harvie, kissed his native slave girl, Anacaona. They both wore worried expressions, but he gave her a brave smile and pressed his palm against her cheek. He buckled his grandfather's sword around his hips, picked up his musket and slipped out the door.

Baracoa, the old Indian chief, called another meeting, this time for Indians only. Jax watched them, lit by a few scattered cook fires, as they filed back into the lodge hut.

He was envious that they had something to concentrate on.

Jax sighed and went into the hut that he and Allie had been sharing. Allie was down on the floor of the hut, smoothing out the grass mats, but she stood and went to Jax when she saw his troubled expression.

"What's wrong?"

"What's wrong?" Jax echoed irritably. "Our one chance to get out of here just got shot down and the pilot murdered. What do you think is wrong?"

Jax shook his head, silent for a moment. Then he looked at Allie and took her in his arms.

"I'm sorry," he said. "I'm just frustrated. We're not getting anything done. I got my boat back, but we're still just sitting around here doing nothing when we could be going back home.

"Meanwhile, the colonists don't have any qualms about killing people, and they keep thwarting our attempts to get help." He caressed Allie's hair as he continued thinking out loud. "I hate to think about what could be taking Beau so long to get himself and Brit out of there."

"Well, you said that colonist back at the cave told you that Beau's helping the rebels."

"I know. And as you can imagine, that doesn't make me feel any better. My sister and my friend in the middle of a revolution?"

"Well, what else can you do?"

Jax let go of Allie and started pacing. "Phil said he found a bunch of automatic rifles and grenades back at the cave. He wants to obliterate the colony, and I said absolutely not. But I don't know. Maybe we *do* need to mount some kind of assault."

"But you hate guns."

"I know," Jax said almost in a growl. "But I'm sure Beau could use the help. If he's mounting a rebellion, what are his chances against Payne's army? God, I don't know what to do!"

Allie went to him and he paused in his pacing. She put her arms around him and laid her head against his chest. "You need to relax," she said softly. "Get some rest tonight and maybe you'll find an answer in the morning. Get your mind on something else for now."

"Like what?" Jax asked with a note of irritation.

Allie turned her head up toward him and kissed him. Jax paused and looked down at her. His face expressed momentary confusion as his frustration abruptly dissolved, and his emotions took a different turn. Allie knew that she had successfully deflected his soliloquy when he held her tightly and began returning her kisses.

Fueled by the tense emotions of the past hour, Jax's heart was hammering in his chest. Their lips pressed together, his hands explored her body, discovering curves and planes that, until now, he had only imagined.

Allie leaned into him, her hands clutching his back. She felt his fingertips trace the gentle curve of her spine, beneath her blouse, and she tingled under his touch. But she pulled away and looked up at him for a moment.

Jax paused, looking into her eyes, their pupils dilated in the dim light of the hut. With his hands on her hips now, his breathing gradually slowed just a bit, but he was tortured by the interruption of his exploration of her body, until Allie raised her arms. Jax slipped her linen blouse off over her head, and Allie returned the favor.

Forcing himself to take his time, Jax held Allie's shoulders as he drank in the sight of her body. Her skin was quite fair from having always been covered in her old uniform of baggy clothing, but was now smooth and warm and perfect in his hands. Her dark hair spilled casually over her shoulders, and Jax gently brushed it back.

He caressed her shoulders and her neck, and he smiled as he leaned in and kissed her again. One arm around her back, his other hand found Allie's breast and he cradled it gently.

She grasped him tightly now, and they lay back on the grass mat, each of them aware of nothing except the object of their love.

§

After the three colonists had shot down James and his plane, natives had been posted as guards around the bay where the two boats were anchored. During the night, Phil knew the native guards saw him as he and Jerry crept to the bay, climbed in the dinghy and started paddling into the bay. But since the natives were posted to guard the boats from the colonists, they did not stop them.

Phil was hoping that would be the case.

He was completely oblivious to the fact that, on numerous occasions, he had irritated most of the natives in the village, so that none of them were sorry to see him go.

They paddled quietly toward the boat, dimly illuminated in the light of the crescent moon, now dipping toward the west. In the silence, they were both lost in their own thoughts.

Jerry was somewhat ambivalent about Jax and his friends. He hadn't really known them for very long, but they seemed nice enough. Aside from that, though, he had not formed any real opinions about them.

But Phil was sick of Jax and his passive attitude toward the colony. Phil had been beaten and tortured by those bastards, and they would have killed him if Beau hadn't rescued him.

Now *there* was a man of action.

Phil had heard from Jax that Beau was orchestrating some sort of rebellion against the colony. But being a typical bleeding-heart liberal, Jax didn't want anything to do with it. The pansy-assed coward was perfectly happy to just wait around for Beau to do all the heavy lifting so they could go home.

After climbing into his boat, Phil tied the dinghy to it, weighed anchor and started the engine. He pulled out of the bay and steered toward the east.

"Are you sure we should do this?" Jerry asked once they were away from the bay.

"I'm not just going to sit around and do nothing. Not with all this firepower at my disposal."

"Yeah, but we're just two guys. And we're going to be right out in the open, unprotected."

"Don't you wimp out on me too," Phil growled. "We have a chance to deliver some much needed retribution to that fucking colony, and by God, we're going to do it!"

"But what can two men do against that stockade?"

"You've never fired an M16, have you?" Phil asked with a sneer. "I'm sure we can do some damage to the lower part of the stockade that's coated in cement or adobe or whatever the hell it is.

"But we can absolutely destroy the upper part, the exposed logs, and the sentinels cowering behind them."

Jerry still seemed hesitant, but he had come too far to back out. Not that Phil would turn around and take him back anyway.

Within a few minutes, as they rounded the southeastern shore of the island, they could see the dark bulk of the colony ahead of them. Phil throttled back to look and to prepare. As they bobbed on the waves, he was happy to see how close the stockade came to the shore at some points.

"Get me one of those rifles," Phil said. "And several magazines. And take some for yourself."

Jerry picked up one of the M16s and handed it to Phil along with a stack of the curved magazines. He picked up another one and examined it in the moonlight. He watched as Phil inserted one of the magazines into his rifle and he followed suit. But he wasn't feeling as enthusiastic about it as Phil was.

"Thank God those gun runners were smuggling thirty round magazines," Phil said. "We won't have to stop and reload nearly as often." He smiled and almost shivered with excitement. "It's been over two decades since I've handled this kind of weapon."

"That was in Kuwait?"

"Yeah," Phil said, caressing the rifle. Then his voice turned quiet and bitter. "But Kuwait was a lot different from this. Always had to do exactly as I was told. Follow instructions to the letter!"

Jerry felt the beginning of a nagging worry while listening to Phil's ramblings.

"What are you talking about, Phil?" he asked. In the dim light of the early morning, Phil couldn't see the apprehension on Jerry's face.

Snapped out of his murmurings, Phil seemed to become aware of his surroundings again.

"Nothing. I just had a few run-ins with the Army. They apparently don't appreciate initiative." Speaking under his breath, he mumbled, "'Conduct unbecoming' my ass." With the waves slapping against the side of the boat, Jerry didn't hear that part.

"But I wasn't in the military, Phil. I've never shot a person before."

"You can't think of them as people," Phil replied, settling into an instructive tone. "They're enemies."

"But they're still people."

"You have to shoot them or they'll shoot you."

"But they don't just have guns up there. They also have cannons."

Phil scoffed and waved it off.

"Sixteenth century cannons are no match for a well-armed, twenty-first century warrior in a fast motorized boat. Those old cannons don't have the speed or the accuracy."

Jerry was still hesitant.

"I don't know, Phil. I just don't think I can do it."

"Ah, fuck it!" Phil finally said, irritated. "Just drive. I'll do the shooting."

He got up from the driver's seat and Jerry took his place, without a word, but seemingly relieved.

"This is better anyway," Phil said. "I'm the one they beat and tortured. It's only right that I be the one to take the bastards out." He looked down at the rifle again and his irritation seemed to quickly dissipate. "I'm just sorry to see that these M16s don't have the full automatic setting. But I'll still be able to inflict some pretty good damage using it as a semi-automatic."

They looked toward the stockade, and from this distance, they could just make out a few individual guards, very small this far away, but awash in light from their torches, and backlit by the crescent moon.

"Just stay out about twenty or thirty yards," Phil said, planning their approach. "Any closer and the sentinels will just be a blur. And we'll be better targets for their muskets, too."

"Okay," Jerry said nervously.

"Are you ready?" Phil asked as he sat down. Jerry took a deep breath, exhaled, and nodded.

Phil braced himself so that he could maintain a good firing position toward his left. He gripped the rifle firmly, took a deep breath himself, then he nodded toward Jerry. His friend pushed the throttle forward and they began speeding toward the walls of the colony.

Phil knew the first pass would be a piece of cake. They would not be expecting it. The sons of bitches won't know what hit them.

As the southeast corner of the stockade came in range, he could see the guards looking his direction. Phil steadied the rifle and looked along the sights.

He squeezed the trigger, heard the rapid "clack-clack-clack" as the rifle fired the burst of three shots, and he saw his first victim drop. He smiled as he took out the second guard before he had a chance to duck down behind the battlement, but the rest, it turned out, were not quite as easy. Having seen what happened, the guards were now taking cover.

Phil was laughing now as he sprayed bullets at the stockade. The magazine was spent before they came to the north end of the colony, and Jerry drove well beyond it to stay out of range before doing a wide turn and stopping.

"That was perfect, Jerry," Phil said. "You're doing great!" He snapped in a fresh magazine, and now facing toward the right side of his boat, they began their second run.

He aimed at individual guards when he had the opportunity, but he knew that the logs of the stockade were not providing much cover any longer, with the damage the shells had inflicted on them already. There were now gaps in places where the logs had already splintered.

Some of the sentinels were attempting to return fire, but their muskets proved to be little threat. By the time their second pass was complete, Phil was certain he had killed at least six men.

Before starting the third pass, in addition to loading another magazine, Phil gathered a few of the incendiary grenades. He arranged them within easy reach, on the seat beside the magazines.

"Did you see those sections where the shore goes up close to the wall?" He asked. Jerry nodded. "Be ready to come in close, if I give you the okay. If we can get close enough to it that I could lob a couple of these babies over the wall, we could *really* do some damage! To see that stockade go up in flames – God, what a beautiful sight that would be!"

Jerry didn't seem to share his enthusiasm, but he nodded again. He opened up the throttle and began their third run. Phil smiled contemptuously as he saw the guards scrambling to shoot at him again. Their puny weapons were nothing against him. Another sentinel dropped from a well-placed bullet.

Then, they heard a thunderous boom as one of the cannons was fired. The gunner's aim was not even close. The cannonball splashed harmlessly several yards ahead, and they felt the spray of seawater as they drove through it. As they passed, Phil was able to shoot the gunner before he had a chance to take cover.

They were approaching a section where the wall came near the water, and Phil was happy to see that the battlement was severely damaged at that area. No guards could be seen there, so he pointed toward it and nodded to Jerry. Jerry jerked the wheel to the left and sped closer to the wall.

Phil put the gun down and picked up one of the grenades. As they started turning parallel to the wall, Phil stood up, pulled the pin and arced it hard over the splintered battlement.

As they headed back out away from the stockade, Phil was watching to see the result. He didn't see the explosion itself, since it was on the other side of the wall. But he cheered when he saw the almost blinding glare as the powdered aluminum mixed with the iron oxide inside the grenade, causing a thermite reaction. This resulted in an eruption of fiery molten metals from the device, and a section of the wall burst into flames.

More cannons were being fired, but the shots were still no threat. They got ready for their fourth run.

§

Beau, Brit and a small contingent of rebels were waiting at the jail for others to arrive. They had gone in through the front door this time, but now, they were just milling about.

Beau had suggested that Brit stay in the Underground, but she insisted, rather, on accompanying him. She felt that, if she allowed him to go without her, something bad would happen.

She had experienced a brief flashback to when her parents were killed, and though the circumstances were entirely different, she feared letting Beau go without her. She didn't want to risk losing him and, to some extent, she felt that if they stayed together, he would remain safe. So he insisted that she at least carry a pistol.

"I wish I had known earlier what our plan was going to be," Beau said, chafing with impatience, his voice quiet and chilling. "We could have held on to Dare the last time we were here, instead of trying to round him up again now."

He had barely finished speaking when the door swung open. Payne was pushed in, his hands tied behind his back, followed by John and another rebel. Payne was in his night clothes and clearly looked flustered.

"Mr. Bannister," Payne sputtered. "Miss Malone. Thou art involved in this?"

"Did you find Dare?" Beau asked John, ignoring Payne.

"No," John replied, "and Payne claims to know nothing of his whereabouts."

"Where is Dare?" Beau asked, now acknowledging Payne's presence.

"As the man said, sir, I do not know. If he is not at his home or in his office, then I have no idea. Of that I swear to thee."

Beau looked at him for a few seconds through narrowed eyelids. Then he pushed Payne down into a chair and glared down at him.

"Why did you order your men to kill innocent unarmed people?"

"I gave no such order, sir," Payne said, seeming to take offense at the suggestion. He looked from Beau to John and back. "To whom art thou referring?"

"You sent a troop of ten armed men into the underground lair of these folks to kill them." Payne was shaking his head. "They killed unarmed people," Beau continued, "including women and children."

"I swear unto thee, sir. I sent those men to gather up the people and bring them in for questioning. I did not order that they be killed."

"That's not the story we heard," Beau said.

Michael Pattenson stepped out from the group and faced Payne. Payne seemed to recognize him.

"Lieutenant Governor Dare presented us with thy orders," Pattenson said. "Infiltrate the rebels' hiding place and kill them."

"Those were most definitely *not* my orders," Payne stated emphatically. "I give thee my word."

"So Dare came up with that on his own?" Beau asked.

"I am sorry to say that I hath been suspecting Mr. Dare of certain heinous activities of late. Of altering

288

my orders." He looked at Brit with an expression of embarrassment, and he lowered his voice. "And of unseemly treatment of certain people." Brit's face hardened with the reminder of her imprisonment and near death at Dare's hands. Looking back at Beau, Payne implored, "I promise thee, sir, I do not wish ill on any of our colonists."

"What about the slavery?" Brit asked coldly.

"Slavery, miss?" Payne echoed, confused.

"I saw your name on bills of sale and receipts, of Indians sold into slavery."

"Well, yes Miss Malone. Witnessing such transactions doth sometimes become a part of my duties. I fear I do not understand thy objection to that." He was still, clearly, confused.

"You don't see anything wrong with buying and selling human beings?"

"We hath always had slaves, miss. Be that not the case with thee and thy people?"

Brit realized that arguing human rights to a civilization existing four hundred years in the past was a useless endeavor. She blew out a frustrated breath and turned her back on him.

Payne turned back toward Beau. "May I ask, sir, what thy plans are?"

"To overthrow your government," Beau replied simply, almost casually.

"A revolution? Why?"

"To allow the people freedom to live as they please, without tyranny. The reason the English came to America in the first place."

Suddenly, they heard the sound of gunfire, distant at first, but coming closer. Beau's head snapped around toward the door at the sound of the shots.

"Get him in a cell," Beau instructed John. As Payne was led away, Beau went to the front door and carefully opened it a crack, and Brit came up beside him. He looked out and saw nobody. But he could hear the gunshots more clearly.

"That's automatic gunfire," he said. "It sounds like we may have help!"

The metallic gunshots sounded in rapid three-round bursts, now interspersed with the distinctive sound of musket shots. As Beau listened, he also began to hear the thunderous reports of the cannons.

He pondered what to do, wondering who could be coming to their aid, and wishing that he could contact them, to coordinate their attack. He eased out of the door a bit more, and was able to determine that the sounds were only coming from the east.

As he was listening, another group of rebels ran toward him, and he moved out of the way to allow them in the door.

"The colony is under attack from the sea," said one of the excited rebels, whose name Beau could not remember.

"Aye," another chimed in, "some form of weapon is wreaking havoc upon the wall and tearing it apart!"

"Not only that," the first one said with eyes wide, "but just before we arrived here, we saw a blinding flash, and the wall erupted in flames from some unknown source, like the fires of hell itself! Many sentinels hath been killed, and those who remain are hard put to defend the colony."

"Well, I don't know who it is," Beau said, "but like the saying goes, the enemy of my enemy must be my friend. How many people have responded to our invitation so far?"

"Many, sir. We hath not compiled a count as yet, but our number be growing steadily."

"Excellent! And what about Dare? Has anybody found him yet?"

"No sir. It appeareth that he may be in hiding."

"Damn it!" Beau said. "I don't want that bastard running around free, able to round up reinforcements and interfering with our goal."

"You think he has supporters?" Brit asked.

"I'm sure there are some who would be loyal to him. But I don't want to wait to find out. Especially now that it looks like he's the main instigator of the mistreatment of the colony. I want the son of a bitch captured!"

Brit realized that she felt a little more strongly about it. She wanted him dead.

§

Jax lay awake on the mat in the quiet darkness of the hut, Allie's head resting on his arm. He could tell from her breathing that she was sleeping peacefully. Their lovemaking of a short time ago was still on his mind. And in thinking about it, he had realized some interesting things.

Jax had not had any romantic relationships in quite a long time. After his parents' death, he was so focused on taking care of Brit that he had no time for outside distractions. She was his main responsibility.

Then Beau came back from Afghanistan and coaxed them out of their self-imposed reclusion, gradually easing them back into society. But even then, Brit remained Jax's primary charge, and the desire for comforting isolation was still a facet of his personality.

Allie was the first person who had managed to elicit any kind of romantic interest from him. And how quickly it had grown! He could scarcely believe that it was only nine days ago that he had consciously begun to pursue her.

And now, she was sleeping beside him, her body resting warm and naked against his. He softly kissed her forehead and she stirred slightly, as if something had tickled her. She snuggled up a little closer to him and moaned softly, and then her breathing settled back into its original rhythm.

Jax smiled and, with a contented sigh, closed his eyes to go to sleep.

He wasn't sure if he had actually fallen asleep yet or not, but his eyes opened when he thought he heard something. He turned his head slightly, straining to hear through the night-time sounds of the forest. He heard it again, and he realized that somebody was tapping on the wood frame of the door of their thatched hut.

Jax eased himself up, slipping his arm out from under Allie's head. He stood up and pulled on his linen trousers. He pushed aside the grass mat hanging over the door and saw Arasibo standing there. The moon was setting and he was illuminated mainly by the stars.

"Cacique Baracoa and our council hath determined that we must away to the high country," he said. "The gods shall be beating upon the earth soon, and we shall be safer up high."

Jax hesitated before speaking, hoping that his feelings about their superstitious beliefs did not show on his face.

But before he had a chance to say anything, he heard another, more distant sound. Arasibo turned his head as if he had heard it too. They waited, and a few seconds later, the faraway cracking of gunshots reached their ears. It was repeated several times, in rapid, three-shot bursts. Almost like a semi-automatic rifle. Jax thought about Phil's revelation to him a few hours before.

The sounds varied, the volume becoming louder or quieter, sometimes vanishing completely, depending on the direction of the breeze bringing it to their ears. Then, the breeze would shift and they would hear the brief staccato reports again.

"Alright, Arasibo," Jax said, turning back to the native. "You and your people do what you need to do."

"Thou wilt come?"

Their conversation was punctuated now by the sounds of musket fire alternating with the automatic weapons. Within a few seconds, Jax heard the faraway sound of a cannon, like thunder from the other side of the island. The sound was distant and distorted, but he was certain that's what it was.

"No, Arasibo. I have to go back to the colony. I have to find my sister!"

"Thou needeth help," the native said.

"No, I don't want to endanger your people any more than I already have. You go ahead and protect your own people."

Arasibo thought for a moment, but then he nodded and quietly turned, disappearing into the night.

Jax let the grass mat fall back into place and turned. Allie was standing there, slipping her blouse on over her head.

"I'm sorry, honey," he said. "I didn't mean to wake you."

"You didn't," she said as she heard the faraway cracking of the gunshots, followed by the resonating thump of a cannon firing.

"I'm going back there," Jax said. "I have to find them and get them away from there."

"I'm going with you," Allie replied as she finished dressing.

"Not a chance! I can't look for Beau and Brit while having to keep an eye on you too."

"Excuse me, Monsieur Chauvin?" Allie replied with a sarcastic edge to her voice.

"I didn't mean that," Jax said quickly, trying to defuse the situation. "I'm not being chauvinistic. I just mean that it's dangerous. The colony must be a battlefield by now. I don't want you to be endangered now along with them."

"I understand," she said, but she said it with a voice that indicated that she was not going to consider any opposition. "But I've been thinking about the natives and about their belief that an earthquake is about to happen."

Jax shook his head impatiently. "What does that have to do with it?"

"There are people who seem to be particularly in tune with natural forces, much more than the rest of us. Often to the point of being considered to possess supernatural abilities. It's not so much anything having to do with religion or superstition, but a real, physical affinity with nature."

"Great. But what the hell does this have to do with what we were talking about?"

"You want me safe – I'll be safer with you. If an earthquake does happen, I'll be safer in a boat on the water than here. In fact, we all will. If you find Beau and Brit before the earthquake, great! We can go out to sea and probably won't even know when the earthquake strikes."

Jax paused, thinking about what she said. He didn't like to admit it, but he could see her point. He still wasn't sure he believed the whole earthquake prediction thing, but in case of a quake, he knew they would be safer on a boat.

"Besides," she continued, picking up on his hesitation, "I can stay on the boat and take it out on the water while you're gone. Otherwise, you'd have to tie it up to a dock where the colonists might be able to take it again."

"Okay," he sighed as he picked up his shirt and began pulling it over his head. "You really believe in that earthquake stuff, though?"

"I don't know, Jax, but it makes sense. We were talking when we first got here about some weird tectonic activity in this part of the ocean where the plates meet. It's entirely possible that seismic stress could be building, which would result in a quake. And maybe Baracoa really is able to sense that."

They were both fully dressed now, so Jax nodded in response.

"Alright, let's get going."

A quick glance into Phil and Jerry's hut reinforced Jax's suspicion. It was confirmed without a doubt when they reached the bay and saw that Phil's boat was gone, and Jax cursed him under his breath. Jax and Allie started dragging the life raft to the water's edge.

They turned when they heard footsteps behind them. Arasibo and about a dozen other native men were coming down the path toward them.

"We will help thee," Arasibo said.

Jax felt gratitude welling up, and he grasped the man's shoulder and said, "Thank you, friends," including the other warriors as well.

There was not room for the natives in the raft, but they didn't seem to mind. They started swimming toward the boat, some of them pushing the raft ahead of them.

§

Phil wished that he could somehow attack the stockade on all sides, but he had to be satisfied with only being able to strike from the sea. It was frustrating knowing that he was only damaging one side of the colony. Still, having unleashed a second and third incendiary grenade, the wall was now an inferno of smoke and flame. It was a gorgeous sight!

He knew for a certainty that he had taken out at least twelve men, and he suspected several more. The flames now illuminated his targets very nicely, and blinded the sentries so that they had a harder time seeing and aiming at him. So he had instructed Jerry to go just a little slower on this latest pass, and he had been able to take careful aim, killing four more men.

As Jerry turned and cut the throttle, Phil turned toward him, smiling from ear to ear. He was panting, not from any physical exertion, but from the sheer excitement of their assault on the colony.

"Did you see that dark part of the wall by the rocks, near the end of this last run?" Phil asked. Jerry nodded. "Let's get another grenade up there."

Jerry nodded again, without a word. He was starting to enjoy this. It was exhilarating. He tried not to think about all the people who had died as a result of their attack, but Phil was right – thinking of them as the enemy, as soldiers who were trying to kill you, really helped.

When they started, he had been hesitant, even afraid, and he had concentrated simply on driving the boat fast and getting themselves out of the danger zone. But Phil had also been right about the colonists' weapons. As they continued their assault and still remained unscathed, Jerry had begun to experience a feeling of euphoria, indeed almost a feeling of invincibility.

Phil loaded another magazine into the M16 and sat back to catch his breath for a moment as they rocked gently on the waves. He looked at Jerry and they both smiled – Jerry reluctantly at first, but nevertheless, he gave in to the feeling of joy that their adventure had unleashed.

"Well, you ready to do it again?" Phil asked.

"Absolutely!"

Phil got into position again as Jerry punched the throttle, sending them speeding toward their enemies. The sentries were now trying to stay hidden as much as possible. Phil could only see the occasional head as someone tried to aim at him, but with the fire burning the wall, Phil could see them much better than they could see him. Heads were all he needed to see.

Phil directed Jerry's attention to the section of the wall that he had spoken of, where it came near some rocks on the shore. So far, aside from some splintering from the bullets, it had escaped the assault and was dark. Jerry nodded in response and turned to make an approach toward the fortress.

Phil put the gun down and picked up a grenade, and then braced himself in a standing position for the best leverage. They were speeding toward their targeted section of the wall, a dark spot in the midst of multiple burns.

The final moments of Phil's life passed in what seemed slow motion as, his perception heightened by fear, he was conscious of everything that led to his downfall.

In the moment he pulled the pin, Phil saw the sentinel. A lone soldier on the dark section of the mangled battlement looked over the side and, his vision unaffected by the fires burning at a distance from him, was able to clearly see them. He took aim. Phil, holding an incendiary grenade instead of a gun, was unable to shoot him, and was just about to tell Jerry to turn when he heard the shot ring out.

The bullet hit Jerry dead center in his forehead. Killed instantly, his body fell to the left from the rocking of the boat on the waves, jerking the wheel. Phil was about to throw the grenade, but now off-balance because of the turning of the boat, he stumbled and fell to his knees, the live grenade still in his hand.

Burning at four thousand degrees Fahrenheit, the molten metal spewed all over Phil. He had never felt anything so painful. His right hand and forearm were almost instantly charred all the way through. The blackened thing broke and fell off of his body from its own weight, but the fiery substance had already set the rest of his body on fire.

Phil, in a desperate panic from pain, frantically tried to brush the burning metal from his shoulder and chest. This had the opposite effect, instead spreading it faster to the rest of his body.

Distracted by the intense sensation, and by the sound of his own screams, he was oblivious to his surroundings. He didn't notice that the grenade, still gripped in the charred remnants of his hand lying on the deck, was also erupting all over the guns and grenades just a few feet away.

The grenades and ammunition exploded in a spectacular fireball that Phil himself would have greatly appreciated, had he not been in the center of it.

In just a few seconds' time, Phil was little more than a charred lump on what was left of the burning deck. The cruiser was now fully engulfed in flames, the cabin blown away. Now entirely covered with the incendiary material, its hull breached by the explosion and the burn, the boat sank in the shallow water by the shore.

Not dependent on external oxygen for combustion, the material continued burning for several minutes underwater, casting an eerie glow on the side of the stockade.

§

Beau looked at his watch. It was nearly 2:00 a.m. He was impatient as the sounds of the battle raged on outside, wondering who was involved. He was even more impatient when the sounds suddenly stopped.

Despite the hour, there were people running in all directions, scared and confused by the noise of the attack. A few seemed to be running with purpose, perhaps to assist in the defense of the colony, but so far, nobody had come to the jail.

Seeing Beau's concern, John approached him, hoping to distract and encourage him.

"There be more support for our cause than we ever dared to hope for." He looked around at their growing number, milling about in the jail and the front lobby area. "Our scouts keep coming, and bringing more friends."

"Yes," Beau replied, "that's good. We'll likely need them."

The door opened and several more armed people slipped inside, and the scouts who brought them found Beau and made their report.

"The eastern wall of the colony hath been badly damaged and breached by some sort of powerful weapon, and is currently in flames."

"Were you able to see who the attackers were?" Beau asked anxiously.

"No, sir. We could not come close enough without being detected. But our people hath taken positions everywhere throughout the colony." The man was beaming. "At last count, we numbered over three hundred!"

"Aye, sir," said his partner, "many of whom be members of the Constabulary."

"Yes, Mr. Bannister. Apparently, many of the soldiers hath seen firsthand the corruption in their leadership."

"Very good! What about Thomas Dare?"

"Our people are asking about and searching," the first man said. "We received a report that somebody thought that they spied him attempting to hide on the south side of the colony. But with so much activity out there, he was having a hard time of it. We hath concentrated more men in that direction, to improve our chances of finding him."

"Do you know if he had any supporters with him? Soldiers?"

"Of that, we know naught, sir."

Beau shook his head and sighed. "I thought that the old man would be the easiest part of the plan. I wanted to have all the leadership of the previous regime in custody."

"What else can we do, sir?" John asked.

Beau looked around the room. There were nearly fifty armed men standing around, crowded into the lobby. "We're not doing any good here." He thought for a moment longer, then nodded his head decisively. "We go out of here, spread out and work our way south. Our number, added to those already searching down there – we'll find the son of a bitch."

The three men nodded. They seemed as if they were nervous, yet anxious to get out of the cramped quarters.

Beau felt a presence at his side and turned to see Brit. For a moment, he had forgotten about her.

"We're heading out, honey," he said. "You stay here and –"

She didn't let him finish. She raised her pistol in both hands, to point upwards, as she had seen cops on TV do when tracking a criminal.

"Not a chance," she said.

§

The crescent moon had sunk into the sea to the west a few hours before, so its meager light added nothing to the smoke and flames that continued billowing up on the eastern side of the island. The echoing sounds of the distant battle had subsided now, but the effects, the fire and smoke, still dominated the night sky.

A line of torches snaked up a path on the western side of the central mountain on the island. The natives had gathered up certain necessities and left the village, quickly but efficiently, and were now marching up to higher ground.

It was not a steep climb, nor a long one. At about 1500 feet, the path widened and leveled into a wide clearing, on the southwest side of the mountain. Rings of stones from previous fires remained, and near the rocky face of the mountain, a raised dais or altar stood, decorated with various talismans.

At this clearing, the natives spread out into family groups. The mountain continued up a few hundred feet more. But this clearing, mostly surrounded by lush vegetation, seemed to be their destination, one which had welcomed them on numerous occasions in the past.

Baracoa, the chief and priest, sat down in the grass near the dais. He closed his eyes and began rocking back and forth, listening for more communication from the gods. Many of the other natives, though, rolled out mats and lay down, extinguishing their torches, hoping to get a couple of hours of sleep.

§

Even before Jax and his band of native warriors reached the easternmost part of the island, they saw the orange glow in the sky. Ominously, the battle sounds had stopped abruptly, but the fires continued to rage on.

Jax drove past the cave where his boat had been kept and then rounded a rocky point. The southeastern part of the stockade rose just a few yards ahead of them. From where they were, they could see the damage to the wall – logs splintered, whole sections of the upper battlement falling down, and many sections of it in flames.

He could not see Phil's boat, though. Only after looking for a few moments did he see a bubbling area in the water several hundred yards north, with a strange glow emanating up from it.

Seeing that there seemed to be no safe place to come ashore, Jax turned around and went back to the dock at the entrance of the cave. The tide was out and the cave was wide open, but he didn't want his boat stuck inside for another twelve hours. So instead of going into the cave, he pulled up to the outer dock, where the path from the colony terminated.

He cut the engines and climbed down from the bridge, as Allie finished tying the bow and stern lines to the posts of the dock.

"Be ready to pull away after we've gone," Jax said. "If anything happens, and you're threatened in any way, you know how to drive the boat. Get away and stay safe."

Allie nodded. "How are you going to get inside?" she asked.

"I'm hoping that our escape route through the river under the wall is still open. But we'll just have to play it by ear."

"Please be careful," Allie said.

Jax found that the shotgun he usually kept onboard was nowhere around, probably taken during the colonists' initial inspection of his boat. However, he did find a flare gun, and he pocketed an extra flare. He kissed Allie, then climbed down onto the dock where Arasibo and his warriors waited.

Allie watched them until they disappeared up the path and into the forest, and she sighed. She didn't want to be left alone on the boat. She didn't want to go back into the colony either, or into a battle, but she had been the one to suggest this excursion.

You and your great ideas, Allie!

She went toward the front of the boat to untie it from the dock. She kept her eyes and ears open for any signs of approaching danger, but so far, all was quiet. The cave, though, was intriguing. She climbed back up onto the *Camilla*, went to the bow, and she turned on a spotlight and shone it into the cavern. Turning it in different directions, she illuminated various sections of the interior.

She saw a few other boats, in various stages of dismantling. And she saw the dead guard with the arrow in his chest. With Phil's attack on the colony, Allie realized that they must have been distracted enough that nobody had thought to send a replacement. So they didn't know that he was dead, or that Jax had retrieved his boat.

Then she saw the musket on the ground at the dead man's side. She remembered Jax, heading toward a battle zone in the colony, armed only with a puny little flare gun.

Leaving the spotlight shining in the cave, she climbed back down onto the dock and followed the light inside.

§

Incendiary grenades, burning at over one third the surface temperature of the sun, are ideally suited to destroying weapons caches, since they can melt metal into a useless puddle. Wood logs, therefore, are no match for them. Thus, the fire in the stockade was spreading.

The molten material from the grenades burned for only about a minute each, but once ignited, the logs provided continuous fuel. Portions of the wall had already been mangled by Phil's M16 assault on it, in many places reduced to splinters and kindling.

Adding fire to the onslaught, sections of the burning wall, as well as a few unlucky sentinels who happened to be in the path of the grenades, fell onto structures below them, helping to spread the fire. Thus almost the entire eastern side of the colony was now a blazing holocaust.

Sentinels were focusing all their attention on battling the fire, now that the enemy had been vanquished. But it was proving to be too much for them, even when civilians joined them.

The populace in general was in a panic, trying to get away from the fire, and these proved to be a hindrance to those who were trying to fight the blaze. Many of the latter were running back and forth with buckets. Some used water to throw on the flames, where the fire was close to a water source. Others shoveled sand or dirt on the blaze to try to douse the fire.

In either case, their efforts, valiant though they were, were not equal to the task of extinguishing the flames.

Beau was pleasantly surprised to find that it was easy to get around out in the open, even armed as he was. With the attack on the stockade wall, many men were armed and running in all directions, hoping to defend their home from an unseen enemy.

The defenders, the fire fighters and the panic-stricken, all worked in their favor. Beau and his little army spread out and were able to blend into the crowd, with nobody paying them any heed. And except for right beside the burning structures, it was still dark enough that Beau's features remained mostly hidden and unrecognizable.

Once they left the jail, they began working their way southward in a sort of phalanx. They didn't want to move too slowly, drawing attention to themselves amid the panicking crowd. At the same time, they didn't want to move too fast and risk missing clues to Dare's whereabouts, so they were careful to strike a balance.

Some of Beau's men, those who would not be hindered by being recognized, knocked on doors, using the excuse that they were checking to make sure that everyone was alright in the aftermath of the attack and the current fire. But their eyes were always seeking alcoves or other places that could be used as hiding places.

Those who could not afford to be recognized, like Beau and Brit, carefully searched alleyways and dark public areas. But despite their relentless sweep toward the south, their quarry still could not be found.

§

Jax and his native accomplices followed the path to the edge of the forest, at which point they could see the stockade. The entire eastern side was engulfed in flames, and the fire was quickly spreading to the southern side.

As they watched, the southern gate began swinging open, apparently to allow many of the residents to escape the fire, as people swarmed out, some carrying a few possessions. As the smoke billowed up, burning cinders drifted down, providing an additional handicap to those trying to flee. The flames were already licking at the edge of the gate, and those who went through it did so wearing expressions of terror.

"I think I can get in easily enough through the gate," Jax said, turning to Arasibo, "and we wouldn't have to try to find the river opening. But I'm not sure about you. You would definitely stand out in the crowd." Arasibo looked up at the battlement.

"There are no guards," he said. "They are all fighting the fire. We will accompany thee, to find thy friend and thy sister." In the darkness, Jax could just see the other natives nodding in agreement, and it was clear that they would not be dissuaded.

"Alright. Be careful. Try to stick to the shadows."

They started forward into the clearing. What starlight there was, the thick smoke now obscured. As they came closer to the structure, the billowing smoke even blocked out the flames to a great degree, which further helped them to remain hidden in the darkness. The benefit, though, was balanced by the burning of their eyes and difficulty breathing.

The people coming through the gate were primarily women and children, most of them dressed in their night clothes, while the men were likely engaged in fighting the fire. Working their way through the crowd in the smoke and the darkness, like salmon swimming upstream, Jax and his friends entered the gate, and they didn't seem to attract much attention.

At least not until Lieutenant Governor Thomas Dare ran into Jax. Here inside the stockade, the flames were more intense, providing more light, and Dare recognized Jax immediately.

"Thou!" Dare said, startled, as he stepped back. Then he saw the band of natives behind him.

In an act of cowardly panic, as a little girl and her mother were running past, Dare reached out and grasped the child. The girl screamed and her mother stopped and turned, looking in disbelief and terror as Dare held the girl in front of him, a dagger to her throat.

"Thou wilt let me pass," Dare barked, "or this child's blood shall be upon thy head."

The mother looked on helplessly, her hands over her mouth, as Dare, still holding the child as a shield, moved slowly to the side to avoid Jax and the natives. He turned as he advanced, backing up so as to continue facing his foes.

Therefore, he was not aware of Allie pointing a musket at his head until he bumped into the muzzle.

"Put her down, Mr. Dare," Allie said. Dare froze in his tracks and allowed the child to slowly slip down to the ground. Jax looked at Allie, feeling pride at her bravery, and a little fear for her safety.

Dare let go of the little girl, who ran to her mother's arms. He raised his hands and, as his left hand neared his head, he took a chance. He quickly reached for the musket which was still against the back of his head.

The risk paid off. Before Allie realized it, Dare was able to wrest the gun from her. In the same movement, he swung around with his right hand, still holding the dagger, and plunged it into her chest.

Allie's face registered surprise at first, as she realized her mistake. The surprise was quickly replaced as she felt a moment of pain. Then she saw the shock and horror on Jax's face as he was rushing toward her, and she experienced a flash of regret that she would not see Jax again.

In that instant, seeing Jax's face, love was the last thing she felt.

It was over in only a couple of seconds. Reacting too late, Jax fired his flare gun as he rushed to Allie's side. The flare struck Dare in the back near the left shoulder, as he was fumbling with the musket, trying to turn it around. The old man felt the searing impact in his upper back, the force of it knocking him to the ground, and he howled in pain as his shirt and vest caught fire.

Jax fell to his knees beside Allie's lifeless body, lifting her head, as the tears streamed down his cheeks. He tried to avoid looking at the spreading stain of blood on her blouse. He was oblivious to all of his surroundings, including Dare's screams.

Jax didn't realize that, in writhing around on the ground, Dare eventually managed to extinguish the flames. Dare lay still, panting for a brief moment, his eyes glazed with pain and shock. He pulled himself up on his elbow, relieving only slightly the pain of his charred and blistered back. He reached for the dagger that he had dropped during his throes on the ground. As Jax rocked back and forth with Allie cradled in his arms, the old man attempted to pull himself toward him.

Seeing what Dare was doing, Arasibo had fitted an arrow to his bow, but before he pulled it back, he heard a gunshot. Dare collapsed on the ground with a bullet in the back of his head.

The natives turned to see a white man and woman sprinting past them, the pistol still raised in the woman's hand. They knelt beside Jax, one on each side of him. The blonde haired woman was crying too, as she put her arms around Jax and buried her head in his neck.

The surface of the earth is constantly moving. The science of plate tectonics is a relatively new one, developed as theory in the early twentieth century, and finally accepted as fact by the scientific community in the late 1950s and early 60s.

Despite the seeming solidity of the earth's crust, it has been mapped as being composed of many distinct pieces. Depending on the scientific definition being employed, the surface consists of either seven or eight major plates, and several minor ones. Their movement is only, on average, an inch or two per year – certainly not detectible to the average human, though there are some, like Baracoa, who seem to possess a greater sensitivity to such events.

These plates move in relation to each other in different ways. Some plates slide past each other in opposite directions, usually unobstructed, but occasionally producing a shock. Some move apart from each other, producing a gap through which magma or lava is released, creating volcanoes or new land masses. At times, two plates may collide, causing either a continental collision or a subduction zone.

About 200 miles northeast of the island, deep on the ocean floor, two plates had formed a subduction zone, in which one plate slipped under the other. In time, the subducted plate would disappear completely under the overlying plate, eventually being taken back into the earth's mantle, where it would be melted down and essentially recycled.

Usually, this movement is unimpeded. Occasionally, though, the edge may stick, snagged on something that prevents the plates from moving freely, building up pressure as they continue their inexorable movement in overlapping each other. This causes the overlying plate to distort, bowing upwards, until finally, the edge snaps loose. The pressure is quickly released and the overlying plate is allowed to flatten once again.

The result on a land mass is an earthquake.

In this case, the shock was not massive, but was eventually felt by those on the island. Baracoa, still sitting on the ground near the dais a few hundred feet from the top of the mountain, had begun rocking more vigorously, and he commenced a sort of moaning. The other natives were roused from their slumber and looked toward the old man.

Following his lead, they all began coming together, hundreds of natives collected around the old chief and priest. Families gathered close together, arms around each other, and began rocking in unison with Baracoa as they felt the ground tremble.

Under the ocean, there was an additional result. When the overlying plate snaps back into place and the curvature abruptly flattens out again, the edge suddenly moves forward, releasing its energy into the water, causing an immediate vertical displacement. This displacement rises quickly to the surface, producing what is commonly known as a tsunami.

Up on the side of the mountain, after the shock of the earthquake, the natives remained, rhythmically rocking with Baracoa, knowing that the event was not yet over.

§

The shock was felt in the stockade as well. It was a minor quake but noticeable. At the southern gate of the colony, Beau and Brit managed to get Jax to his feet. Only then did Jax realize that his friend and his sister were safe, and he hugged Brit tightly as Brit sobbed against his chest.

Jax looked around and saw Arasibo and his friends looking very nervous. He thought he understood why as, through the smoke and dust, he saw nearly a hundred armed men surrounding them.

"It's okay, buddy," Beau said. "They're with me." Jax looked at Beau, then at the militia that he had assembled, and he nodded.

"We cannot remain here," Arasibo said. "It be not safe."

"Don't worry, Arasibo," Jax said. "They're friends."

"The danger is not from them, but from the sea. We must away to high ground."

Jax looked at Beau as a flash of insight broke through his grief, and he started pulling him and Brit toward the gate.

"He's right," Jax said. "Come on, we have to get up the mountain! That's where all the natives went during the night. Baracoa, the old chief, knew this was going to happen."

"You go," Beau said. "I still have a lot of people in here to get out."

"I'm going with you, Beau," Brit said.

"No you're not, honey," Beau said, his voice softening. "Jax especially needs you right now. Head up to higher ground. I won't be far behind."

Beau turned to his men and issued a brief instruction. Immediately they turned and spread out in all directions, to warn people and get them out. Beau looked quickly over his shoulder at Brit, then ran into the stockade.

Jax, his face streaked with soot and tears, put his arm around Brit's waist. After a regretful glance toward Allie's body, lying still in the sand, he guided Brit out the gate.

"Lead the way, Arasibo," he said.

§

Beau sprinted through the colony, watching as his men went off in different directions to warn people. He made several turns until he reached the hidden door in the abandoned alleyway. Opening the door, he raced down the now familiar stairs and corridors, not bothering to close the doors behind him, until he came into the Cathedral.

There were still several people there, though they seemed somewhat shaken. Coming through the group, he saw Bethany approaching him.

"How goes the battle?" she asked.

"There really wasn't much of one," Beau replied. "But we're still in danger. Gather up everybody and get out. I don't have time to explain, but everybody has to get out of the colony."

"How can we do that?"

"The walls are on fire and the gates are open," he said urgently. "Get everybody out and head west, up the mountain. Hurry!"

He waited only long enough to see that the warning had been taken seriously. Bethany turned and began collecting everybody and preparing them to make a fast escape. Then Beau turned and headed back up to the surface.

His next stop was the jail. Nobody was left there except for Governor Payne who was locked in a cell. Beau unlocked and opened the door. Payne looked at him cautiously.

"Come on out, Payne," Beau said.

"What art thou going to do with me?"

"I'm letting you go."

Now Payne appeared suspicious.

"If you really don't wish ill will on the colonists as you said," Beau continued, "then prove it. Listen to the rebels and their complaints, and let them have a say in reforming your colony."

"I shall indeed, sir."

"For now, though," Beau said, adding some urgency to his voice, "we're in danger here. We have to go outside and head up to high ground."

Payne hesitated, looking confused, and Beau got impatient. "Come on, man, get going!"

Payne was quickly on his feet and out the door.

"Head west, up the mountain!" Beau called after him.

Beau followed him out the door and looked around. The sky was lightening as the sun was preparing to rise, but smoke and flame still billowed up from the walls and other structures. People were still rushing about, but now with more purpose. Some were leading children, others livestock, but all were heading toward the gates.

Beau started to follow them, but then he saw a group of three men still trying to put out the fire on one section of the wall, a nearly futile gesture considering that section was almost completely burnt already.

"You men!" he called toward them. Unable to hear him, they kept working, trying to smother the flame up on the battlement. Beau ran toward the steps and scaled them at full tilt. He hurried to where the men were working, but before he could say anything, something in his peripheral vision caught his attention over the wall.

On the open sea, a tsunami can travel over 500 miles per hour, though with its low amplitude and long wavelength, it would likely go undetected if it passed under a boat or ship. However, as it nears landfall and the seabed rises, the wave slows down dramatically. What it loses in speed, though, it gains in height.

Thus, as the seabed rose near the island, the wave was growing, and when Beau looked over the battlement, toward the northeast, the crest of the wave was nearly at eye level, and rising.

The men looked up, surprised to see him there. Then they noticed what he was looking at and their eyes bulged. There was no time to climb down. The wave was almost upon them.

"Over here!" Beau called, directing them to where he was standing, a rare section of the wall that had not burned. Hoping that the log structure, sunk into the earth and the concrete base, might withstand the wave, he was beckoning to them. They were racing toward him when the wave struck the wall, shaking the platform they stood on.

Beau wrapped an arm around the pointed top of a log and reached his other toward the men. He grabbed the first man and helped him secure a hold on one of the logs as he himself had. The second man was in front of a charred section, which gave way immediately as the water crashed into it, but he was close enough to the first man that he was able to grab onto his arm, and from there, gain a grip on the wall.

The third man was not so lucky. He was washed away as the charred wood crumbled, sweeping him off the battlement and into the churning maelstrom down below, within the walls.

The force of the water rushing over Beau was tremendous, and it was all he could do to hold on. The sea forced itself, not only over the logs but between them. Beau lost his footing as the sea drove relentlessly over him, pushing him into an almost horizontal position. It tried to force its way into his mouth and nose, threatening to drown him, and still it kept coming.

§

Jax and Brit, and their native guides, were climbing a trail up the side of the mountain, attempting to reach safety. Scattered groups of fleeing colonists had joined up with them, though they were cautious about the natives. Arasibo led them up and around the south side of the mountain.

It was even darker in the forest, surrounded by the dense foliage. Most of the people were holding on to others in an effort to stay together in the inky black of the unfamiliar forest.

Then they heard the thunderous crash of the wave behind them.

The wave continued relentlessly past the colony, the force of its forward momentum driving it on. The colonists scrambling up the mountain tried desperately to stay ahead of the water, and the broken trees and other debris, but many were too slow.

In the eerie darkness, the roar of the advancing sea mixed with a cracking sound as small trees and limbs snapped under the force of the wave. Those fleeing could hear behind them the screams of those overtaken, but the screams were quickly extinguished as the water engulfed the victims.

Some had escaped the walls of the colony, but had not made it to the hills when the wave struck. Most of these were overtaken by the water before the energy of the wave was depleted. Floundering in the surge of water along with the debris, they were then washed away when the water drained back down.

"We should go back for Beau," Brit said as she hesitated, her voice quivering.

"He'll be here," Jax replied. "He said he'll be right behind us."

"Yeah, I know." Jax heard the quiver in her voice. "He told you that once before, but he stayed behind to save me. I don't want to lose him too."

Jax put his arm around her shoulders and squeezed her, kissing the top of her head. Jax was relatively confident about Beau.

Allie, though. Jax had a burning in his gut and a pain in his chest about Allie. He could still see her lying on the ground with a vacant stare, the bloody wound on her chest.

He shook his head and sighed, squeezing Brit's shoulders again.

They finally emerged from the forest into a large clearing where hundreds of natives were gathered together. In the torchlight of their camp, the natives saw all of the white people accompanying Jax and Brit, and they rose, many of the men taking up their bows and arrows, spears and knives.

"If it please thee, my brothers," Arasibo said, addressing his countrymen, "these people shall join us here."

The Indians looked at each other doubtfully, but they relaxed their bows. They were suspicious of the host of white people, and as a group, they turned for guidance toward their leader. Baracoa, apparently emerging now from a sort of trance, looked up at the white people, smiled, and nodded his head, stretching out his hands toward them.

§

Beau was thinking that he couldn't fight it any longer. His arms had slipped under the force of the water, despite his mighty grip around the log, and he dug his fingernails into the wood. Exerting his entire body to hold on just a little bit longer, he could feel scattered pains from his old war wounds. He fought the urge to take a breath, knowing that air was out of reach.

Then, just when he knew he couldn't hold on any longer, the wave was spent and Beau was able to find his footing again.

Later, he realized how fortunate he was to be on the battlement. At least there, the main danger was just water. Had he been down on the ground in the stockade when the wave struck, he would have been at even greater risk from the debris.

He realized this as he was gulping in great lungs full of air, and he looked down into the stockade. There, in the dim light of the rising sun, the bodies of those who had not been quick enough bobbed in the still churning water. The corpses bumped into fragments of buildings and carts floating in the water, or against stones, cannons and other heavy wreckage which had been lodged in the ground just below the surface.

He looked at the two men next to him on what was left of the battlement. Panting for breath, their fingers bleeding from their grip on the rough wood, they were unable to speak, but nodded their thanks. They started for the steps, but Beau put his hand up, still panting for breath and coughing up water. They waited for a bit, occasionally glancing at Beau, wondering why he was detaining them.

Then, after a few minutes, the water came surging back, washing downhill, further agitating the debris below them, and doing more damage to some already weakened structures. Even after the wave had passed, the water inside the stockade below was still restless, seeking egress from its enclosure, and it was finding a few areas in the damaged wall where it could retreat back to the shore.

Shakily, Beau started down the steps, holding tightly to the railing to keep from stumbling. His legs felt wobbly as if they were made of rubber. But they also felt heavy, requiring a great deal of strength to move them, and his arms even more so. He reached the base of the stairs, stepping down into the water which was up to his waist.

He looked behind him as the other two men splashed off the steps. Then he looked up at what was left of the stockade wall.

"Fire's out," he said.

"Aye," one of them replied with a chuckle.

"Good job." Beau took another deep breath and sighed. He began slogging through the murky water, pushing aside debris and bodies, looking for any survivors.

In time, the stockade was drained of water and the cleanup work began. With their new, albeit apprehensive, relationship with the natives, they focused first on rebuilding homes. They would decide later what to do about the wall.

Some of the colonists were reluctant to give up their slaves, but they were in the minority. With much coaxing from Beau, the majority ruled that they should be allowed to rejoin their people.

Payne, also with a great deal of coaxing, agreed to reconsider their views on slavery.

The natives were happy to receive many of their loved ones back, and this went a long way in salving their relationship with the colonists.

The sun was sinking in the west as Jax stood on the southern beach, looking out to sea, the *Camilla* once again anchored in the bay. A few days after the tsunami, there were still occasional bits of debris bobbing in the calm water here and there, or washing up on the shore, but for the most part, it had all washed away.

The island's central mountain had blocked much of the wave. Aside from getting soggy from the sea's surge, and some minor damage to a couple of huts, the southern side of the island, and the native village in particular, had pretty much escaped the ravages of the tsunami.

Jax felt a hand on his shoulder and he turned to see Beau, looking at him with a sympathetic look in his eye.

Jax was getting to the point where he hated that look.

He had received it several times when they reached the high clearing early in the morning when the tsunami struck, and the Indians saw that Allie was not with them.

He received it from the Hemmingtons who had, coincidentally been among the party climbing to high ground with them.

And he kept getting it from Brit and Beau.

Jax knew that they all meant well, and he couldn't fault them for it. In their position, he would probably do the same thing. But that look, he found, seemed to reinforce the sadness that he already felt.

Just a few days ago, Allie had been alive, sensuous and warm in his arms. He could scarcely believe that she was gone.

And the sympathetic looks were just constant reminders of her loss.

He didn't need reminders.

"How's the *Camilla*?" Beau asked. Jax had retrieved her from the dock outside the sea cave shortly after the tsunami passed and brought her back to the bay.

"She's fine," Jax replied, looking back at his boat. "A few scrapes on her hull from being battered against the dock, and a few things onboard shifted around a little. But that rocky outcropping at the cave sheltered her pretty well."

"That's great." Beau stood there, silent, trying not to say anything that might make his friend feel worse.

"I still can't get over Phil and Jerry and that stupid stunt they pulled," Jax said shaking his head.

"Yeah, well it helped those of us still stuck on the inside. But you're right, it was pretty stupid."

"How did your meeting with the colonists go?" Jax finally asked after a pause.

"It went very well," Beau said, brightening up. "They're a sad bunch – they lost almost five hundred of their number the other night. But they're very receptive to a change. When we first got here, you called Roanoke 'the Lost Colony.' Well, they really are kind of lost, now. Even Payne has expressed an interest in trying to develop more of a democracy."

"When that many of their population openly rebels, that has to be something of a wake-up call," Jax said as he looked back out to sea.

"Hmm. Turns out Payne wasn't involved in the conspiracy to keep us here after all." Jax looked at Beau curiously. "At least, that's the way it seems. It was all Dare. And his little network of spies, including his son-in-law Henry Hewet. Dare had a tidy little 'self-help' operation going on right under their noses, even including a couple of different love nests. Payne was tripping all over himself apologizing to Brit about the way Dare treated her."

"Must have been going on for quite a while," Jax said. "You told me Bethany's boat was taken thirty-three years ago."

"And that was probably the first. Nobody seems to recall an occurrence like that before then. He got away with it and kept it up. Not that boats came around here that often, but when they did, they were fair game."

"So, what about Dare's network? Are they still around?"

"I don't think so. It was pretty small. But Hewet's wife died in the tsunami, and with Dare dead too, Hewet has been spilling his guts. Payne thinks they've broken up the whole ring."

"Good to know. So they want a democracy, huh?"

"Yeah, I was able to describe a little about the States, how the early English settlers drafted the Constitution, established the government. You know, Truth, Justice and the American Way."

"That's Superman."

"Whatever. All the things that make America the model of perfect political balance and unity we see today."

Jax scoffed softly.

"But they wanted to know," Beau continued. "They really want to do it right. And interestingly, almost none of them are saying they want to leave now. Except for a few of the modern hostages, the ones kept here against their will, they all seem to want to stick around and rebuild their lives and their colony."

A few more moments passed between them before Beau nervously broke the silence again.

"Brit tells me that you don't want to leave either."

"Yeah." Jax turned to look at Beau. "Not for a while, anyway."

"Don't you think it would be better, at a time like this, to immerse yourself in something you love?"

"That's what I intend to do. I've been fascinated with Indians since I was a kid."

"Well sure, what boy wasn't? Cowboys and Indians and all that. But what about shipwrecks?"

"Shipwrecks are dead, Beau. I've realized that I'm tired of digging up dead things. These natives are real and alive, and I have a chance to live among them. And to study their new and shaky relationship with the white colonists as it develops."

"You'll be missed on the *Camilla*. I mean, she *is* yours."

"I know you and Brit will take good care of her. If I spent much time on the *Camilla*, I'd constantly be reminded of the fact that my love is gone. In fact, we lost two of our people. I think seeing Ron's and Allie's empty work stations daily would just be too much for me right now."

"Well, I think we'll be around for a while, just in case you change your mind."

"Oh?" Jax was only mildly interested in what Beau was saying, and he turned back to look out to sea.

"Yeah. Brit and I were thinking we might start with the wreckage we found a couple of weeks ago. Since you found Ananias Dare's musket there, it's obviously the ship that brought the colonists to this island. We know there's no treasure on the ship, so we won't get rich from it. But from what you and Brit have said about the mystery of Roanoke, we *will* likely receive a fair bit of fame. That could certainly help us drum up more business."

"No!" Jax said, turning his attention fully onto Beau. "You can't tell anybody about this."

"What the hell are you talking about?"

"Beau, if word got out we found the lost colony of Roanoke alive and well on a tropical island, it would be ruined."

Beau looked at him incredulously.

"You were talking the other night about how cool it was to be the ones who finally solved the mystery of Roanoke."

"It *is* cool, but it has to be something that we keep to ourselves. I mean, I promised Arasibo a few days ago that if we get off the island, we'd send people to help them. But now that the colony is not a threat to them, we can't do that."

"This is huge, Jax!" Beau said with an irritated edge to his voice. "Keeping it a secret kind of makes the coolness factor take a nosedive. How would telling people about it ruin it?"

"Come on, Beau. You know how 'civilized people' exploit anything new, the same way they rape natural resources with no thought to the big picture. A year or less after being immersed in modern civilization and these people could be a bunch of burned out drunks, if they're even still alive. I can just see it now: *Survivor: Roanoke!* Or some other stupid reality show."

"Oh, quit being such a goody-goody bleeding heart liberal."

"Well, you quit being such a selfish, money-grubbing conservative." Jax paused and sighed when he realized that their conversation had digressed into their old argument. "I'll grant you that may be a worst-case scenario. But at best, in time their civilization will be lost."

"You know how much money this could make us?" Beau asked, but with a little less volume as he realized his argument was losing steam.

"Money isn't everything, Beau."

"Which is something usually said by people who have plenty of it."

"You know, you don't have to make money off of these people. I have a feeling you'll be marrying into money soon."

Beau hesitated for a moment, at once taken aback by Jax's little joke, and encouraged by it. He silently pondered what Jax had said. Then he snickered and shook his head.

"Just my luck!" he grumbled. "Being related to a damn hippie liberal."

"I think you'll survive," Jax teased.

They were both silent for a while.

"You know, I can't guarantee that the people who were forced to stay here against their will won't talk when they're finally able to go home," Beau finally said.

"Well, we should do what we can to try to convince them. But as far as it depends on us, this place needs to be kept a secret."

They watched as the sun touched the horizon, to begin its exit for the day. Then Jax, hearing soft footsteps behind him, turned around.

"Jax," Yahima said with a gentle smile as she approached him, "wouldst thou care for some refreshment?" She offered him a hollowed coconut shell with some liquid in it. Almost as an afterthought, she handed one to Beau as well.

"Thank you, Yahima," Jax said as he accepted the cup from her and tried it. It tasted like a fermented tropical fruit punch. "Mmm. It's very good."

She smiled shyly, looking at him for a moment. Then she turned around, walking back up the path to the village. She turned once to look back at him before disappearing into the forest.

"You know she's kind of sweet on you, don't you?" Beau asked.

"What?" Jax looked at him, surprised.

"Yeah, Brit's noticed it too."

Jax glanced back toward where Yahima had faded into the forest moments before.

"I don't know that I'm ready for that yet," Jax said, and he took another drink.

"I know," Beau said quietly. "But maybe someday."

A few quiet moments passed as they watched the sun set.

"These sure have been a couple of crazy weeks," Jax sighed, shaking his head.

"To say the least, my friend."